_Th._
being such a
supporter of my books
and me!

Killing
Kindness

Lisa Sell

First published in 2022 by Red Dragon Publishing

RED DRAGON BOOKS

ISBN: 978-1-7391036-9-9

Cover Design by: Emmy Ellis @ Studioenp
Promo: Red Dragon Publishing

Killing Kindness

For Belinda, whose friendship overflows with kindness.
Thank you for always being there for me.

PART ONE
KILLING KINDNESS

An Invitation

You are invited to a celebration of our beloved

Simon Pritchard's life.

Since his disappearance in 1992, we have cherished

our memories of Simon.

Now we want to celebrate the sixteen years we had with him.

Please bring your photographs, stories, and love for Simon.

Buffet and drinks provided.

Date: Friday 20 August 2021

Time: 2pm

Location: The Mill Bed and Breakfast, Trillhaven, Dorset.

RSVP: Charlotte Pritchard, cpritchd@gmail.com

A Directive for The Six – Minus One

Your attendance is expected, not requested, at The Mill Bed and Breakfast in Trillhaven, from Friday 20-Monday 23 August 2021, inclusive. Your rooms and meals are covered.

As Simon's former friends, this is the time to reflect on your part in his life and death. No need to RSVP. You will come. Consider the enclosed information detailing your damning secret as an incentive. Failure to stay at The Mill for the entire long weekend will result in your secret being made public.

Non-attendance will be dealt with accordingly.

CHAPTER 1

Three long, hot weeks ended in death. Teenage temperaments boiled over. Humidity slicked their skin with sweat. Blaming the heat for the group falling apart was too convenient. More than mugginess made Simon Pritchard snap.

The Six were united in a common purpose. Every summer holiday, activities took place, giving parents the chance to offload their offspring. Six sixteen-year-olds, fresh from finishing GCSEs, were the chosen ones. Selected teens earned cash helping to run Trillhaven's holiday club alongside adult supervisors. The Six was hardly an inspired name, but the adults found it helped the assistants to bond. Being in a group made them feel elite. Those only a few years younger respected their authority.

Alex, Kat, Joe, Stevie, Erin, and Simon formed the gang of 1992. Kids hung around them, desperate to be a favourite. The adult helpers admired the teens' work ethic while ignoring their night-time shenanigans. Young adults need to let loose, particularly when preparing for further education or work. A disused mill on the outskirts of Trillhaven became a playground. There they learnt how to tip from childhood over the cusp into adulthood. The Six discovered the joys of alcohol, accompanied by a love of music and sometimes each other. The owner of the mill watched from her cottage across the way. She stayed out of their business until she had no choice.

On the last evening of the holiday club, children danced to a DJ's cheesy tunes. Nearly every local entertainment event was led by him. The Dorset town of Trillhaven lacked social opportunities. Everything was small, including the locals' closed minds, overpopulated residential areas, and crammed schools. A blanket woven with community gossip and judgement spread wide over them all.

The pressure of small town life weighed on Simon. From experience, everyone expected him to be nice. If the dictionary had a visual representation of kindness, Simon's photograph would be on display, not that he would've appreciated it. The young man hated his babyish face and impish grin. Sharper, more mature features might have allowed him to say *no* more often and for it to be accepted.

Simon's friends believed his cup of kindness would always run over. That summer, they received it in abundance, until the boy broke. We all have darker natures we try to suppress. For a while, Simon kept his demons hidden.

Then came Friday 21 August 1992, when The Six disintegrated. Fights, betrayal, disappointment, and damning allegations signalled the end.

Kindness isn't infinite. That night, Simon killed kindness. He might have murdered a man, too. Simon can't tell anyone what happened. He was never seen again.

CHAPTER 2
Charlotte, the Sister

Friday 20 August 2021

When Charlotte Pritchard bought the flour mill and renovated it, the residents of Trillhaven considered it weird. She knew pleasing locals who fear change was impossible, even when improving somewhere covered in graffiti and neglect. Wealth meant Charlotte didn't need the profits or hassle from running a business. Even though her father had insisted she lacked the intellect and confidence, she was a powerhouse barrister. She dared to state how she was better in the role against her dead father, but only in the company of her mum. A spectre of cruelty loomed over the Pritchards.

After the mill's closure in the 1970s, machinery and fixtures were stripped away. Trillhaven's residents expected it to become a similar type of business. Instead, the building became a concrete shell. It was given a temporary revival when The Six claimed it in August 1992. Later, the mill became a memorial to Simon. Then Charlotte took over.

Her mother thought it ridiculous to resurrect what should be left alone. She only visited because Charlotte stayed at The Mill when she wasn't in London. Trusted managers ran the place, although Charlotte regularly returned to Trillhaven. Being there brought her closer to Simon and nearer to discovering what happened in 1992. Her motives weren't sentimental. Working in law makes a person a realist.

When the previous owner agreed to sell the building, it heralded a new beginning tinged with hints of the past. Green slimy tracks on the bricks and broken windows disappeared. Under new ownership, the mill offered comfort and light.

The builders and interior decorators rolled their eyes at Charlotte's demands and overseeing of the work. She refused to relent. Every detail had to be right. Although a cliché, an image of the phoenix rising from the flames was *the* motivation. She had risen from her father's ashes. As soon as he was dust in an urn, Charlotte purchased the mill. It signified her recovering not only the building but also trying to make sense of Simon's disappearance.

Much had changed at The Mill. Modern sat comfortably with the rustic. Sleek lines, spacious windows, and futuristic lighting should have seemed out of place against older fixtures. Somehow it worked. Rough bricks scrubbed clean were foundations likely to remain for centuries to come. Charlotte welcomed the new and still acknowledged the past. While she had her memories of Simon, he remained with her. The Mill, version 2.0, signified hope.

Charlotte shook away her thoughts and focused on the memorial. She couldn't wait to see what was left of The Six: Alex, the Farm Boy; Joe, The Leader; Kat, the Princess; Stevie, The Clown; and Erin, The Thinker.

By the end of the long weekend, Charlotte would have the answers to questions she'd been asking since her brother disappeared. Someone had to pay.

CHAPTER 3
Alex, the Farm Boy

Friday 20 August 2021

Alex vowed to hide his guilt at the memorial. The former Farm Boy knew he was responsible for Simon's disappearance in 1992.

Alex glanced over at the bed and breakfast. Even though the drive from Burton Farm was only ten minutes, he'd arrived early. As a farmer, rising before the lark was second nature. Farm Boy had grown up to become, simply, a farmer. It was never in doubt.

While Alex had stayed local his whole life, he hadn't seen the mill since 1992. Clean bay windows, creeping ivy, and fresh, grey tiles made him struggle to remember how it used to be. Painted words preserved on brick, stating a former life as *Bartlett & Sons Trillhaven Flour Mill*, confirmed he was in the right place.

Memories flooded Alex's mind faster than the sound of the river forcing through the sluice gates. To be at the river was to remember Simon's anger at Alex. Looking at the riverbank triggered a memory of Simon's backpack abandoned there, a sign he had nowhere further to go.

Alex shut the window and turned on the car radio, hoping for a distraction. Anything was better than thoughts of Simon's body buffeted by crashing water.

CHAPTER 4
Joe, The Leader and Kat, the Princess

Friday 20 August 2021

Joe and Kat vowed to hide their guilt at the memorial. The former Leader and Princess knew they were responsible for Simon's disappearance in 1992.

Joe grimaced as the passenger door slammed. His wife's continual lack of respect for the Audi wore thin. He wondered if Kat hated his possessions out of jealousy. A child's shrieking echoing from the past reminded him there were more serious reasons for Kat to despise the vehicle. She scowled as he pushed the driver's door shut with a gentle click.

'That's how you do it,' Joe said, 'not like a raging bull.' He still tried to be The Leader he used to be as a boy, although it proved difficult with a stubborn wife who often retaliated.

Kat slapped her palms on the car roof. 'You can't tell me what to do with the car after what you did. Making a dig at my size by likening me to a bull is a low blow, too.'

'Why does everything have to be about you? You can never stop being the Princess.' Joe kicked at gravel. 'Lose weight and stop moaning.'

Kat pulled down her top to cover her stomach. Having cycled through clothes sizes over the years, she could've kept her older, better fitting clothes. Keeping baggy tents passing for larger ladies' clothes felt like giving up, though. Somewhere inside her she was still Princess; the pretty, slim girl everyone wanted. As she stretched her top further, the elastic hem protested it had little left to give. Kat related. Joe also stretched her patience. Decades of living with a bossy man who loved himself more than her took a toll. The perfect couple show had to continue, though. They would never confess the teenage dream descended into an adult nightmare. Lying was their shared talent. Joe's devastating mistake offered plenty of practise.

The long weekend at The Mill was an opportunity to confirm the Andinos had succeeded. They had successfully raised five children. In 1992, Joe and Kat broke Simon's heart, but everyone would see it was worth it, at least on the surface. They sacrificed Simon for their life together, not that anyone else knew.

The Leader and his Princess weren't bound by wedding vows. Their part in Simon's disappearance chained them together in misery and deceit.

CHAPTER 5
Stevie, The Clown

Friday 20 August 2021

Stevie vowed to hide her guilt at the memorial. The former Clown knew she was responsible for Simon's disappearance in 1992.

She ended the call and sucked in a breath. The recent eyebrow piercing dug in whenever her face moved. After checking the swelling in the car mirror, she hoped for healing. Other piercings in her body were making themselves known, too. Perhaps she was too old for rebellion. Stevie wouldn't be herself without trying to get a reaction, although anarchy wasn't part of her life anymore. For a start, she was married. No one was more surprised than her. Her husband loved her as she was. He'd also checked on her for what felt like the hundredth time. As guilt nipped at Stevie for being ungrateful, she muttered an apology into the universe.

When they met at a fundraiser, Stevie knew the man she chatted with all night was a gift sent straight from God. Perhaps God had a sense of humour. Her husband never disposed of toilet roll tubes and believed the floor was a laundry basket. Despite this, Stevie believed the best gifts are often the most unexpected.

Previously, she never believed she'd meet a decent man. The Clown was the butt of everyone's jokes. Stevie often made jokes at her own expense, getting the jibes in before anyone else did.

Since 1992, she'd made many changes. It had to happen. Old habits might have killed her or someone else. Maybe they had. No. Stevie shook her head. It was a day to celebrate Simon's life. The shame remained, though, of what she did to him. Guilt coiled around her chest. She took a breath and applied scarlet lipstick. The Clown remembered how putting on a face could hide her guilt.

CHAPTER 6
Erin, The Thinker

Friday 20 August 2021

Erin vowed to hide her guilt at Simon's memorial. The Thinker knew she was partly responsible for Simon's disappearance in 1992.

Looking up at the ceiling, Erin tried to place which part of the former mill she was in. As The Six's teenage headquarters, they avoided the upstairs floor. Rickety stairs were an accident waiting to happen.

She plumped the pillow and congratulated herself for arriving well before the memorial. With each passing week, her body needed more rest. Noticing her weariness on arrival, the receptionist allowed Erin to check into her room early.

With the mill of her younger years so changed, Erin couldn't get her bearings. She willed her mind to go back. A memory unleashed: staring at holes in the roof, drunk on cheap cider and intoxicating friendship. Erin would lay her head on Kat's lap as alcohol surged through their veins. Stevie slurred the lyrics of "Lithium" by Nirvana, playing from Joe's stereo. Alex and Simon played drinking games, trying to prove themselves more men than boys. GCSEs were done. Summer's grip held autumn at bay.

They were The Six: Alex, Joe, Kat, Stevie, Erin, and Simon. Once, they'd been invincible. Then it was over.

Simon disappeared by the river. A bloodied corpse was found nearby.

CHAPTER 7

Friday 20 August 2021

'Simon was kindness,' Charlotte began. 'He lived the values I keep striving to learn. Not only was he my brother, he was also a role model to many.'

Stevie shifted in her seat, wondering why people elevated those who were gone to sainthood, not that anyone was sure if Simon was dead or not. After *her* death, she wanted an honest eulogy. Her husband was horrified when Stevie demanded her shady past featured in the funeral tribute. Portraying her as an angel was ridiculous. People relate to those who admit their mistakes. Stevie had written the eulogy for her husband to give. He asked if she could, just once, give up control. She couldn't. The mistakes she'd made wouldn't allow it. After her death, Stevie had to get the last word in.

She reflected on the day the police turned up at her house. No teenager wants to hear a close friend has disappeared. Stevie could tell the police officer with the gentle voice was trying not to say he believed Simon killed himself. The hints Simon's disappearance was linked to a man's violent death were horrific, too. Stevie couldn't look the PC in the eye. She knew more than he did, and it wasn't good.

Charlotte continued. 'Today we've chosen to celebrate Simon's life rather than to mourn it. Goodness knows we've grieved for him for so long.' After a pause, her eyes flitted towards her mother, who was trying to stifle her sobs.

'We all have theories about what happened to Simon,' Charlotte added. 'As a family, we've accepted he's gone. It doesn't mean we've let go. He's always alive in our memories.'

Love, Alex thought, *what is it?* He couldn't feel it there in The Mill's dining room. It was beautifully decorated, but suited a wedding more than a memorial. White paper lanterns burst from the ceiling. White roses entwined in trellises on the walls. Alex wanted to paint it all black, black as the day his friend disappeared, black as their last argument, when Alex imagined killing Simon. It wasn't the time for an archway enclosing speakers as they shared stories. The cover of interrogation under the arch wasn't for him. Alex's secrets would stay locked inside.

Alex, the Farm Boy, went to the fields after being told of Simon's disappearance. Along with his father, Alex sat on a mound of earth and watched birds swooping across the land. He hoped Simon was as free as them. More than this, Alex hoped Simon took Alex's secrets to the grave or wherever he went.

Joe didn't recognise the woman addressing the audience as his wife. While he should have applauded her bravery, Joe felt the balance between them shift. The fallen Leader squirmed in his seat. Kat, who rarely gave eye contact, entertained with her stories. There she was; the Princess Joe loved and fought for, the girl who should've been Simon's.

After hearing Simon had disappeared, Joe felt like a part of him had been wrenched from his body. He had won the prize, but at what cost? Simon could have killed himself because of his best friend's selfishness.

As she shared a memory, Kat savoured the looks of approval. For once she didn't consider her appearance, planning to eat little at the buffet, or her unhappy marriage. Although she couldn't swear to it, Kat wondered if she'd spotted a shock of red hair and a wide grin at the back of the room. A hazy image of Simon offered kindness. Kat's happiness soon disappeared. She didn't deserve his approval. She was convinced she was the reason Simon disappeared. Finishing her speech early, Kat searched for Joe. A face familiar after many years caught Kat's attention. Erin's smile almost outshone imaginary Simon's grin. Seeking friendship, Kat took a seat next to Erin.

Stevie's phone buzzed. Heads turned. Her eyes cast heavenward, asking for the ground to swallow her whole. The former Clown no longer sought attention. A woman – the only person wearing a hat – tutted. Stevie suppressed the urge to tell her she was at a memorial, not a christening. The devil and angel on Stevie's shoulders continued their eternal war.

Erin approached the archway. There she could share how kind Simon was to her. When returning to Trillhaven after those disastrous months away, Erin feared rejection. Many people were casualties of her recklessness. 1992 was her year of change. Simon helped make it happen. She could never thank him enough. Knowing she wasn't able to made The Thinker struggle to put her thoughts into words.

Words escaped Erin back then, too, when she gave a statement to the police about Simon's disappearance and a man's death. She knew she'd brought trouble with her. Returning to Trillhaven was the wrong choice.

Charlotte scanned the room and noted they were all there: Alex, Joe, Kat, Stevie, and Erin. The Six reunited, except for one. Hypocrites gathered together. Charlotte, the sister, resolved no one would forget Simon. The long weekend at The Mill was set to be a blast from the past.

CHAPTER 8

Monday 3 August 1992

The boy's bottom lip quivered. From the other side of a square of glass within a closed door, Stevie raised her middle finger. 'Wait until opening time. There's ten minutes left, loser!' she shouted.

'Bit harsh. He's desperate for the tuck shop.'

Stevie span around. 'Bloody hell! Don't creep up on people.'

Simon leaned on the counter of the youth centre bar, converted into the holiday club's tuck shop. The bright green bar and matching booths made for a nauseous atmosphere. Not the best combination, along with kids full of sugar and fizzy drinks.

'You can hardly miss me.' Simon ruffled his spiky red hair. 'Although you're outdoing me in the colour stakes.'

Stevie checked her peroxide streaks in the mirror spanning across the back of the bar. Along with rainbow tie dye dungarees and red biker boots, no one could miss her. Whenever the school bitches called her The Clown, she wore brighter colours. She wasn't a pattern cut-out of the fashionable girls. The daughter of hippie parents who named her after Stevie Nicks believed she was destined to shine. Besides, being called The Clown wasn't so bad. They were fun and entertaining, exactly what Stevie wanted to be.

'Surprised you're doing the holiday club.' Simon filled a container from an enormous cash and carry tub. Flying saucers puffed sherbet as they cracked upon landing.

Stevie grabbed a strawberry lace from an open jar. 'Why are you surprised?'

'This isn't your kind of thing.'

Simon didn't mention how Stevie didn't respect authority. For the past academic year, she was hardly at school. When she *was* there, smoke signals from joints made her traceable. Teachers gave up on disciplining her. Stevie was smart and knew she'd aced the exams with hardly any revision. The only reasons to attend school involved scoring skunk, causing trouble, or attending exams.

The rest of her time was spent at illegal raves and hanging around with the townies. She figured rebelliousness was a phase. Turning into her parents would never happen. They were losers, more interested in saving trees than caring for their child.

Stevie vowed to leave her village as soon as possible. It being called Artinghole was reason enough. Anywhere sounding similar to *arsehole* wasn't a place to thrive. She planned to go to college, gain some 'A' levels, and move on. Staying on in the sixth form at Trillhaven School wasn't an option. Telling the head teacher to stick the school up his arse on the last day had something to do with it.

'Doing the holiday club will look good in my Record of Achievement,' Stevie began, 'although I'm not sure where mine is.'

Simon's eyes widened. 'Don't lose the Record of Achievement. All the teachers say we'll use them for the rest of our lives.'

'Chill out. I've got it covered. Even *I* know you don't get a job based on an expertise in skinning up and chugging shots.'

'Looking, er, colourful, Stevie. You're really adopting this Clown thing, aren't you?' Kat's catty tone matched her smirk.

Kat tolerated the other girl because she wasn't a threat. It was well known Stevie settled for popular girls' sloppy seconds. The school's toilet walls confirmed it.

'Looking like a perfect princess, Katrina.' Stevie shoved her aside.

Kat checked her baby pink velour tracksuit for damage. She congratulated herself for getting the entire outfit from Top Shop. Stealing tops *and* bottoms wasn't easy in Bournemouth's shops, teeming with security guards. She copied the body language of a casual shopper with money to spend. The thought of being caught for the sake of keeping up with others made her feel sick. Not that Kat needed a reason to vomit. It was how she dealt with food and its perceived effect on her figure.

'Hi, Si.' Kat flicked her curls from her face. The discomfort of sleeping with rags in her hair was worth it to channel Mariah Carey's look.

'Hi.' Simon's scarlet cheeks almost matched his hair.

Stevie grinned at the boy's blushing. Signing up for the holiday club had seemed lame, but she needed the money. After promising the adult helpers to behave, Stevie knew she'd only appear to be doing so. She was intelligent enough to have fun at others' expense. Simon's crush on Kat offered Stevie mischief gold.

'Where can I put this?' In her hand, Kat swung a bag barely able to hold lipstick and loose change.

'Must be heavy.' Stevie laughed. 'Mind you, don't hurt your arm lifting it.'

'It's from Warehouse. Ever considered getting stuff from proper clothes shops?' Kat sneered at the Army Surplus rucksack on Stevie's shoulder.

'We've got our own room.' Simon led the girls towards a room near the bar and opened the door. 'This is the team room. It's a bit manky, though.'

When he learnt The Six had private space, Simon looked forward to getting to know the others better. While he knew the group members from school, not all of them were friends. Stevie was someone to chat to when she bothered to turn up. Kat was, well, she was everything. Simon couldn't confess, though.

Kat opened a window. 'It smells of wet dog in here.' A sucking sound came from each foot as she lifted them in turn. 'Gross! I bet this carpet's never been cleaned.'

'You won't catch anything,' Stevie replied. 'Don't take your shoes off and avoid the crap in the corner. It's probably a biohazard.' She pointed at mouldy footballs and cracked PVC gym mats, guaranteed to be soaked in sweat.

Kat took out a small bottle from her pocket and spritzed it in the air. Stevie batted her hands against Body Shop's Dewberry eau de toilette.

'It reeks like a tart's handbag in here.' With the swagger and sway of a born leader, Joe entered the room.

Simon and Joe joined in a hug, obeying the rules of crotches not touching and a pat on the back for a job well done of being male. It was the best they could do, considering they both lacked height and facial hair.

'All right?' Joe scanned Kat's body while raking fingers through his quiff. Everyone knew he tried to live up to the manly warrior meaning of his Greek surname, Andino.

Kat fanned her reddening face. Simon threw a football to his friend. Joe focused on bouncing the ball on top of his feet, counting each one while trying to break Simon's record in keepy-uppies. Kat balanced on the edge of a sofa; a seventies brown and orange paisley hangover. A spring *twang*ed in protest as Stevie jumped on the sofa.

'Oi, Oi!' Alex shouted an entrance.

A deep tan made his teeth even whiter. Months of working on the family farm around school hours made him nature's poster boy.

'It's not fair how tanned you are.' Kat held out her arm next to Alex's, comparing skin colour. 'I reckon you've grown in the past week, too.'

Alex slapped the ball from Joe as he braced to bounce it again.

'Al, I was onto a winner there!'

'Get over it. How's it hangin'?'

Joe cupped his crotch, Michael Jackson style. 'Pretty well.' He gave a cackle while winking at Kat. Her eyes darted away, focusing instead on Stevie rolling a cigarette.

'You can't smoke in here!' Kat backed away. 'I swear I'm getting asthma.'

Despite having six children, her parents ignored the dangers of passive smoking. The family was bundled up in a three bedroom council house. Adding chip fat and tobacco odours to the mix didn't help Kat in downplaying her humble roots. The girls from The Pink Posse always smelled like perfume counters. Kat was obsessed with odours and what they represented.

'There's a quiet spot behind the building to have a ciggie,' Simon said to Stevie.

She headed for the back door. 'Cheers, Si. I need a nicotine fix before registering the kids. Bugger me…' Stevie moved away.

As the door opened, the others turned towards the visitor.

'Sorry I'm late. I couldn't find the room as I didn't come here for primary school.'

Kat's hand whacked her chest. 'Bloody Nora! It's Erin Sullivan.'

'This is a surprise.' Alex said.

'Thought you moved?' Joe did little to hide the suspicion in his voice.

'We had to come back.' Erin sniffed. 'Mum's boyfriend turned out to be a criminal. If he finds us, we're dead.'

CHAPTER 9

Friday 20 August 2021

At the buffet following the memorial, they skirted around each other. Questioning looks darted across the room. No one wanted to be the first to approach. After the other guests left, The Six-minus-one gravitated towards each other. They gathered around a table in The Mill's bar. Conversation centred on the effects of the passing years.

'You've all aged far worse than me.' Joe gave a megawatt grin.

'Quite the silver fox nowadays, aren't you, Leader?' Alex said.

Kat groaned. 'Don't call him that. I'll never hear the end of it. He's not Leader nowadays and certainly not foxy, although he's boasted about being a catch for years.'

'You caught me ages ago. We've been together since we were sixteen.' Joe's fingers clenched Kat's upper arm. 'I could've done less time in prison for murder. It might've been more fun.'

A collective hush descended. Kat shifted in her seat. The others busied themselves with nervous glances and fiddling with their phones. The sight of Charlotte approaching offered a welcome distraction.

'Thanks for coming.' She opened her arms as if offering a group hug. 'This means a lot to Mum and me. As Simon's closest friends, it's only right to have you all here.'

'How come you didn't have the memorial on the actual date Simon disappeared?' Joe asked.

Kat slapped his arm. 'Don't be disrespectful.'

'I'm only asking what everyone else is thinking!'

Charlotte smiled. 'I thought it best not to do it on the anniversary. Mum still struggles on the day and likes to be alone. Anyway, you'll all be here tomorrow. Perhaps we could have a quiet drink together to remember Simon then.'

'You should've waited until next year,' Joe continued. 'A nice round thirty years since Simon disappeared.'

Charlotte grimaced. 'Point noted, but every day is one where I miss my brother. I'll be honest. Covid lockdowns and restrictions haven't helped my business. Having you staying here is a boost. I know we're all still trying to get back to normal, whatever it's going to look like.'

'You really must let us pay, rather than giving free bed and board,' Erin replied.

'I didn't do it.' Charlotte frowned. 'I thought one of you had.'

'What do you mean?' Stevie asked. 'The note stated everything was paid for. It insisted we be here.'

They searched each other's faces, no doubt wondering if they'd all received an extra "incentive" to stay at The Mill.

Charlotte coiled her auburn hair around her finger. Her reflection was either welcome in having similar features to Simon's, or painful in seeing her brother reflected as female. They shared the same brown eyes and red hair, although she was taller than Simon before he left. Having her father's height made Charlotte angry. She wanted nothing from him.

'A man paid for your rooms in cash,' Charlotte said. 'He booked the whole B&B with you as the only guests. The man told the receptionist it was for a reunion.'

'What's the bloke's name?' Stevie asked.

Charlotte shrugged. 'John Smith. Yes, I know. There are a few "Smiths" who stay here.'

'I don't like the sound of it.' Kat's voice trembled. 'Why would a stranger pay for all this, let alone add what was in the invites?'

'What was added?' Charlotte asked. 'Do you have it here?'

Kat fanned a hand over her scarlet face. 'I threw it away. I reckon one of you has paid for all this and is being coy.'

Charlotte assessed each of the five. 'Perhaps spending time together will help lay some ghosts to rest. I assume none of you have stayed in contact.'

Kat crossed her arms. 'We follow each other on social media.'

'Not me,' Alex said. 'I can't be doing with people knowing my business.'

'Did you all stay in Dorset?' Charlotte asked.

'I'm still at the farm; forever Farm Boy.' Alex let out a long belch. 'Pardon me.'

Joe laughed. 'Bet you're still gassy after a curry, right?'

'Don't remind me!' Stevie cried. 'Our team room stank after Al used the toilet!'

Kat addressed Charlotte. 'I'm surprised I haven't seen you around Trillhaven. Joe and I still live in the family home.'

'A step up from the council estate.'

Kat wrung her hands around each other.

'Sorry!' Charlotte said. 'I didn't mean it like that. I remember you saying how much you hated living in a council house.'

Joe narrowed his eyes. 'Good memory. We'll need to watch your sharp mind. You might bring up things from the past we'd rather forget.'

Within a tissue covering her mouth, Kat caught a nervous giggle.

'What's been happening with you, Stevie?' Charlotte asked.

'I'm living in Thame in Oxfordshire. I have a lovely house which comes with the job.'

'One of us broke away from Dorset, then,' Erin said. 'What's your job?'

Joe smacked his knee. 'She probably has a market stall, selling neon tie dye clothes.'

'Dressing like a clown isn't my thing anymore.' Stevie smoothed her blouse. 'Does this look colourful?'

'To be fair, we're all wearing black to be respectful,' Joe replied.

'Nowadays, black is my uniform. I don't feel the need to make jokes to cover my insecurities, either.'

'Where do you live, Erin?' Charlotte kept the questions coming. 'I expect a famous author has a beautiful house. I'm picturing a beachside property in Sandbanks.'

'I'm in Christchurch. I've been there for years. Don't be fooled into believing authors make millions.'

'Bullshit!' Joe's volume had increased with his alcohol consumption. 'From the amount of novels you've churned out, you must be rolling in it. Although, Kat says it's been a while since the last book.'

'I've been busy. Also, I'm mentoring new authors. It takes up a lot of time.'

Charlotte smiled. 'What a lovely thing to do. Simon would've approved. I'm sure you're all living well in memory of my brother. I'll leave you all to catch up.'

After she left, Joe banged a fist on the table. 'What does she mean? I live my life for me, not for anyone else.'

'Don't we know it?' Kat replied. 'Charlotte's likely out of sorts, with this being Simon's memorial. It's the anniversary tomorrow. Show some compassion and stop checking out her backside.'

Alex nudged Joe. 'Still got an eye for the ladies?'

'Looking, not touching.' Joe's snigger ended as he turned towards Kat's stare. 'What about you, Al? Is anyone in the running for a farmer's wife?'

As Alex leaned his elbows on the table, his shirt sleeves strained against thick biceps. 'I've been busy sowing my oats, on the land and in the bedroom.'

Stevie, Kat, and Erin looked at each other and shook their heads. They used to have Simon to defuse Alex and Joe's attempts at being macho. Simon was the centre of the gang, maintaining the balance. At the beginning of the holiday club, the teenagers soon became good friends. They recognised each other's personalities and gave themselves nicknames. Simon was the only one who didn't get a new label. They struggled to find another word for someone who symbolised being kind. To be called by his name was to call Simon kindness.

Despite the group's closeness, they kept their worries from each other, which led to an explosive last night together. They'd been behaving for too long. When Simon lost his sense of kindness, The Six fell apart.

'Talking of sowing oats,' Joe began. 'You've certainly been busy.' He pointed at Erin's stomach.

'I wondered when someone would mention it. You won't offend me. I'm pregnant, not fat.'

Joe glanced at Kat.

Waiting for another joke at her expense, she scowled. She expected the others were wondering where the attentive boy of 1992 had gone. Kat knew the answer. He'd never existed. Her husband turned on the charm when it suited him.

'You haven't mentioned the pregnancy on Twitter,' Kat said.

'I like keeping my life private.'

'How far gone are you?' Kat had found her voice and confidence in being with old friends.

'Nearly five months. I'm feeling it.'

'Got a fella then?' Alex asked.

'It was hardly divine intervention,' Stevie said.

'Women can raise children alone,' Kat began, and then mumbled, 'Sometimes, I wish I had.' She looked over at Joe, who was focused on downing a drink.

'Actually, I'm a surrogate,' Erin replied. 'I'm doing this for my cousin, Gemma. Remember her?'

Stevie gave a loud sigh. 'Ah, yes, the snotty kid who wouldn't piss off. She nearly had me chucked out of the holiday club.'

'You *did* push Gemma's head into the apple bobbing bucket.' Joe grinned.

'She was getting on my nerves, along with Charlotte.' Stevie scanned the area. Charlotte was nowhere to be seen. 'They kept hanging around the team room. Gemma lived to tell the tale after I dunked her, didn't she?'

'Yes, she did, and she's much nicer nowadays. Gemma and her husband were trying for a baby for ages. I offered to carry it for them.' Erin shrugged. 'No biggie.'

'It's a wonderful thing to do,' Kat said. 'Especially as it's a geriatric pregnancy. They can be risky.'

'The term *geriatric* is so degrading,' Erin replied. 'We're not old yet.'

Alex raised his glass. 'I'll drink to that; to the teenagers inside us!'

'Sounds filthy!' Joe sniggered. 'Fancy having a teenager inside you, Stevie?'

She raised an eyebrow. 'You've not changed.'

'Enough.' Kat swatted at Joe. 'Erin's telling us about the pregnancy.'

'This is the only child I'll have,' Erin continued. 'I'm single and happy. Life is good.'

From under the table, Kat picked up a handbag resembling a holdall.

'Wow.' Stevie pointed. 'It's different to the thimble holders you carried in the nineties.'

Kat chuckled. 'With five kids, you learn to have all the space you can get.'

'And money,' Joe added. 'My battered wallet confirms it.'

'Stingy sod.' Kat pulled a book out of her bag. She offered it to Erin. 'I hope you don't mind.' Her voice lowered. 'Could you sign this?'

'Of course.' Erin took a pen from her pocket and wrote.

'Our friend, the author,' Stevie said. 'It makes sense. The Thinker became a writer. You must have loads of ideas in your head for stories. Got to confess, I haven't read any of your thrillers yet. Work's so hectic I've hardly got time for anything else.'

Kat opened the novel to the first page and read Erin's personal dedication.

To Kat AKA Princess,

My dear friend, may you always know you're loved just as you are. With love from Erin.

'That's sweet. Thank you.' Kat clutched the message of hope to her chest.

'No problem. I'm grateful to be with you all. I wish Simon was here, too.'

'We're not The Six anymore, are we?' Alex lowered his head.

Joe straightened. 'Bollocks. We'll always be The Six. No matter what happened to Simon, he's part of our gang. Here's to Simon.'

Their glasses clinked, signalling a new chapter.

CHAPTER 10

Friday 14 August 1992

Despite how nice Charlotte was to them, The Six rejected her. Although they were only two years older, she couldn't bridge the age difference. Simon was the exception. He'd told Charlotte to give up on being friends with the others because of the hurt it caused her. Simon always had time for his sister. They stood together against a common enemy; their father, Thomas.

'Go away, stalker!' Stevie shouted after Charlotte knocked on the teenagers' team room door.

Being visible through a square of glass put Charlotte at a disadvantage. Throughout the holiday club, she had worn out The Six's patience. None of them, apart from Simon, understood why she needed friendship. Those in her academic year called her a snob. They didn't understand why she never invited anyone to the Pritchards' enormous house and land in the village of Orwick. Charlotte couldn't risk them meeting Thomas. Even when he was in London for weeks, she feared his return. The Pritchards hid his behaviour. If anyone from school saw the cruelty, Charlotte would've died on the spot.

People already thought her weird for calling her father by his name. Charlotte couldn't tell them *Father* or *Dad* were labels he didn't deserve. Simon called him *Father*, but only to make their mum happy. Charlotte refused to do it.

She questioned why Simon had friends when she didn't. Deep down, she already knew the answer. No one could dislike someone so friendly and kind. If anyone needed a friend, Simon was there. His kindness was a conscious act. Kindness fought back against Thomas mocking Simon's ambition to work in computing, rather than following in his father's footsteps.

Since telling Thomas *she* wanted to be a barrister, Charlotte regretted it. She'd foolishly believed the abuse would end because she wanted the same career. As soon as she shared her dream, the mistake became clear. He laughed so hard he spluttered; at risk of choking. Instead of helping, Charlotte wished for it. Without Thomas, the rest of the family could be happy. She never mentioned becoming a barrister again. Instead, she studied harder, vowing one day Thomas would look up to her. It would be a change from him glaring down at the daughter he'd made fall to the floor.

Waiting for Simon, Charlotte stood outside the team room. Inside, the stereo's volume rose. Ugly Kid Joe sang how they hated everything about you. Stevie's snarling face through the glass in the door confirmed the song was for Charlotte. She turned away, hoping Joe hadn't seen her humiliation. Despite his cult of female followers, Charlotte's crush on Joe grew. She vowed not to become a Joe disciple. Eventually, he'd work his way around most of the girls. When Charlotte was older, Joe would see she was a potential girlfriend and not only his best friend's sister. She looked down at her chest and begged her boobs to grow. While lost in thoughts of a womanly body, a hand clamped on her shoulder.

'Did you want me?' Simon asked.

Charlotte jumped back. 'You know better than to make sudden moves. It's like when Thomas…' She looked around her and then leaned towards Simon to whisper. 'When he sneaks up to catch us doing something he reckons is wrong.'

Simon stroked her arm. 'Sorry. I should've thought. Kat said you were looking for me.'

'Bloody Stevie made me leave. She needs to sort out her anger issues. I came to see you. I wasn't bothering anyone.'

'Stevie has a crap life. Her parents are away with the fairies and she's pretty much brought herself up. It makes her snappy sometimes.'

'We have Thomas, but it doesn't mean we're nasty.'

Hordes of zombie-like children, seeking the lifeblood of sugar, headed towards the tuck shop. Simon steered his sister away. Behind the building, they sat on the grass in the shade. It was as private as they could get in a place full of kids and nosey adults.

Simon leant back on his elbows. 'What's wrong?'

'Doesn't matter now,' Charlotte mumbled.

He lifted her dipped chin and smiled. 'It matters to me.'

'I'm sick and tired of being an outsider.' She gulped down a sob. 'Everyone hates me!'

'No, they don't. *I* like you.'

'I want friends, not a brother.' She noted his expression. 'Sorry, I didn't mean it that way. You're the best thing in my life. I'm lonely. I wish I belonged to a gang.'

Simon stared into the distance. 'Careful what you wish for. Not everything's as perfect as it seems.'

'What do you mean? The Six are tight.'

'Sometimes. In any group, people fall out with each other. Six people aren't always great friends. Personalities clash. Secrets come out as people get closer. I think the gang will end.'

'Of course it will,' Charlotte replied. 'The holiday club is over soon.'

Simon wrenched a fistful of grass from the earth. 'The Six is fracturing. We'll shatter. It will be horrific when it does.'

CHAPTER 11

Friday 20 August 2021

Nostalgia overload and a lot of alcohol made Alex decide to go for a walk. The others were too caught up with colouring the past with a rosy tint to notice his silence. He needed space to think.

Alex leaned over the bridge railing, watching the river burst forth. Rusted cogs above the sluice gates reminded him of his dad, who made farm machinery last until it broke. After his dad's death, Alex inherited the farm and bought new equipment. His dream of progress worked alongside tradition. From birth, his destiny was to be Farm Boy and then the eventual owner. Leaving the place with an assistant for four days was difficult. Alex had no choice. Someone had demanded he be at The Mill.

Seeking privacy in the dusk, Alex took a photograph from his wallet. No one else was around. Fencing closed off Charlotte's land. A gate with a key code known only to staff and guests gave access to the rest of the area. Despite being alone, Alex shielded the paper image with a cupped hand. *There* was the proof of his secret. He thought he'd hidden it well. The photograph proved he hadn't. Had the rest of the group been threatened with the exposing of their secrets? The photo was ammunition and blackmail.

Alex had considered not staying at The Mill, as instructed. He'd previously wondered if he could make a confession. Whenever he came close, a barrier of fear slammed into him. Maybe people wouldn't accept the real Alex. He wasn't ready to test the theory.

Back in the bar, he almost told his old friends. Perhaps they were wiser and kinder. No. He needed to be cautious. Trust is fragile. He couldn't view them as anything other than selfish teenagers. Back then, Alex didn't dare reveal his true identity. It would only lead to trouble. Simon tried to force the matter and it ended badly.

Alex looked across the river. Shame and sorrow rose as he reflected upon Simon's disappearance. It didn't have to happen. Simon might be alive if he'd kept his mouth shut.

CHAPTER 12

Monday 17 August 1992

A net sack of basketballs strained over Joe's shoulder. 'Al, are you helping in the sports centre this morning?'

Alex stretched along the sofa. Springs sounded underneath his bulk. 'I'm supposed to be doing paper crafts in the craft room. Not in any hurry to get there, though.'

'Swap with one of the girls,' Joe said. 'Crafts aren't for fellas, especially strong farming stock. To be honest, I'm surprised you're doing the holiday club. I never thought your parents would go for it.'

'I was lucky to get time off from the farm. Dad wanted me to work. Mum insisted I did other stuff this summer than being covered in sheep shit.'

Kat flapped a hand in front of her face after closing the toilet door. 'Please note, I didn't make the stink. Can't you boys use the gents' toilet in the other block?'

'Sorry, Princess. I had a vicious curry last night.' Alex laughed as he laced his fingers behind his head. 'It's gone right through me.'

'Your sheep aren't the only ones that pong.' The net threatened to slip from Joe's grasp as he laughed.

Stevie returned from smoking outside. 'It smells like a rat crawled up someone's arse and died in there. Blokes are pigs.' She flicked the kettle on.

'I'll have a brew.' Joe said.

As he dropped the sack, balls tumbled around the room. Kat booted one away. The ball flew into the air and struck Joe's face.

'I'm so sorry!' Kat stroked a mark forming under his eye.

Joe squirmed. 'Ruddy hell. You've got a kick to rival Les Ferdinand.'

'Oh, your poor face!' She held up a pocket mirror. 'I hope it doesn't bruise badly.'

Joe prodded his cheek. Instead of checking the damage in his reflection, he fixed his hair.

'It's all right,' he said. 'I'll tell everyone I was boxing and you kissed the pain away afterwards.'

'Right. Ha ha.' Kat hurried to the kitchenette and turned on the tap over a heap of dirty mugs. 'Tea, anyone?' She concentrated on the washing-up bowl's contents.

Stevie blocked Kat's access to the sink. 'I was doing it.'

'Of course.' Kat flicked water from her fingers. 'Love the purple streaks, by the way.'

'On the packet, it was blue.' Stevie inspected strands of her hair. 'It'll do for now. I can't let The Clown image down.'

'I'm leaving before Kat shows off more football skills,' Joe said. 'Hey, as an apology, can you swap duties with Alex?'

'I'm in the sports hall with you today.'

Joe placed his chin on Kat's shoulder. 'Al hates doing crafts and you're brilliant at it.' He offered his best puppy dog eyes. 'Please, for me?'

A girlish giggle erupted from her mouth. 'OK.'

Stevie pushed between the couple. 'Get a room; preferably not this one. I'm trying to make a cuppa here.'

Alex stood. 'I'll check on Simon and then meet you there, Joe.'

Stevie tapped a teaspoon against her palm. 'Have you left Si doing registration on his own again? You lot are taking liberties with him.'

'He doesn't mind and never complains,' Alex replied.

'Because he's so nice. Stop abusing Si's good nature. If you keep taking advantage, he'll snap.'

'Chill out.' Kat said as she added tea bags to cups. 'Simon's a sweetie.'

'Be careful.' Stevie frowned. 'A person's well of kindness can run dry if they don't get any back.'

****

Despite Stevie's warning, Alex was glad to have escaped helping Simon. Registration was worse than a rugby scrum. Kids swooped, desperate to be registered so they could crack on with activities. Parents asked countless questions, checking on their little angels who turned into devils behind their backs. Simon dealt with everything. Guilt stabbed at Alex. He had to apologise.

Further up the corridor, Alex heard sobbing. The sound carried from the open doorway of what was usually the admin office. The primary school where the holiday club took place insisted offices were out of bounds.

'I don't want to like boys! It isn't normal. Dad will be so angry.' A boy's voice stumbled over the declaration.

While trying to stay upright, Alex's hands slid down the wall outside the office.

'Being gay isn't abnormal,' Simon's soothing voice replied. 'Ignorant people say nasty things, but they're lies. I get you don't want your parents to know. Believe me, I know dads can be difficult.'

Of course, Simon has a key to the office, Alex thought. None of the rest of The Six had the privilege and weren't aware their friend had access.

'I'm only thirteen,' the boy said. 'Perhaps I'll change and fancy girls.'

Simon cleared his throat. 'Maybe you will, maybe you won't. You have a long life ahead of you. Try not to live it in fear. I'm getting an adult helper so we can talk some more. Is that OK?'

Alex took the cue to leave. An undone shoelace had other ideas. He tilted and slammed against the wall.

'Are you all right?' Simon appeared outside.

'Should've done my boots up better.' Alex set to lacing them up. 'Sorry about not being there for registration.'

'No problem.'

Alex straightened. 'I feel bad about how you do all the stuff the rest of us hate.'

'There's one way you could make it up to me.'

'Which is?'

'A kid in there is struggling with his sexuality. I'm going to ask one of the adults for useful info. Reckon you'd be helpful, too.'

Alex forced a laugh. 'Not sure I'd be any use. Besides, I'm already late to meet Joe for the sports activities.'

As he turned to leave, Simon caught his arm.

'Please, Al. The boy doesn't have to know you're going through something similar.'

'We. Are. Not. The. Same.' Alex punctuated the five words with jabs at Simon's chest.

Simon stepped aside. 'Remember what happened in the changing rooms last term?'

'*Nothing* happened.' Alex bashed his fists against his thighs.

'You were kissing a lad.' Simon's voice dropped to a whisper. 'I haven't said anything, but I think–'

Alex's fist connected with Simon's face. He toppled to the ground. Blood trickled through Simon's fingers as he cradled his nose. Alex swung back his foot, ready to hurt a traitor. Screams made him stop. The boy Simon was helping wouldn't stop wailing.

Alex forced a smile while pulling his victim up from the floor. As Simon stood, Alex whispered into his ear. 'If you ever tell anyone I'm gay, you're dead.'

CHAPTER 13

Friday 20 August 2021

Alex stared at the photograph of him kissing a man in a club. The sweet peck between lovers made him smile. Tim should've been the man he settled down with, if only in private. Tim, however, refused to live a lie and had left the farmhouse for good. He didn't want to be known as only a farmhand any longer. Tim struggled to understand why Alex guarded his sexuality. Alex yelled at Tim as he was leaving not everyone can be loud and proud.

The ghosts of his father, grandfather, and the men before kept Alex straight, if only as a fantasy. He wasn't a city dweller, gaining confidence in a large gay community. Alex was a farmer living in a tiny village where people dictated how to live. In the past, he wondered if he'd misjudged the locals. Maybe they wouldn't care about him being gay. Perhaps some of them also hid their sexuality.

Another church visit killed Alex's hope of acceptance. He listened to another sermon from a sanctimonious vicar on the sins of homosexuality. The church was the social hub of the village. The Burtons always attended. Therefore, Alex did, too.

Gatherings after services became tests of endurance. Women praised the vicar for condemning "the gays" in a sinful, pleasure seeking world. Men gathered in packs; their masculinity challenged by the usual pint glass being replaced with a cup and saucer. While cracking homophobic jokes, they congratulated each other for putting up with perversion.

Tim attended the church only once. Alex shoved his angry partner outside before an argument began. Later, they discussed God and homosexuality. Tim tried to convince Alex not all Christians were backward and unloving. Tim's church in Bournemouth was an open and loving place, where sexuality rightfully wasn't a barrier to faith or acceptance. Alex didn't dare trust it. He declared having a private life made him happy. Even to his ears, it sounded false, let alone Tim's.

Alex's decision to stay in the village and at the farm meant he had to hide his true self. As the last remaining Burton, he'd let his ancestors down. There was no son; a new Farm Boy to inherit the farm. Years ago, he considered marrying a woman and going through the motions of making a family. It wasn't fair to make another person's existence a misery. Insomnia took hold as he worried about the future. Without an heir, Burton Farm was dead.

The river crashed below the bridge, demanding Alex's attention. The gut-churning thought of finding escape in the water entered his mind. Was Simon right to kill himself, if that's what happened?

In the last week of the holiday club, Simon was unsettled. No one knew why. The release of teenage angst and revealed truths caused an explosion on the last night. The shame at helping to set the fuse never left Alex. If he hadn't hit Simon, things would've been different. When the adult leaders threatened to throw Alex out, Simon said the fight was mutual. Alex didn't argue. Both agreed to supervision and staying away from each other. Alex was happy to do so until the fateful night at The Mill.

Inky dusk shunted pink tinged clouds from the night sky. The steel bridge railing cooled in Alex's grip. He held the photo, contemplating throwing it into the river. It wouldn't stop the blackmailer. There would be copies, no doubt put through the locals' letter boxes. He wondered if it could be to his advantage. The thought of forcibly coming out was terrifying, though. When a person had kept their life private for so long, it wasn't as simple as blurting out the truth. Alex hated himself for not being able to claim his true self. Ancestors who wouldn't have approved, an unforgiving village, and news of homophobic attacks kept him quiet. Alex was born too long ago, into a world that had taken too long to catch up. He vowed to see out the long weekend and keep his secret. Anyway, being with old friends wasn't a chore.

As Alex turned towards The Mill, he noticed a movement. Across a sprawling lawn stood a familiar house with a familiar woman outside. She was still alive. The former owner of the mill raised a hand. Alex rubbed the goosebumps rippling along his arms. He headed back across the bridge.

CHAPTER 14

Friday 20 August 2021 - The Witch

She'd been called The Witch for so long she only answered to the label. Even the postie who knew her real name called her The Witch. Those who dared to ask wondered if she was offended. She threw her head back and held onto her frail body until the laughter subsided. Why would she be hurt? Witches are powerful. They create magic and mystery.

Many tried to solve the mystery of her age. After entering her forties, her face had barely changed. Perhaps she *was* magical; preventing further wrinkles. The rest of her body, unfortunately, was immune to witchcraft and continued to fail.

Children sometimes knocked on her door as a dare. When The Witch appeared with a snarl, they ran. She enjoyed playing up to their fears. If people are afraid, they will stay out of your business. She was glad she didn't live in Burley where witchcraft was steeped in its history and being a witch made you a tourist's dream. The Witch was happy to be the only living legend in her area.

The name was given to her on account of her grey, frizzy hair and a hooked nose. It hardly meant she was a full-blown hag. She played the game, though. Decorators questioned her colour choice when painting her thatched cottage overlooking The Mill. She snapped at them to get on with it. Let the house be gingerbread. Let them make links with "Hansel and Gretel". Being a witch could be useful.

Fading hues of red, tinged with pink, covered the sky. Night came to claim the day. Being outside gave The Witch energy. The river running nearby was part of her daily flow. She refused to allow Simon's death to ruin it. The Mill, however, still cast a shadow of death. It once contained six people who each played a part in a boy's disappearance. The Witch had often listened outside to their conversations and arguments.

Despite her not wanting the building, inheritance is stubborn. She left the mill to ruin, ignoring The Six making it a playground. Applications for cafes, museums, and even demolition were refused. For years, The Mill stayed the same. The Witch didn't need money. She hardly ever left home and preferred simple pleasures.

All offers were declined until a barrister offered something more valuable than cash. Charlotte revealed the answer to a question The Witch had been asking since 1992. When she learnt the truth, worry vanished. After Charlotte became the owner of The Mill, The Witch found some peace.

She looked over at the bridge. Although he was larger, she recognised the broad shoulders and jutting ears. The man turned around, confirming his identity; Alex. Of course, she knew his name. For a while, she'd lived through The Six, enjoying friendships she'd never had.

Older Alex stared back. Their eyes locked. Although the approaching darkness made it hard to see his expression, Alex's nervousness was clear. The Witch considered it wasn't her he should fear. The person approaching him was the monster.

The Witch retreated inside her cottage. She wouldn't be a witness to horrifying events again. 1992 nearly finished her. She didn't tell the police the truth about Simon and Dylan. After exposing a killer, she would've surely been the next to die.

While some of it was the truth, the gossip about Dylan spiralled out of control. From the moment he arrived, searching for work, he was polite. She avoided strangers, but the man was mesmerising. Sure, he was handsome. Looks were never important to her, though. Dylan was a kindred spirit; seemingly dangerous, but with a well-intentioned heart.

In the shack by her house, he made it his own and did jobs on the land. After building the goat shed, he lovingly tended to the goats. The Witch paid him well. She enjoyed his company, although she didn't confess it. Since Dylan's unsolved murder, she remained alone.

The Six were back, minus Simon. She needed them to leave. Terrible things happened when they were around.

From her kitchen window, she took a last look at Alex. He smiled at someone he should've been running away from. The devil has many guises, including a person greeting Alex with open arms.

Closing the curtains, The Witch hoped it was enough to keep evil outside.

CHAPTER 15

Wednesday 5 August 1992

Kat swung her handbag at the towering nettles. She yelped. 'I've been stung!'

'Woman down!' Alex shouted.

Stinging nettles had been left to grow in the fields leading to the mill. It was obvious The Witch used them as a deterrent, but she hadn't figured on a determined bunch of teenagers.

From the front, Joe turned around. Concentrating on further nettle swashbuckling, Kat collided with him. He caught her in his arms, where she practically swooned; the rescued maiden in distress.

'Can you two get off with each other another time, please?' Stevie shouted from the back.

Kat jumped away from Joe's hold. 'Don't be rude. Joe's only helping.'

'Rub a dock leaf on it,' Erin said, standing behind. The overgrown path meant they could only walk in a line.

'I'm not putting plants on my skin.' Kat's eyes widened. 'A dog might've peed on it.'

'We told you to lift your arms up,' Alex added.

'I did.' She pouted. 'My arms aren't as long as yours.'

'Kudos, short arse.' Stevie pushed forward and raised her hand. Kat completed the high-five.

Maybe this girl isn't a complete airhead, Stevie thought. Kat was a member of The Pink Posse, a group of catty bitches who judged everyone. Stevie knew they'd originally created her nickname, The Clown. She didn't retaliate, caring little about anything, including herself. Stevie would never admit to anyone, let alone the bullies, her self-hatred. She embraced being the fool; the one who wore bright colours and kept everyone amused. At least no one would forget her.

Her hedonistic parents focused on free love. This should've meant their daughter received love in abundance. Unfortunately, they directed their affection towards the environment. A blade of grass received more attention than Stevie. Her parents only noticed her when it suited. She supplied food when they were chained to trees and painted placards for protests.

Kat thought she saw something in Stevie's expression; recognition. Being seen was usually threatening. For two years, Kat had worked hard to be part of The Pink Posse. Their humiliating demands confirmed her lowly place. Fetching drinks, doing their homework, and stealing were some of the orders. Kat had believed being a dogsbody was better than being known as the council estate girl.

'Let's get a move on before The Witch sees,' Simon said. 'She'll be angry with us for breaking in.'

Alex patted his shoulder. 'Chill out. She's seen Joe and me go inside before and said nothing.'

'I reckon she can't speak.' Joe stood at the front, leading them once more.

'Of course she can,' Simon replied.

Joe halted. Intent on checking the rising sting bumps on her arm, Kat slammed into him. Simon stepped aside before the domino effect continued.

'How do you know The Witch can speak?' Erin asked. 'Have you spoken to her?'

'A boy from school's dad is the postman here,' Simon began. 'He says The Witch always snaps at him for making her sign for parcels.'

'Bet those packages contain body parts.' Stevie cackled like the proverbial witch.

Kat looked at the gingerbread house and then over at the mill. 'I don't want to go in there now. Let's go to Bournemouth instead. I'd rather be at the beach, anyway. A load of people from school are down there tonight.'

'The last bus went ages ago,' Stevie said. 'Pisses me off how shit the bus service is here. It's what we get for living in a backward town.'

'Don't worry.' Joe pulled Kat close. 'I'll protect you from The Witch.'

Ignoring the nettles, Simon pushed past them. 'She's not a witch, so there's nothing to be afraid of. Get over it.'

The others were silent. Simon had become snappy recently. Whenever they mentioned it, he bit back. Instead, they focused on the mill. Although Joe and Alex had visited before, its ability to stay standing was impressive.

The Witch had taken measures to board over broken windows. Recently, fencing appeared around the building. Joe couldn't swear to it, but he believed she liked them being there. What he thought was a secret entrance hadn't been closed off. Alex and Joe had found a note nearby stating they could visit as long as it didn't disturb The Witch.

Reluctant to admit the woman frightened him, Alex hid his relief. He didn't believe she was an actual witch, but she made him nervous. When The Witch stared, her eyes drilled into his core. Alex always looked away.

Joe removed the rocks covering a hole dug under the fencing. So far, no one else had discovered the tunnel. Lying on his stomach, he shimmied through a dip in the earth. On the other side of the fence, The Leader beckoned to the rest of the group.

'I'm not crawling in the dirt like an animal!' Kat clutched the fabric of her baby doll dress. 'The satin will tear.'

'Why is your underwear on the outside?' Alex sniggered.

Kat put her hands on her hips. 'It's fashion, dickhead. Haven't you seen Kylie Minogue's videos?'

'Many times and not just for the songs, right lads?' Joe laughed. 'Kylie's hot.'

Kat grinned as if she was the singer, accepting the compliment. 'I bet you'd never tell a popstar to cover up.'

'As if I'd meet Kylie in Trillhaven,' Alex replied.

Stevie untied a jumper from around her waist. 'Put this on, Princess. I don't care if it gets dirty.'

As Kat handled the garment, her upper lip curled.

Stevie shook her head. 'You only have to wear it to tunnel through. No one else will see you wearing something so awful.'

Before pulling it over her head, Kat sniffed the jumper. She stroked the sleeves, softer than the itchy polyester The Pink Posse favoured.

'Thank you,' she said before lowering to the ground. 'No one look at my knickers!'

'Damn it.' Joe's smile stretched across his face. 'I should've gone after to appreciate the view.'

'Don't be a perv,' Simon said. 'Go ahead, Kat, we'll turn away.'

Scuttling like a sea lion, Kat whinged throughout. Upon reaching the other side, she whooped. 'I did it!'

'Careful,' Stevie replied. 'You're in danger of enjoying yourself.'

Stevie dropped to the dusty earth and crawled commando style. Her harem pants were filthy. It didn't matter, considering she did the washing at home. Her parents wore the same clothes until they fell apart. Their suspicions about harmful chemicals in toiletries, particularly deodorants, meant Stevie never invited anyone home.

Erin remained silent as she pushed through the tunnel. She needed The Six. Making a fuss would make her look pathetic. After leaving Trillhaven to live in Blandford, she realised how spiteful she'd been. Even The Pink Posse avoided her.

No one understood Erin wasn't inherently bad. Tina, her mum, was a promiscuous alcoholic who used her looks to get what she wanted. Devoid of parental love, Erin sought affection elsewhere. A pixie haircut highlighting razor cheekbones and full lips made her a catch. Like her mum, Erin had used boys and humiliated girls to boost her self-esteem.

When Tina began a relationship with Dylan, Erin expected disaster. Naturally, they met in a pub. What should've been a one-night-stand stretched further. Dylan was staying with friends, although he spent most of the time at the Sullivans' house. Tina's attraction to him was obvious. He was more handsome than her usual rough-and-ready type. She ran her hands through his thick hair and cooed over dreamy brown eyes.

At the end of the fortnight, Erin braced herself for Tina's tears and drunken tantrums at saying goodbye. Instead, Tina announced they were moving to Blandford with Dylan. Erin didn't protest. A fresh start couldn't come soon enough. She became a model student. Friendships were lacking, though. Teenagers often set relationships in stone from primary school.

Despite the circumstances, returning to Trillhaven offered a chance to try again. Dylan had committed a crime. Erin wouldn't pay for it. She already knew the other members of The Six in varying degrees. Thankfully, only one of them had been on the receiving end of Erin's previous mischief. She decided to make amends with Stevie. Before, they'd competed for the role of school slut, a label both once viewed as a compliment. Erin needed to kill the reputation. She deserved better. She had a feeling Stevie could relate.

Erin viewed Kat as a friendly prospect. She was obviously lost and searching for somewhere to belong. The boys were nice enough, although Alex's and Joe's laddish behaviour could be tiring. Simon was kind to the core. Erin craved kindness.

After taking Simon's hand, he startled at her touch. They waited while the group stepped through a low window, visible underneath a partially pulled away board.

'Are you OK?' Simon asked. 'Stay with me if you're worried about the dark.' He held up a torch.

'It's not the dark that's scary,' Erin replied. 'I'm afraid I've blown it with everyone. They'll never forget how awful I used to be.'

He squeezed Erin's hand. 'They're already giving you a second chance. Sometimes, you let the scary thoughts take over.'

Erin gave a bitter laugh. 'I'm The Thinker, right?'

'Stick with me.' Simon clasped her hand tighter. 'Nothing bad will happen to you.'

Erin knew Simon couldn't be her rescuer. No one could fight Dylan, let alone a boy who wasn't quite a man. Dylan refused to let go of Erin and her mum. Although Dylan and Tina never married, he swore an oath: only in death would they part. Tina and Erin would pay for leaving him on 3 July 1992.

CHAPTER 16

3 July 1992

Tina was a whirlwind, shoving things into bags and suitcases. 'Hurry up, Erin!' she yelled from the kitchen. 'He'll be home soon.'

The clock confirmed they had an hour at most. Dylan stayed at the pub longer than before. Tina couldn't rely on guesswork. As soon as he'd left the house, she sprang into action. Not telling her daughter the plan in advance proved to be a mistake. Tina feared Erin might have let something slip. Erin's confusion at the sudden departure slowed them down. She demanded answers.

As Tina entered the lounge, she sighed at the girl lying on the sofa.

'I'm not moving,' Erin began. 'Not until you explain why we're going.'

'Dylan ain't innocent. He killed Nick.'

Erin sat up. 'But… but… You were together that night. You drove to the beach to go for a walk.'

'I'm sorry. I lied to the coppers to give Dylan an alibi. He begged me to do it, swearing he was helping a friend when Nick died. Stupid bastard wouldn't say who it was.'

'Perhaps he *was* helping someone,' Erin mumbled, while chewing her thumbnail.

Dylan often helped waifs and strays. Tina despaired at the dodgy people he brought back for a meal. While keeping his past secret, he claimed to have something in common with such people. Dylan wasn't a saint, though. The habit of losing his temper after a few drinks increased. He'd never lashed out at Tina or Erin. With them, he was always sweet, maybe too sweet. The relationship had moved fast. Tina was paying the price for infatuation. Nick's death had cleared her love-blinded vision.

After delivering the local paper each evening, Nick lingered at their house to chat. Being in between jobs, Dylan grew bored and enjoyed the company while Tina worked at the supermarket. Since leaving the army, Dylan hadn't caught a break. The dream he sold Tina of security and contentment never materialised. While she dealt with irate customers, he worked on projects, usually involving parts scattered everywhere. When they met, she thought he was The One. Dylan promised a new life, a different town, and a better future. Like the gadgets he pulled apart, he tinkered with the Sullivans' lives and left them in pieces.

Many times Tina warned Dylan spending time with Nick wasn't healthy. Dylan accused her of having a twisted mind; making friendship with a boy into something sordid. On one occasion, when Nick was still there hours past delivering the paper, Tina told him to leave. Jealousy made her mad. Dylan didn't laugh like that with her anymore. Eventually, she realised she had nothing in common with him. Their relationship was based on attraction and lacked a deeper connection. Tina couldn't end it, though. She'd given up so much, uprooting her child from their hometown.

Tina now despaired at her daughter not moving fast enough. 'Erin, you need to accept what everyone's saying. Dylan killed Nick.'

'The police didn't charge him after the questioning.'

The mother smiled at her child's innocence, hoping she'd hold on to it in the coming days. In her bedroom, Tina took out the item hidden in the wardrobe. She gagged at its feel in her hand.

'I found this,' Tina said as she returned to the lounge.

Erin stood. 'Why have you got that?'

The colour drained from her face. Her mum held the cap Nick always wore. They often teased him about wearing matching clothing bearing his initials.

Tina pinched the cap's peak between two fingers. 'I was trying to sort out the crap in the garage. The cap fell away from behind when I shifted the filing cabinet.'

'Is it...' Erin leaned in to get a closer look. 'There's blood!' A rusty stain was on the peak of the cap. 'We have to get rid of it and then leave.' Erin headed for the stairs. 'Really, we should go to the police, but I don't feel safe. Wily would go nuts if we shopped his brother.'

Both shuddered at the thought. Everyone called him Wily because of his devious behaviour. He was on his third wife and seventh child, officially anyway. The handsome, rugged looks he shared with Dylan guaranteed Wily female attention. His love of violence and misguided family loyalty meant he had a revolving door to prison. If Erin and Tina had given the police Nick's cap, they would've signed their own death warrants.

'Where are we going?' Erin asked as she reached the top of the stairs.

'Back to Trillhaven. My sister said we can live with her for a while.'

'Seriously?'

Tina threw her hands up. 'It's the best I can do. Be grateful someone's putting us up. I don't have any savings and now, no job.'

'What about Paige? She'll let us stay at hers, what with being your best friend.'

'Her gaff is full of the kiddies she keeps popping out. Trillhaven will have to do.'

'Won't Dylan go there?'

'I'm fairly sure he'll leave us alone. I know enough about the jobs he's been doing with Wily. They won't want the coppers learning about it.'

Tina was wrong. Nothing stood in Dylan's way. He would have followed them to the ends of the earth. Thankfully for Dylan, he only had to go as far as Trillhaven.

CHAPTER 17

Saturday 21 August 2021

After breakfast, the group met outside The Mill. The temperature soared, threatening a record for the hottest day of the year. 1992's summer days were perfect for working at the holiday club, followed by cooler evenings in the mill. As adults, the heat wasn't as welcome. The group prepared to go for a walk, hoping to find one of their missing friends.

'Alex isn't answering his phone.' Joe flicked the Aviator sunglasses from his head and onto his nose. 'The receptionist has also tried and I've knocked on his door.'

Erin sought shade under the awning attached to the building. 'I've messaged him. No reply so far.'

'Are we going for this walk or not?' Stevie wiped her hand across her forehead, trying to sort out her sweat-glued fringe. 'I'm ginger and standing in one place makes me a sun trap. I'm not made for a heatwave.'

Joe gave a wink. 'I said to Simon back then I reckoned you were ginger. He wondered why you were embarrassed, as he didn't care about being a redhead. Did you dye your hair weird colours to hide the natural colour?'

LISA SELL

Stevie placed a straw hat on her head while glaring at Joe. 'Hardly. I enjoyed being the colourful Clown. I'm covering up now because I don't want to frazzle. Not ashamed.'

As was their way in 1992, Joe led the rest of the group. Gone were the high nettles and weeds overtaking the narrow path. Under Charlotte's ownership, her grounds were full of neat gardens and freshly mown lawns. The path was only used by staff and guests. Joe paused on the bridge while the others waited behind him. Once again, they followed The Leader.

Erin shielded her eyes from the sun's glare to look at the gingerbread house. 'I wonder if she still lives there. Surely, she isn't alive.'

'Who?' Joe asked.

'The Witch. Remember how she often watched us? Alex was terrified of her!'

They joined in laughter.

'The giant Farm Boy being scared of an old lady was hilarious.' Kat chuckled. 'Apart from making me swear I'd never allow my hair to go grey, The Witch never bothered me.'

Joe leaned on the railing. 'You might not be grey, but you've let the rest of you go to seed. No longer the Princess, eh?'

'What a horrible thing to say to your wife!' Erin nudged her elbow into Joe's ribs.

Kat forced a smile.

'She knows I'm only teasing,' Joe said. 'It's what we do, right, darling?'

No, Kat thought, *we don't. If I mentioned you're balding, have a beer belly, and a forest of nasal and ear hairs, you'd sulk for weeks.*

70

Erin touched Kat's arm. 'You're beautiful, Kat. You always were and still are our Princess. I wish I had your gorgeous eyes. Your smile is infectious. Seeing your face helped me make it through the memorial.'

'Thank you,' Kat almost whispered to her feet.

Joe slammed his hands on the bridge's railing. 'Enough of the mutual appreciation society.'

'I'm surprised you haven't smothered him in his sleep,' Stevie whispered to Kat.

The women grinned. Joe was an egotistic teenager, but he still had cheeky charm. The older version had changed.

Joe ramped up the mean man act for a reason. He didn't want to go on the walk or be at The Mill. Although they were once good friends, he was in no hurry to find Alex. His absence was a blessing. Despite their earlier banter, Alex's presence was an uncomfortable reminder of The Six's last evening together.

Teenage Alex had approached Joe, who'd drifted into drunken sleep. Joe misunderstood the boy's intentions in leaning over. Ever outspoken, Joe wasted no time shouting that Alex tried to kiss him. Ignoring his friend's obvious hurt, Joe made a string of homophobic jokes and poked fun. Later, Joe destroyed Simon's dreams. It was quite the night. The events of a few hours impacted upon all of them forever.

Now, Joe pretended to care about searching for Alex. The past should stay there. Damning evidence sent in the post with a command to stay at The Mill meant he had to stay. If the others discovered what he'd done, Joe would lose everything.

CHAPTER 18

Saturday 21 August 2021

Kat typed the key code into a box next to the gate, allowing access beyond Charlotte's property. As Kat entered the last digit, Joe clamped his fingers around her forearm.

'I was about to do it,' he said.

Kat shoved him aside. A strange boldness had taken hold of her. At The Mill with the gang, she rediscovered elements of her younger self. Although not a highly confident teenager, she had felt secure. Having real friends in The Six rather than the fake Pink Posse gave her a sense of belonging.

Watching the others walk through as she kept the gate open, Kat assessed them. They were older and possibly different people. Were they still friends after this long? The gate clanged behind her as she let go.

'Flaming hell!' Joe yelled. 'Why don't you announce to The Witch we're nearby?'

Kat folded her arms. 'You've done a good enough job by shouting your gob off.'

'Oooh, are you afraid of the big, bad witch?' Stevie made claws of her fingers, digging into Joe's shoulder.

Adjusting his shirt, he moved away. 'The Witch didn't scare me then and certainly doesn't now.'

'I'm boiling.' Erin swiped her forehead with her hand. 'Perhaps we should see if Alex has turned up at The Mill instead?'

'Are you getting tired of being on your feet?' Kat asked. 'Carrying a pregnancy load is exhausting. If you want, I'll go back with you.'

Joe kicked against the dry earth. 'Make up your minds what you're doing.'

Erin touched Kat's arm. 'I'm fine. I brought a bottle of water. Exercise is good for the baby and me.'

'You carry it better than I did,' Kat replied. 'I was huge with all my kids.' She turned to her husband as he held up his hands in mock surrender.

'I didn't say a word!' Joe grinned.

'I know what you were going to say.'

Joe kept his arms up as he backed away. He stopped, looked at the ground, and shook his foot. 'What the…? I don't sodding well believe it!'

'Ew!' Stevie scurried away. 'He's stepped in horse mess.'

The others stopped laughing at Joe to turn towards Stevie.

'Horse *mess*?' Erin repeated. 'What happened to sweary Stevie?'

She grinned. 'Nowadays, I rein it in, although the occasional swear word slips out. Someone's always watching.'

'Sounds like a conspiracy,' Erin replied.

Joe swiped the side of his shoe on a patch of grass. 'Stop gassing and help me sort this literal shit out.'

'You'll have to bin those.' Stevie pointed at beige suede shoes blotted brown.

'They're bespoke from Rome!' he wailed.

Stevie shrugged. 'Go to Primark. If your clothing's only a few quid, you don't care when it gets ruined.'

'Let's keep moving.' Kat looked behind her. 'Joe, stay at the back so we don't have to smell you.' She hid her smile at taking over from The Leader.

Wild grasses, trees, and weeds filled the landscape. The wilderness seemed even wilder against The Mill's gardened land. This was the area they'd known and loved; The Six's former paradise.

Erin stopped and pointed. 'It's still here!'

They looked over at a shed made of corrugated iron, held together by rust and luck.

'What is that heap?' Joe asked.

'The Witch's goat shed,' Erin replied.

'Oh, yes!' Stevie cried. 'The goats often ran at us. Remember when one butted Simon and he landed on his backside?'

'The waft of goat stench was strong in the summer.' Kat tilted her nose and sniffed. 'I can't smell them.'

'I shouldn't think so,' Erin said. 'Nothing could live in there. It looks ready to topple.'

Joe pushed ahead of the women. 'Maybe Alex went in to see his old friends. He loved those goats.'

Kat watched the others move ahead. 'I'm not going in there. It looks set to fall down.'

After booting one of the metal walls, Joe grinned. 'Still standing. Whoever constructed this did a good job.'

'Probably Dylan.' Erin's voice dropped to a whisper.

Stevie squeezed her hand. 'Sorry. It's insensitive not checking if you're OK being here, especially in your condition.'

'I'll be all right. This long weekend is for making peace with the past. Unfortunately, Dylan is part of it. I don't want to go inside, though.'

'I'll stay here with you,' Kat said.

Joe squared his shoulders. 'No problem. I'll check. If Alex is sitting inside this shithole rather than enjoying The Mill's bar, I'll be the first to take the piss.'

He wrenched open the battered metal door. In the gloom, broken furniture, paint pots, and building materials came into view. There was no need for a lock when storing rubbish. A line of light appeared over Joe's shoulder.

'Where did you get that from?' He pointed to the pen light Stevie was holding.

'I'm a proper girl scout; always prepared. This may be small, but like me, it's a pocket rocket. Not the size that counts, right? It's what you always said, and not only about your height.'

He grimaced, likely remembering the rumours about *Small Dick Joe*. Such things happened after sleeping with girls and dumping them the next day.

'Alex isn't in here.' Joe headed for the doorway. 'Let's join those two nattering outside.'

Stevie caught his arm. 'Wait up,' she said.

The torch revealed a double wardrobe. Whoever lugged it into the shed must have been strong. Along with its huge width, the wardrobe almost reached the ceiling. Mould infested the wood. Stevie moved towards a note tacked to one of the wardrobe doors.

'What does it say?' Joe watched her unpin the piece of paper.

She held the light above the note and read aloud, '"Finally, I can come out of the closet. To have lived with this secret wasn't fair on me or others. To die is a kindness. I'm killing with kindness."'

'What the hell does it mean?' Joe gave a shaky laugh.

Stevie reached for the wardrobe handle, telling herself she would not be afraid. She would fear no evil. Yet, she did.

She opened the door. The torch clattered to the ground. Stevie fell onto her back. Darkness embraced her. Her chest was heavy. Fear wasn't the only dead weight on her body. A corpse was lying on Stevie, too.

CHAPTER 19

Wednesday 19 August 1992

Simon scowled as he read the phrase written on sugar paper. 'Killing with Kindness? That's not the theme.'

Alex looked at his group's banner. Kindness Day wore on his nerves. Many kids tried to outdo each other in volume. He wasn't sure if his tetchiness was due to having a hangover or because everyone was being so nice. An adult helper decided a day dedicated to kindness was overdue. Continual fights between the locals and neighbouring village kids were getting out of hand. The kindness lessons were undoubtedly also for Simon and Alex after their argument. Simon let everyone believe he'd fought back. Since then, they'd stayed away from each other. Evenings with The Six were uncomfortable. Alex ignored his former friend's efforts to make up. The pathetic boy was unbearable sometimes. No one was ever that nice. Simon's sneering at Alex's group's slogan: *Killing with Kindness* proved it.

A girl held up the banner. 'It *is* about kindness. We discussed how kindness has different meanings. Some animals have to be put down because they're poorly and it's kind to kill them.'

A boy threatened to burst into tears again, despite Alex explaining earlier his cat would probably live a while longer. Perhaps the concept of killing with kindness was too deep for the youngsters. Alex couldn't back down. Simon didn't have the monopoly on defining kindness.

Alex prodded a girl. 'We also discussed how killing with kindness can mean what else, Whitney?'

There were many children at the holiday club whose names came from their parents' love of music. At registration, Alex tried to keep a straight face when signing in Elton and Sting. He never mentioned this to Stevie, named by Fleetwood Mac fans.

Five-year-old Whitney cleared her throat as she prepared to give her rehearsed line. 'Killing with kindness is when we can be too kind and...' Whitney's bottom lip wobbled, '... mother people with kindness.'

'*Smother*, you dickhead!' an older boy yelled while the rest of the group laughed.

Whitney ran out of the hall, bawling at getting the word wrong again. An adult supervisor chased after the child.

'Brad.' Alex congratulated himself on not calling the boy *Brat* again by "accident". 'Remember, we're being kind today. Apologise to Whitney.'

Erin, Stevie, Kat, and Joe were occupied with their groups, staying out of Simon and Alex's unusual feud. The past few evenings at the mill had been tense, filled with either spiteful comments or them ignoring each other.

Alex followed Simon as he went back to his group. Their chosen slogan, *Kindness Wins,* shone in neon on the banner. Alex grabbed his ribs as he chuckled.

'What?' Simon forced a smile.

'Does it really?' Alex jabbed at the words. Fluorescent orange paint covered his finger. 'Does kindness win if it's all a fake act?'

Simon was silent. The children in his group looked to their expert in kindness. He concentrated on scuffing his trainers against each other.

'That's a low blow.' Simon's voice quivered.

'Look, I'm fed up with arguing. I'm sorry I–'

'Get off my case! I won't allow you to keep riling me. Why are you always trying to prove you're such a bloke?'

'At least I don't have pink flowers.' Alex pointed at the fresh blooms arranged in a vase. 'Bit poofy, isn't it?'

'Knock it off with the gay bashing. Besides, pink tulips signify caring.'

Alex folded his arms. 'We'll stick with our bad ass version of kindness, thanks very much.'

Simon approached him and leaned in towards his ear. 'You may be right,' Simon whispered. 'Maybe killing with kindness *is* the way to go. Being nice is getting me nowhere, especially with you. Perhaps I should smother *you* with kindness. Maybe then you'll see who I really am.'

CHAPTER 20

Saturday 21 August 2021

Stevie rolled away. If the body stayed on top of her a minute longer, she would never recover. Her screams pounded the metal walls. Erin and Kat ran inside.

'Please God, no!' Stevie rocked on the dusty floor. Her cries became whimpers.

Joe remained silent. The body demanded his attention. Alex was lying on his back. Blood stained his clothes. Open arms splayed across the floor exposed slashed wrists.

'No. Not him!' Erin clasped her stomach.

Kat adopted mother crisis mode. It was way beyond a child with colic or a teenager's issues, though. All she could do was call for paramedics who had no chance of reviving Alex.

As she lowered towards Stevie, Erin grunted against the weight of her belly. 'Come on, sweetheart. Staying here won't help.'

Emerging from a nightmare, Stevie blinked several times. 'Yes, of course. There are things to arrange.' She stood to take out her mobile from her pocket.

Erin placed a hand over the phone. 'Kat's contacting the emergency services.'

'Good, good.' Stevie paced. 'Does anyone know who Alex's relatives are?'

'I'm not sure,' Erin replied. 'Who's at the farm? We need to tell them.'

'Shut up!' Joe threw his hands up. 'Stop spouting useless crap when our friend is dead!'

Erin stroked his shoulder. 'We're devastated, too.'

She glanced at her old friend and decided not to remember him that way. Whenever the image entered her mind, she would replace it with the wide smile of friendly Farm Boy. The thriller fiction Erin wrote coming true made her shiver. Alex's death had happened recently. They'd been with him the previous evening. Decay wasn't the only thing assaulting Erin's nostrils. Alex's earlier pain and fear lingered in the air.

Joe held the note removed from the wardrobe door and began reading it aloud. '"Finally, I can come out of the closet."'

'We have to leave,' Stevie said. 'Talking about Al while he's there isn't right.'

'He can hardly be offended now!' Joe yelled.

Erin clasped his arm. 'Let's wait for the services with Kat.'

Outside, the three stood together, joining in grief and shock.

'Alex was gay.' Stevie broke the silence.

Joe moved away. 'Of course he was. Doesn't take an expert to figure it out.'

'I wasn't aware, not that it matters,' she replied.

'When we were younger, he tried to hide it,' Joe began. 'Simon and I suspected. Alex changed the subject whenever anything about being gay was mentioned.'

'None of us would've had a problem with it,' Erin added.

'Alex's village, which is stuck in the Dark Ages, might have,' Stevie said. 'I remember what it was like there. It probably hasn't changed much. I've seen it from working in those kinds of places, too. They're so backward, judgemental, and cruel. Did Alex think this was his only option? We've failed him.'

'Like with Simon.' Erin clutched her arms at her waist.

'We don't know for certain Simon committed suicide,' Joe said.

'Please don't use the word *committed*,' Kat began. 'It harks back to suicide being wrongly viewed as a crime.'

He flicked a hand at her as if swatting a fly. 'Whatever. I couldn't give a shit about being politically correct. I just want Alex to be alive.'

Stevie turned to Erin. 'I'm surprised he did it inside the wardrobe, but I guess it makes sense with what the note says. Still, it seems dramatic for Alex.'

'The flower is weird, too,' Erin added.

'Damn it!' Stevie smacked her forehead. 'I think I touched it when, you know... Alex was holding it.'

A memory of kindness banners at the holiday club popped into Erin's head. She'd tried to keep out of Simon and Alex's argument. It ended with Alex's snide remark about Simon's pink tulips. As she considered the same flower lying by Alex's body, Erin tried to remember what pink tulips signified. Surely it was a coincidence. She retreated to share with her unborn child how she hoped Alex was at peace. He was a good person. Simon was decent, too. Both were gone; two out of six. No. Erin, The Thinker, couldn't consider the connection. It was too horrific.

83

CHAPTER 21

Saturday 21 August 2021

Charlotte watched the police car leave. Everyone had shared what they knew about Alex, which was little. The old friends had been apart too long. When she was younger, Charlotte liked Alex, but he seemed distant.

The group struggled with thoughts of their friend suffering because of his sexuality. Charlotte knew how difficult coming out of the closet could be. Considering Alex's suicide note, perhaps it was in poor taste to use the term. She decided to phone Harriet before going to bed. There was comfort in knowing her wife waited in London. Until then, Charlotte had work to do; resurrecting the past and making others acknowledge it.

She considered how Simon also possibly died because of a secret. Throughout their questioning, she wondered what the police were trying not to say. Being an accomplished barrister made her a skilled reader of body language. The police officers' questions regarding Simon confirmed they'd also recognised the connection. The rest of The Six attending the memorial and staying at The Mill were catalysts. It wasn't the end. Charlotte knew she couldn't stop things from happening. Closing the B&B and sending the group home would be traitorous to her brother. She needed answers from the rest of The Six.

After finishing another scotch, Joe's hand trembled. He slammed the tumbler on the bar and clicked his fingers. The steward's eyes shifted over to Charlotte, watching from the entrance.

'I don't need permission!' Joe drawled. 'Pour me a drink.'

While he faced the bar, Charlotte nodded to the bar steward. Under her boss's gaze, Donna straightened her collar and obeyed.

With his glass filled, Joe stumbled towards Kat and Erin sitting in a corner. 'Where's Stevie?' He landed on the sofa, slamming against Kat.

'She's getting changed.' Erin was sitting opposite. 'She couldn't bear being in the same clothes.'

Joe looked down at his shirt and sneered. 'Who cares? Death never goes, no matter how much you change and scrub.'

'How do you know?' Charlotte joined them.

'Ask the famous author.' He pointed at Erin. 'She got rich writing about people's deaths.'

'Fiction is fantasy. This is real and bloody heartbreaking.' Erin dragged the back of her hand across her tear-filled eyes.

Kat reached over to a table set for the next day's breakfast diners. She removed the ring holding a linen napkin, flicked it out, and offered it to Erin.

'Ignore him, Erin.' Kat glared at her husband. 'I understand you're devastated, Joe. We all are. Ease up on the drinking and the nastiness. Now is the time to pull together, not fall apart.'

Joe slumped over the arm of the velvet sofa. 'The Six were never a team. After what we did to Simon, you and I are aware of it, Katrina.'

Kat glanced at Charlotte and then Erin. 'We were silly teenagers.' A nervous laugh trickled from Kat's mouth. 'One minute we fancied someone, the next, someone else. It was all nonsense.'

'Our marriage is nonsense?' Joe's volume rose.

'Simon really liked you, Kat.' Charlotte avoided Joe's stare. 'He confessed when I caught him staring at you. When I mentioned it, he was so embarrassed. Hey, you might have married my brother if The Leader hadn't turned on the charm.'

Joe banged a fist against his chest, Tarzan style. 'That's me; dazzling ladies with my Grecian good looks and sparkling personality.'

'Whatever.' Kat rolled her eyes. 'Go to bed. You're drunk.'

Joe swayed as he stood. Standing upright on the smooth oak floor had already proved to be a challenge. 'I'm not staying here a second longer! The police can't tell *me* what to do. I'll leave whenever I want.' He turned out empty trouser pockets.

Kat grabbed his wallet and phone from the table. She jingled a set of keys. 'You're not going anywhere. The police asked us to stay so they can take full statements tomorrow. They spared us by not doing it today.'

'Alex killed himself!' Joe's face drew close to his wife. Spit flew from his mouth and landed on her. 'Case closed. Give me the keys!'

Kat hid them behind her back. Joe lunged. Charlotte shoved him aside. She backed away from the snarling man and looked over at the bar steward. 'Donna, call security.'

Kat shouted over. 'Please don't. Sometimes, he drinks too much, particularly when under stress. Unfortunately, it makes him behave like a dick.'

Donna put down the phone and gave her boss an intense look. Charlotte nodded.

'I've had enough of this,' Joe slurred. 'I'm off to bed.'

As he swerved around the furniture, the others grabbed their glasses. After holding up a hand, Joe headed for the stairs.

'I'm glad I closed the bar to the public tonight.' Charlotte took a seat. 'He'll probably be ashamed facing us tomorrow. Please excuse me for asking this, Kat. Does Joe hurt you? He looked like he was ready to punch you.'

Kat gave a jaded laugh. 'My husband has *many* faults. Domestic violence isn't one of them. Sometimes, he can't let go of The Leader image.'

'What the hell happened to the cheeky and likeable lad?' Erin asked. 'Even before we found Alex, Joe seemed on edge. The way he talks to you isn't right. When we were younger, he treated you like, well, a princess.'

'Joe knocked me off the pedestal. With every child, I lost him a little more. He can't cope with responsibility and wants to be sixteen forever. I worry Alex's death is going to cause Joe a lot of harm.'

'I can't believe Alex is gone,' Charlotte added. 'Although Simon fell out with him at the holiday club, they were such good friends before. Whenever Dad wasn't around, Alex and Joe came over to play on our console. Alex was so sweet, making sure I didn't feel left out.'

Erin leaned back to check towards the stairs. 'Where on earth is Stevie?'

'Give her a few more minutes,' Kat said. 'She's struggling. I would too if a body fell on me.'

'I'll never un-see it,' Erin replied, 'of Alex, like…'

Charlotte frowned. 'I can call for a doctor if you need one.'

'We're doing fine. There's a fighter in here.' Erin stroked her bump.

'It's such a wonderful thing you're doing,' Kat said. 'Being a surrogate with a first pregnancy is amazing. Do you worry you'll struggle to hand over the baby to Gemma?'

'I've never been maternal, but I'm not unfeeling. I love this child because it's part of me and will be in my wider family. Long ago, I decided not to have kids. You know how awful my mum was, particularly with the whole Dylan thing.' Erin's voice softened. 'None of the men I've met have been worth settling down with. Being single means I can focus on *my* needs. I'm selfish, I guess.'

'No one who's a surrogate is selfish,' Kat said. 'Simon would be so proud of your kindness.'

'Thank you.'

Charlotte pointed behind them. 'Here she is.'

'We were worried about you!' Erin cried. 'Come and join us.'

'I'm feeling better now.' Stevie adjusted her clothing. She moved her hands away. A slipped halo ringed her neck. Wearing the work uniform gave Stevie more control. The rebel Clown became a vicar.

CHAPTER 22

Thursday 20 August 1992

Dylan snatched the bottle of vodka after Simon took a sip. 'Enough booze for tonight. I can hear the noise from here. I understand kids want to have fun. Alcohol isn't always the way. I've seen the damage it can do.'

Simon looked around the shack. His garden shed was bigger, but somehow Dylan made the place homely. A poster of Iron Maiden's *Number of the Beast* album cover gave a clue about the man's musical taste. There were a few photos above the bed; strangers Dylan wouldn't name. The mysterious man gave little away. He didn't hide his past with Erin, though. A picture of her smiling, along with Tina, was central.

Before they'd left for Blandford, Simon sometimes saw Tina staggering around Trillhaven. If anyone saw her in public with her mum, Erin always scarpered. Tina's alcoholism and wild behaviour was often the subject of town gossip. Simon didn't judge Erin for being ashamed. He would've given anything to have a different father.

'Do you believe in God?' Simon asked.

'Why are you asking about that?'

'The Six were talking about it tonight.'

'It's a deep conversation for a bunch of teenagers.' Dylan sat on a rickety wicker chair and rested his feet on a crate. Everything in his home was mismatched or at the point of breaking.

'God talk makes a change from listening to Joe perving over girls. Stevie said God probably doesn't exist, but if God is real, she's definitely female.' Simon chuckled.

'Stevie sounds like quite a character. I'm not sure about religion.' Dylan leaned back and scraped his hair into a ponytail. 'If there is a God, He or She hates me.'

'It's not fair you have to hide when you've done nothing wrong.'

'I might've killed the boy and be lying. Why do you believe me?'

Simon shrugged. 'Intuition. Everyone reckons I'm a pushover because I'm nice. Earlier, the others joked if God exists, I'd be made a saint.' Simon kicked out at a nest of tables in front of him.

'Easy!' Dylan shouted. 'There's hardly anything in here as it is. Don't wreck it.'

'Sorry. I don't know who I am anymore.' Simon flushed. 'This anger is scary. My whole life I've been decent to people and barely get anything back. You're not supposed to be kind and expect anything from it, though.'

Dylan rested a tobacco tin on one knee and a packet of Rizlas on the other. 'I bet even Mother Teresa had days when she thought people were ungrateful bastards. No one's totally good. We all have darkness inside of us. Some are better at hiding it. Skilful liars can make people believe anything.'

'Do you think I'm a liar?' Simon clasped his hands together.

After licking the paper, Dylan sealed the cigarette. He brushed off curls of tobacco from his jeans.

'Everyone lies,' he said, 'even you. Only The Witch and I know about your visits here. I haven't told anyone how I found you stumbling, drunk as a skunk.'

Simon blushed. The second night at the mill, Erin brought some strong gin from Tina's stash. Simon drank more than he'd intended. After leaving, he struggled to stand, ending in tripping over a tree root. Someone stood outside the shack. A strange boldness took the boy over as he approached. Dylan's height was imposing, matched with a penetrating stare. Simon saw something else, something softer, and allowed the man to help him up. Inside the shack, Dylan cleaned Simon's wounds while he made drunken comments about living in a hovel.

The next night, Simon visited again to apologise. On the sober occasion, he wondered if being with the stranger was safe. When he learnt Dylan was trying to reconcile with Tina and Erin, Simon was touched.

Later, Dylan said he had been questioned by the police about a paperboy's murder. Erin and Tina believed he was guilty. Simon wondered if he should stay away from Dylan. Loneliness kept the teenager coming back. Despite being part of a group, he was lonely. Obsessed with appearances and who fancied who, teenagers didn't care about deeper issues. The wiser man listened and advised. Yet Simon felt a tingle of fear whenever they met. Every time he went to the shack, he looked to the river and wondered if he was treading out of his depth.

'You're lying, too.' Simon flinched at his foolish bravery.

After kicking away the crate footstool, Dylan stood. 'I was forced to lie! Look where it's got me.' He flung out his arms. 'Tina stole the life I wanted. I gave her everything. I was like a father to Erin. She needed it, considering her real dad did a runner. Those bitches betrayed me!' The cigarette bent between his nicotine-stained fingers.

'I better be off.' Simon edged closer to the door.

'Don't be scared of me. Grow up and face your fears.'

'I'm not afraid.' Simon cursed his high pitched voice. 'It's getting late.'

'It's getting too late to be your true self.'

As Dylan's eyes narrowed, Simon's insides churned.

Dylan continued. 'By all means, be kind. The world could do with some kindness, but don't ignore your anger. Use it. Look out for number one. Make those who've hurt you realise the damage they've done. Take revenge. Never, ever, let kindness be your undoing.'

Maybe he's right, Simon thought. *Perhaps I need to show them who is the boss. Kindness is to my advantage. They'll never expect lovely, kind Simon to take charge. What a shock it will be when I do! Tomorrow will be the perfect ending for the summer of The Six.*

CHAPTER 23

Saturday 21 August 2021

After learning Stevie was a vicar, Kat claimed tiredness and went to bed. She pushed Joe onto his side, cursing herself for forgetting to pack earplugs. The drunken snoring resembled a pig being violated by a chain saw. Add on stale alcohol fumes, and Kat wondered why she hadn't killed him in his sleep.

Bolstered by pillows, she sat up in bed and turned on her Kindle. When he was sober enough, Joe complained about the light. After receiving an invitation for Simon's memorial, Kat began re-reading Erin's novels. When the first book was published, Kat found it such a thrill. She often told customers at the shop where she worked about her famous author friend. Kat never mentioned she hadn't spoken to Erin since 1992. Even though time had passed, they were still friends. The Six were bound together, mainly from what happened to Simon.

Earlier, Erin had been so kind. When she challenged Joe's criticism of his wife, Kat felt seen for once. She hoped Erin would stay in touch. Images of sitting in the front row of author events as a special guest filled Kat's mind. She hadn't asked when another book was being released. Surrogacy was Erin's main concern, as it should be.

Words on the Kindle screen blurred. Guilt clouded Kat's focus. She should've been a better friend to Alex. If the gang hadn't gone their separate ways, maybe he would be alive. Thinking of Alex, scared of disclosing his sexuality, was painful. With the others in contact, perhaps Alex could've gained the confidence to tell them. Kat was certain everyone would've offered a positive reception, apart from one person. On cue, Joe flopped onto his back. The snoring continued. She hated Joe's alcoholism. She hated him more, knowing he wouldn't have accepted Alex being gay, no matter what Joe told the others. The Leader's fragile masculinity couldn't bear it.

Kat wasn't a better person compared to her husband. In lying to him, she was also a hypocrite. Panic fluttered in her chest as she checked the bank account on her phone. While the amount was pleasing, the regret wasn't. Whoever had sent the demand to stay at The Mill used her secret account as a reason for her not to refuse. The letters were individually addressed to Joe and Kat. When she opened her envelope and saw a copy of her bank statement, the room span. Joe's own letter kept him too preoccupied to notice her trying not to faint.

She questioned who had accessed the account. To avoid questions, she didn't receive paper statements. The letter from a blackmailer detailed her crime. They knew she stole from her employer. Despite stealing for months, she wasn't good at lying. One accusation and Kat would've crumbled. Keeping Joe's secret wasn't as difficult because it wasn't hers. Joe said his letter was just an invitation to stay at The Mill after the memorial. While Kat knew better, she didn't push it further. His actions and making her keep what he did secret were wrong. She did it, though, needing to keep her family together. The Andinos decided to stay at the bed and breakfast. Being exposed would be worse.

If Joe found out about Kat's bank account, they would argue. From the moment they met, The Leader took charge of her life. At first she hadn't realised it was happening. The naïve sixteen-year-old considered it a win; dating the boy many girls wanted.

Kat reflected on how Joe often decided where they went. He showed her off like an expensive bracelet hanging from his arm. She couldn't deny it was a buzz. Appearance meant everything to Joe. Kat, too, if she was honest. On her eighteenth birthday, he paid for her to have a tattoo on the nape of her neck. By labelling her permanently as *Joe's Princess*, he staked a claim. Years later, she always wore her hair down.

Joe came from a humble background. His family had created a successful chain of Greek restaurants across Dorset. Kat's parents' only ambition was to keep having children.

Kat stole clothes and accessories to fit in with the other girls. If she had asked, her parents would've offered money. She knew it meant them going without, though. When questioned, she claimed new outfits were hand-me-downs from The Pink Posse. She didn't tell Joe about shoplifting and how nice clothes helped her face the mirror. From childhood, she developed an obsession with body image. When puppy fat set in, she despaired. Even when she lost weight, she still saw a non-existent roll of fat on her stomach.

As an adult looking at photos from her teens, Kat was stunned. She was thin, dangerously so. A damaged mind distorted her reflection. Unfortunately, she took it into adulthood.

After telling Joe she had an eating disorder, he laughed. He claimed five babies and meals in the family restaurant were Kat's issues. Joe suggested she got off her backside, eat less, and go to the gym. She didn't bother telling him what she'd already tried: diets, fasting, binging, vomiting, over-exercising, and much more.

One afternoon, surrounded by chocolate wrappers and crisp packets, Kat sobbed so hard her body ached. She sought help and soon realised counsellors didn't come cheap. A GP placed her on a waiting list, warning it could take a year. Kat would rather be dead than live with disgust. She couldn't ask Joe for the money. Despite attempts to hide it, she knew his conservatory business was suffering. Family handouts wouldn't keep it going forever.

When cashing up at the newsagents, Kat occasionally stole money. It was a small independent business, owned by an elderly couple. When they praised her for working hard, guilt gnawed at her gut. It didn't stop her from stealing, though. Her wages just about covered the household bills. Whenever she altered the newsagents' takings, she promised she'd pay it all back.

The counselling sessions helped Kat learn to like herself a little more and be more confident. When she returned from the weekly "Book Club" Joe commented on how happy she seemed. Although counselling had changed her life, she knew it had to end. A knife of remorse stabbed her conscience.

A message pinged on Kat's phone. After reading it, she flung back the duvet and got dressed. She was always willing to do a good deed, trying to make right her sins. When she saw Stevie's clerical collar, Kat almost fell to her knees and confessed. She could never do it, though. Instead, Kat focused on helping a friend, still knowing it wouldn't be enough to receive forgiveness. Kat and Joe destroyed The Six in 1992. After what they did to Simon, they deserved to suffer.

CHAPTER 24

Friday 21 August 1992

Joe prepared for another kiss. Kat moved aside to check behind the tree they were leaning against.

'We have to be careful.' She took a glimpse from the other side of the trunk. The Witch's house was shrouded in darkness. Kat shivered.

Joe groaned. 'You and I being together isn't an issue. Sneaking around is doing my nut in.'

Kat straightened her top, removing the evidence of his roaming hands. Joe caught her chin in his hand and aimed for her mouth. Focused on looking into the shadows, she edged away.

'I'm starting to think you're a prick tease.' Joe's bottom lip dropped into a sulk.

'Piss off! Not everyone's a tart like you.'

After grabbing her bag, Kat marched towards friendlier people in the mill. As she swung her arms, Joe seized her wrist.

'Sorry, Princess. Please forgive me. When it comes to how I feel about you, I act like a love-sick idiot.' He led her back to their hiding place.

Throughout the school year, Kat resisted Joe's advances. The Pink Posse encouraged her to go for it, wanting their gang to get with the popular boys. Kat had standards. Having the others' sloppy seconds wasn't a badge of honour. While Kat's parents always needed more money, love filled their home to the rafters. A relationship like the one her parents had was her goal. She wanted to believe Joe was genuine. Their flirtation increased throughout the holiday club into something more solid, but secret.

'They must be suspicious,' Kat said as the sound of their friends laughing carried over. 'Going outside together as much as we do is so obvious.'

'Let's not sneak around anymore. I want to make it official.' Joe lowered to one knee. 'Will you be my girlfriend?'

She giggled. 'I nearly had a heart attack. Flipping heck! I thought you were going to propose!'

'Reckon it's coming up next. I've never felt this way about anyone. You're The One, forever.'

Kat pulled Joe up to meet her mouth.

'Of course I'll be your girlfriend. Let's keep it to ourselves for a while.'

Joe dropped his arms from around her waist. 'For crying out loud! Simon will get over it. I'm fed up with you worrying about what he thinks.'

'He's your best friend! You know he has a crush on me. I don't want to hurt him.'

'Si's a big boy. He'll move on.'

Kat picked at the varnish on her fingernail. 'I'm not so sure. Haven't you noticed how snappy he's been recently? Fighting with Alex was out of character.'

'I heard Alex started it. Neither will say why they scrapped. I'm getting fed up with them not talking to each other.'

'Erin saw them. She hid as she thought the boys would have a go at her.'

'Did she hear what they said?'

Kat shrugged. 'Erin couldn't hear much. She said Alex's anger wasn't surprising. Simon's rage terrified her, though. Erin couldn't get away fast enough.'

'He has problems with his dad. The bloke's a right bastard. Si's just lashing out.'

'We should help him, not make things more difficult by flaunting our relationship.'

Joe cradled her face in his hands. 'Simon will have to learn he can't have you. He'll find someone else to fancy and stop being such a wimp around girls. If he'd made a move on you, I would've backed off. You snooze, you lose. I got the girl.'

A twig snapped. Kat sprang from Joe's hold.

'What's that?' she asked.

A light came on in the shack. Kat slapped a hand over her mouth to stifle a yelp. She'd never met the person who lived there, and it was obvious he didn't want company. The others didn't mention the man. Kat figured his mysteriousness made him more frightening. She had no intention of meeting him, particularly late at night.

'No one's there,' Joe said before drawing her in.

They almost connected. A thud sounded. Joe fell against the tree, groaning as he slid downwards.

'A wimp, am I?' A snarl replaced Simon's usual smile. 'How dare you laugh at me!'

Joe rubbed the back of his head and then inspected his palms. 'What the hell? Think yourself lucky I'm not bleeding. If that branch was any heavier, you could've done some real damage.'

'I wish I had!' Simon dropped the weapon. His body visibly shook.

'I'm sorry,' Kat soothed. 'I wanted to let you down gently. Joe and I love each other.'

Joe snapped his head towards Kat. 'You love me?' He grinned.

'This isn't the time.' Her eyes focused on the branch lying nearby.

'I've had enough of people taking the piss!' Simon yelled. 'You only had to be honest. Like everyone else, you took advantage. No more!'

'Shit, it hurts.' Joe clutched his head and moaned. 'Good job you're a mate or I would've decked you.'

Simon grabbed the branch. Kat gasped. She caught a glimpse of the old Simon as he frowned at her fear. He hurled the branch into the river.

'I hope you have a wonderful life together,' Simon said. 'Our friendship is over.'

Kat began to follow him. Joe pulled her back from entering the forest of weeds, already claiming Simon.

'You haven't got a torch,' Joe said. 'Don't worry. He'll be fine.'

'He was so angry. I've never seen him behave like that.'

Joe wiped a tear from her cheek. 'Let's go home, Princess. I'll call Simon tomorrow and smooth things over. It'll be OK.'

It wasn't. Joe didn't speak to his best friend the next day. By then Simon had disappeared.

CHAPTER 25

Sunday 22 August 2021

After waking, Joe's mind whirled through his usual morning-after-drinking list:

Did I embarrass myself?

Did I embarrass Kat?

Did I embarrass other people?

Did I say something I'll regret?

Did I do something I'll regret?

On the last point, Joe grabbed a pillow and held it over his face. He had already done something he regretted. Blackouts after heavy drinking worried most people. Joe enjoyed the temporary oblivion. He considered keeping the pillow in place and drifting into permanent sleep. As he visualised Alex, taking a final breath, Joe threw the pillow across the room.

The water was stale. Kat always left a glass by his side of the bed. There weren't any painkillers, though. Being somewhere else disrupted their usual routine. Perhaps Kat was so upset about Alex she'd forgotten Joe's needs. He peered behind. She had gone to breakfast without him. Whenever he drank, his wife sulked the next day. The party girl had become a party pooper. Joe headed to the bathroom for a shower. He couldn't make clean what was inside, but the charade had to continue.

****

'Just the two of you?' the server asked after taking breakfast orders.

'For now,' Stevie replied. 'Hopefully, the others will be here soon.'

'Thanks.' Erin watched the server leave. 'I'm at a loss for words today.'

'Not helpful for an author.'

Erin scowled. 'I'm having time off.'

'I didn't mean anything by it. A break is a good idea. You have enough going on with the surrogacy. My husband makes sure I have breaks, although it isn't easy. Sunday services, christenings, funerals, and weddings never end.'

'I hope you're not offended.' Erin paused. 'When you turned up wearing a white collar, I was speechless.'

Stevie fiddled with salt and pepper pots. 'No one was more surprised than me when I joined the clergy. I was a pain-in-the-backside teenager who continued into early adulthood. Sad to say, I searched for acceptance in the wrong places. Sex was my self-harm.'

A woman at a nearby table leaned back in her chair. Deep breathing tickled Stevie's ear. The Mill was busy with public diners who weren't guests. Listening to Stevie and Erin, the woman received more than breakfast.

'In my job, I'm used to dealing with nosey buggers.' Stevie turned her head towards the woman and coughed. The woman shifted back onto four chair legs and resumed eating.

Stevie continued. 'My parents had a shit fit when I said I was becoming a vicar.'

'Are vicars allowed to swear?' Erin asked.

'God sees everything I do. There's no hiding from Him, although I try not to swear much. So far, I haven't dropped the c-bomb in a service. I'm a work in progress.'

'I expect you're great at your job. When we were younger, you were a brilliant listener. You helped me through the dramas with Mum.'

'You and I fell out a few times, though. Remember how we fought over the same boys? Wow, we were brutal.'

'Thankfully, we're both older and wiser. I'd love to stay in touch after this.'

'Definitely. After what's happened to Alex, I appreciate my old friends even more. Hey, maybe in your next thriller, the hero will be a female vicar.'

Joe's shoes tapped across the wooden floor as he approached. 'Nice to see you're laughing and have forgotten Alex so quickly.'

'We're grieving, too,' Stevie began. 'Laughter's sometimes a defence mechanism. I guess it's something I learned from my Clown days.'

Joe poured orange juice from a crystal jug. A trembling hand meant more juice landed on the tablecloth than in the glass. Noticing Erin looking, he placed his arm over the mess. He winced as his Ralph Lauren shirt sponged the linen cloth.

'Have you seen Kat?' Joe asked.

'We thought you'd come to breakfast together,' Erin replied. 'I haven't seen her since yesterday.'

'Me neither,' Stevie added.

'She's probably annoyed, as usual.' Joe clicked his fingers. 'Oi, you!'

The server approached them. His grin was more Hammer Horror than happy to help. 'What can I get you, sir?'

'Full English and a pot of coffee, not a cup. I need caffeine and lots of it.' Joe turned to Erin and Stevie. 'After this, Kat and I are leaving.'

'The police are coming this morning to take our statements,' Erin said.

'They have my address. It's not far. Don't know why we ever agreed to stay here.'

'Don't you?' Stevie drew out her question. 'Nothing was added to your invite?'

'Why would there be?' Joe lifted his arm. He would change before Kat saw the stain, remembering her moaning at him for not packing T-shirts.

'Did you receive anything in the envelope, along with the invitation?' Stevie addressed Erin.

'No.' Erin used her brightest author's back cover smile. 'What was in yours?'

'Nothing much. Anyway, I have a plan. Shall we have a picnic later? We'll remember Alex and share memories of him.'

'Is the cordon still there?' Erin asked. 'It was sealed off near where it happened.'

'Charlotte said it's open,' Stevie replied. 'I don't want to go by the shed, though.'

Erin took a breath. 'Why did such a lovely man kill himself? I've realised I knew pretty much nothing about Alex. We should've done more to help him.'

'Don't torture yourself,' Stevie replied. 'That's our Erin; forever The Thinker.'

The three were silent for a moment. Classical music competed against diners' conversations.

Stevie cleared her throat. 'Let's go to the stream behind The Mill. It's a private area for guests. We'll work through our feelings and remember Alex.'

'None of your happy clappy church stuff.' Joe seized a coffee pot from the incoming server.

'I've said my prayers already and I respect it isn't for you. This is for *us*; The Six together again.'

Erin clutched a napkin, twisting it between her hands. 'We're not The Six anymore.'

'We'll *always* be The Six, no matter what,' Stevie said.

Erin grabbed her phone from the table and scrolled through. 'Kat hasn't posted on Facebook since last night.'

'Now I *am* worried.' Joe snort-laughed. 'She's glued to her mobile. When I come home, she's often upset at some troll. Posting her weight issues is asking for trouble.'

'Actually, it's good for Kat to be so open,' Erin said. 'From what I see here, she's moved on and is more about self-acceptance.'

'That's good,' Stevie added. 'You're lucky to have her, Joe.'

He focused on shovelling the meal that had arrived into his mouth.

'I could do with a lie down before talking to the police.' Erin stood. 'This little one needs to be as stress free as possible.'

Stevie moved her seat back. 'I'm going to phone my husband. Let's meet at reception at twelve.'

Joe grunted acceptance while chewing a hash brown. The morning after drinking demons hadn't won. He decided to forget his troubles, including Kat. It was all too easy to make her vanish. He wondered once again if he should leave her. The shame of what Joe did was terrible, let alone making someone else carry the burden too. Kat was losing it and becoming a liability. He had to stop that from happening. If she revealed Joe's crime, it would be the end of them both.

CHAPTER 26

Sunday 22 August 2021

The Witch took a deep breath. She longed for the cooler temperatures of autumn. Summer's humidity was unbearable, but nothing compared to the tension of recent events. Death was once more a visitor. After spotting Alex on the bridge the previous evening, she knew it wouldn't end well.

Previously, The Witch considered having the goat shed demolished. Nostalgia kept it standing. The building became a dumping ground for broken items and a memorial to Dylan, stacked with his furniture. When the police allowed, she would knock down the shed and cherish fond memories instead. She remembered how Dylan tended the goats, laughing as they nibbled everything, including his clothes. After his death, The Witch gave the goats to a farmer. Their bleating for their missing master became unbearable. The animals weren't the only ones hurting. Dylan's death meant The Witch was truly alone. She regretted placing her faith in another person. For a recluse, it was stupid to give a man a home with few questions asked.

Dylan was a puzzle who made The Witch feel both happiness and fear. She recalled the stray chicken incident. The owner, a woman living up the road, didn't stop the birds from escaping. One afternoon, Dylan knocked on The Witch's door. He held a chicken in his arms. Guttural squawks came from its weakened body. After checking over the bird, they discovered its leg was bent out of shape. When lowered to the ground, the chicken wobbled and collapsed. The Witch doesn't remember giving instructions. She went inside and tried not to hear a neck snap. Forever, she wished she'd never looked out the window. Dylan grinned at the bird hanging limp in his grasp.

Because of Dylan's friendliness, The Witch became less suspicious of people. She should've been wary when his brother, Wily, arrived. Maybe the resemblance to Dylan made her forget to be cautious. The brothers shared the same thick dark eyebrows; half-moons rising over intense eyes. Wily was either the older brother or he'd had a hard life. Streaks of grey peppered his version of the brothers' thick, wavy brown hair. Although the siblings had similar features, unlike Dylan, Wily was pure menace. He smirked like the proverbial cat devouring the cream. Wily was obviously the type who used violence to get what he wanted.

The Witch kept her distance from Wily. She knew not to let a stranger into her home. Wily still made a move. Grasping arms clutched her waist. Scents of greasy hair and stale cigarette breath made her stomach churn. The Witch reeled around with a spade, always leaning against her house, and hit her attacker.

When he returned, Dylan's mouth was wide open. He found Wily moaning on the ground, holding his crotch. The Witch updated Dylan on what Wily did before she went inside. From the window, she watched the brothers arguing.

Dylan shoved Wily. 'How dare you touch her? You're an animal.'

Wily staggered, off balance from protecting his wounded assets. 'No more than you, little brother. At least I don't hurt paperboys and–'

A fist in the face interrupted Wily. The man landed on his back, holding up his arms in defence.

'I didn't kill Nick!' Dylan stood over Wily, placing a foot on the attacker's chest.

The Witch startled. She was aware Dylan had run away from trouble, but not murder. She knew he'd lived with Tina Sullivan and her daughter Erin in Dorset. When Dylan was out, The Witch sometimes rifled through his belongings. Giving him somewhere to stay meant he'd given up the right to privacy. Nothing she found revealed a murderer lived nearby.

After noticing Erin going to the mill, The Witch hoped Dylan would approach the girl and reconcile. Instead, he hid whenever The Six appeared. The Witch pondered on Wily's statement about a dead child called Nick. Perhaps Erin and her friends had a lucky escape.

Wily scrabbled in a muddy puddle, formed earlier from watering the dry lawn.

'If you're innocent, you should've stayed,' Wily began. 'I'm ashamed of you for running away. The police stopped considering you as Nick's killer. Confess. Was the kid's death accidental? I would've covered for you.'

'How many more times? I didn't kill Nick! I didn't run away either. This is where Tina lives. When it's the right time, I'm going to see her.'

'You're a stupid bastard.' Wily sneered. 'Tina's a slut. She's probably pissed and shagging half of this backwards town. Goldilocks only has to flick her hair to get the fellas hot.'

Dylan advanced. Wily dug his heels into the mud and slid backwards.

'I came here to bring you home,' Wily said. 'We're family, even though you hit me. You'll always have my loyalty. I'll find a place for you to hide from the pigs. We're good at not getting caught, right, bro?'

'I don't need to hide!' Dylan sat on a bench.

'What are you doing here, then?' Wily managed to stand. He checked his stonewashed jeans and shrugged. 'Little bit of dirt hurt no one. Bro, when you come to your senses, I'll be waiting. Say the word and I'll give Tina a little scare for abandoning you.'

'Don't you dare touch her!'

Wily grinned. 'Never forget your *real* family. If Tina or Erin rat me out for my business enterprises, I'll take action. Speak soon.' Wily thumped Dylan's shoulder before leaving.

'Quite a performance.' The Witch came outside after Wily left.

Dylan dropped his face into his hands. 'I didn't kill him.'

'Your brother's lucky he's still breathing.'

'I mean Nick, the kid from Blandford.'

The Witch took a large gulp before speaking. 'Is that the truth?'

'I can't believe you're asking!' Dylan rose from the bench and paced in front of her.

'Seeing as you're living here, I have every right to ask.'

'I'm not responsible for the boy's murder.' Dylan's voice trembled.

'Your brother scares me,' The Witch began. 'Believe me, I don't say that about many people.'

'He's got a misplaced sense of loyalty. Stupid bastard wants to defend me, even when he thinks I'd killed Nick.'

'Want to talk about Nick?'

'No. I can't do this anymore today. I'm going to fix the fencing by the river. The goats have been chewing it again.'

Watching Dylan strut into the wilderness, The Witch considered what she'd heard. A boy died. Her tenant was a suspect. Wily said the brothers weren't exactly angels.

The Witch considered Simon's visits with Dylan. She didn't want to draw nasty conclusions. A man and teenager could be friends without anything untoward going on. Now she wasn't so sure. Simon was a considerate youngster who never shied from her. They'd had some good discussions. She later told the police she'd seen Dylan beckoning Simon into the shack. It was all she'd dared to tell the authorities.

The Witch noted three of The Six, now adults, leaving The Mill. They carried a hamper and blankets. She headed to the kitchen and began making tea she didn't want. What she didn't see couldn't hurt her. Silence was golden, especially concerning Simon, Dylan, and Alex. The Witch knew what had happened to them all. Nothing could make her confess. Death wouldn't darken her doorstep again, especially if it came knocking.

CHAPTER 27

Sunday 22 August 2021

Erin spread a tartan rug on the ground. Joe lingered on the riverbank above Erin and Stevie. Recessed areas with steps leading towards the stream were new. Much had changed from when they were teenagers. The stream was once a trickle, with banks formed of muddy sludge.

'This is better than sliding on my backside,' Stevie said as she sat. 'Remember the night I wanted to skinny dip?'

Erin laughed. 'Trying to stop you was a mission. You wouldn't accept the water barely covered our ankles and being naked was a terrible idea.'

'I'm glad I slid in the mud and twisted my ankle before getting my kit off. What a nightmare I was.'

Joe joined them. 'Alex and I took turns giving you a piggyback home. Al did most of it, what with him being built like a brick shit house.'

'I miss him so much already.' Erin fiddled with the buckle on her sandal. 'Although we haven't seen each other for years, you're all important to me. When I returned from Blandford, you gave me a second chance. For the first time, I felt I belonged.'

'Because you did,' Stevie replied, 'and still do. We may be a smaller group, but we'll always be The Six.'

The three shared a peaceful moment, focusing on sunlight dancing in the rippling water. A swan glided past, followed by its young. White tinged their grey wings.

'Swans are clever creatures,' Joe began. 'Whenever we came here fishing, Alex told me about them. When swans know their youngsters are ready to leave, the parents distance themselves. Al called it tough love. It reminds me of Kat. Despite our arguments, I can't deny she's a brilliant mum. There's nothing she won't do for our kids, although she lets them make mistakes, too. Even now they have their own children, our kids ask us for advice. I throw money at the situation. Kat tells them to dare to try, knowing we're there as back-up. She's a mother swan, encouraging her young to spread their wings of independence.'

'That's beautiful,' Erin said. 'Perhaps there's a writer in you as well.'

Joe rubbed his thumb and finger together. 'The only thing I'm interested in seeing in print is money.'

'Business going well?' Stevie asked as she unloaded the hamper.

'It's booming. Can I interest you in a conservatory?'

'Not unless your fellas will come to Thame. Besides, I don't own The Manse. It comes with the job.'

'Not being rude,' Joe began. 'You're the least likely person I'd expect to be a vicar.'

'That's because you still think of me as The Clown. The lost are searching for something. I didn't know what I needed until I finally realised it was God.'

Joe cleared his throat and looked away.

'I won't bore you with the details. The church isn't everyone's cup of tea.'

'I'm pleased for you.' Erin poured lemonade into a tumbler. 'Knowing who you are and having a sense of purpose is a good thing.'

'Like you being an author,' Stevie replied.

'I wonder where Kat is.' Joe checked his phone. 'I've sent loads of messages and no reply. This time I must've really pissed her off.'

Erin picked up her mobile. 'I've messaged her on Facebook. Let's see if she's responded. Oh, this is weird.'

'What?' Joe leaned over to look at the screen.

'Kat posted earlier. It says, '"Today's top dieting tip: drown your appetite with water. Kill your hunger with kindness."'

Joe leaned his elbows on his knees. 'I thought she was finished with posting diet crap.'

'Alex's death might've made her escalate,' Stevie said. 'Feeling vulnerable can make people revert to old behaviours.'

'I could do without it.' Joe shook his head. 'When Kat obsesses about weight, I lose her.'

Erin scrolled further through the Facebook feed. 'From her older posts, it's obvious she's crying for help. Does Kat have an eating disorder?'

'She mentioned it once and then refused to talk about it again. If I talk about food or weight, she kicks off.'

Joe grabbed a glass of wine. 'Hair of the Dog,' he said, before knocking the contents back.

'The wine is for toasting to Alex,' Stevie said.

Joe held out the plastic glass. 'Better have another then.'

After giving him a refill, Stevie raised her glass. 'To Alex; our gentle giant Farm Boy. You'll always be in our hearts. May you rest in the peace you didn't have in life.'

'How lovely.' Erin dabbed sweat trickling down her nose with a tissue. 'I bet you're a great vicar.'

'Thank you. Are you OK? You look like you're boiling. It's hotter than I expected.'

Erin laid back and tapped her stomach. 'This little one is creating a furnace. With this heat, it's not the best combination.'

'Kat carried a few of our kids in the summer,' Joe said. 'With the amount of ice she sucked on, I expected our babies to be champion swimmers.'

Erin blew her fringe from her eyes. 'I'd love to go for a paddle, but I can't be arsed.'

Stevie offered a hand. 'I'll go with you.'

'No skinny dipping.' Joe winked.

'The bishop would strike me off. Are you up for it, Erin? We'll head over there into the shade.' She pointed to a tree a little further downstream.

'We should've set up there,' Joe said.

Erin sighed. 'You go, Stevie. Test the water. I might join you in a bit.'

'It's freezing!' Stevie shouted as the water nipped at her feet.

After the initial chill, the water soothed Stevie's troubled soul. Putting on a face for everyone – what her husband called Uber Vicar – was tiring. Years of supporting grieving families, troubled people, and demanding parishes made her resilient. Still, she didn't block her emotions. A vicar taking a funeral service couldn't weep with the mourners, though. With Alex's death, Stevie had become the bereaved. That morning, she questioned God, asking why her friend died. Something inside told her to run from The Mill. She couldn't. Abandoning the others wasn't an option.

Something about Alex's death scene niggled in Stevie's mind. As the water lashed against her legs, she chased the missing details. Perhaps she was searching for clues that weren't there. The evidence suggested suicide. Slashed wrists were an obvious sign. Even so, something about Alex's death didn't add up. She wished she knew what it was.

The sun prickled Stevie's uncovered head, reminding her of the hat she'd left behind. She headed for the tree, deciding to stay underneath it for a while. Flutters travelled overhead as a trio of birds landed at the top of the tree. The threesome lined along a branch. Stevie took pictures of them on her phone. The birds cawed at the unwelcome guest. She shivered when remembering crows signified death.

As she lifted her foot, something pulled it back. Seaweed seized her ankle. Stevie realised seaweed doesn't belong in streams. She didn't want to look down. She knew she must.

Snakes of brunette hair floated in the water. Stevie recalled the legend of Medusa. Looking further wouldn't turn Stevie into stone. Instead, it would shatter her like a smashed rock.

A body laid face down. A pink tulip rested in its hand. Spread-eagled arms and legs performed a reverse snow angel. She *was* an angel and a dear friend. A tattoo on the back of her neck confirmed it. *Joe's Princess.*

CHAPTER 28

Sunday 22 August 2021

A police constable holding Joe's elbow tried to lead him. Although Kat's body had been removed from the stream, he wouldn't leave. The picnic blanket kept away a chill, despite the glaring sun.

'Get off me!' Joe shoved the PC's hand away. She stumbled and slid on wet pebbles.

Stevie ended her conversation with a detective. She ran down the steps leading to the riverbank. The almost upright PC appeared grateful to have support. Since the emergency services arrived, Joe had become increasingly volatile.

'I understand you're distressed,' Stevie said to her friend. 'You can't lash out at people, though. They're trying to help.'

Joe allowed himself to be guided up the steps. After throwing off the blanket, he fell onto the grass.

Stevie sat with him. 'Let's go inside,' she said. 'The police need to get on with their work.' Every word she spoke was an effort. The wedge in her throat threatened to break, along with her spirit.

'I won't leave Kat!' Joe yelled.

'She's gone, sweetheart. The police are trying to find out what happened. They can't do it with us in the way. I get you don't want to leave the place where Kat died. She isn't here, though. She's there.' Stevie placed her hand over his heart.

A paramedic approached them. 'Hi, Joe, I'm here to see how you're doing.'

Stevie pulled Joe up. Sobs wracked his body. The paramedic guided him towards an ambulance. Looking up, Joe halted.

'No, I'm not going in there! You took my wife in one of those. Bring her back!'

The paramedic kept a hand on the man's shoulder. 'You don't have to go anywhere you don't want to, Joe.'

The paramedic looked at Stevie. She shook her head. 'I'll look after him. We're old friends and I'm a vicar used to dealing with people in distress. If he needs help, I'll call.'

The paramedic addressed Joe. 'Are you OK with that?'

He offered a slow nod while staring at the stream.

'Your friend is going to take care of you now,' the paramedic added. 'We're always available if you need us.'

Stevie and Joe shuffled to The Mill. As they walked, she regretted screaming after seeing Kat. Horror made Stevie lose her mind. Perhaps she could've saved Joe from seeing his wife's body. His desperate cries, earlier, to resuscitate Kat were painful. After Joe turned the body over, Erin left, and could be heard vomiting.

Stevie was torn between helping Joe, Erin, or Kat. The first choice was horribly easy. Kat was dead. The bludgeoned mess on the back of her head confirmed it. Stevie's usual cast iron stomach turned into molten metal.

The next decision was harder. Joe sank into the mud, trying to resuscitate his dead wife. After becoming tired from doing compressions and giving breaths, he begged Stevie to take over. She knew it was useless, but had to try, for his sake. Looking at the vacant stare, she covered her mouth over Kat's cold lips. While doing so, she sent Joe to call for an ambulance.

As they waited, Stevie couldn't pray. Words wouldn't come. She refused to look at the pink tulip Kat held. She would have to recognise the link with Alex's death. Both had the flower by their bodies.

Stevie knelt by the stream and sung to Kat. "Stay" was a dedication to the girl who copied the smudged eyeliner favoured by Shakespears Sister. Stevie's voice cracked as she sang of begging a loved one not to leave. She didn't stop singing until a PC appeared.

****

Inside The Mill, Stevie seated Joe in the bar. It wasn't the wisest move, given her suspicions regarding his alcoholism, but he refused to go anywhere else.

'Are you OK?' Stevie asked Erin as she joined them.

'I'm sorry for abandoning you. When I saw… I couldn't take it.'

'Don't be so hard on yourself.' Stevie rubbed the woman's shoulder.

Charlotte approached their table with a tray of brandies. 'I'm sorry for your loss, Joe.'

The newly widowed man looked at his empty hands before seizing the lifeline of alcohol.

Charlotte turned to Erin. 'Damn it. I forgot you're pregnant. I'll get you something else.'

'No thanks. I've been guzzling so much water I'm drowning in it. Oh my…' Erin slapped a hand over her mouth.

'It's OK,' Charlotte soothed. 'Joe knows you don't mean anything by it.'

He raised his head. 'What are you babbling on about?'

'Nothing,' Charlotte sighed. 'Look, I'm not myself at the moment. These deaths are dreadful. Yesterday was even tougher than it should've been. I didn't mention it because of poor Alex.'

'I'm so sorry,' Stevie said. 'Yesterday was the anniversary of Simon's disappearance. I hadn't forgotten. It's just Alex, and then…' She nodded towards Joe.

Charlotte frowned around a smile. 'I understand. These deaths feel too close to my brother, though.'

'This is nothing like him!' Joe shouted. 'It's obvious some bastard killed my wife. Alex's death can't be suicide either. I'm not shocked enough not to notice the pink tulips. How can you compare Alex and Kat's deaths to Simon going off in a strop? The only thing they have in common is water; the river and the stream.'

'Remember what Kat wrote on Facebook?' Erin added. 'Oh my God.' She looked at Stevie. 'Oops. Sorry.'

'No problem. Blasphemy is the least of my worries.'

'Kat's last Facebook post was about dieting, specifically water,' Erin continued. 'Alex's note also connected killing with kindness.'

Charlotte reached for Erin's phone. 'Show me the post.' Charlotte read aloud. '"Today's top dieting tip: drown your appetite with water. Water is good for you. Kill your hunger with kindness." Given what's happened, it's not a coincidence. Have you told the police?'

Erin rubbed her forehead with the heel of her hand. 'I was so upset I forgot. After Alex's death, I looked up the meaning behind pink tulips. They didn't seem right, being with Alex there. Pink tulips signify caring. Remember Simon using them for Kindness Day at the holiday club?'

'Nope.' Joe stared into the empty brandy glass.

'Oh, yes!' Charlotte said. 'He used to give Mum pink tulips, too.'

'The connections between Alex and Kat's deaths with Simon are there.' Erin stood. 'I have to tell the police!'

Charlotte made her sit. 'Take it easy. Stress isn't good for you or the baby. The police will be here tomorrow. We'll tell them then. They're probably looking through Kat's social media already. They will figure things out.'

'True,' Erin replied. 'I should've thought of it.'

Joe smacked the glass on the table. 'Kat's not one of your defendants or a victim in a novel! She's my wife! The state she was in, it's obvious someone killed her. I won't rest until I find the bastard.'

'Please let the police take care of it,' Stevie said. 'I'm worried you'll hurt yourself or someone else.'

Laughter burst from his mouth. 'Me, hurt someone? You don't know the half of it. *I* deserve to be killed, not Kat. She died being faithful to me and my disgusting life. Without her, I might as well be dead, too. The guilt will eventually kill me, anyway.'

CHAPTER 29

Saturday 15 August 1992

'Caught you!'

At the sound of the voice, Joe leapt from the mill floor. 'What are you doing here?' His eyes looked everywhere but in the visitor's direction.

'I might ask you the same question,' Simon replied.

'Just chilling. It gets hectic at home with all the family there.'

Simon chuckled as he approached Joe's stereo. 'Since when do you like Shakespears Sister? Whenever Kat puts it on the jukebox at the holiday club, you take the mickey.'

Joe rushed over to lower the volume. 'It's on the radio.'

The *Play* button was pushed down on the cassette function. Simon decided not to mention it. When his ego was dented, Joe could be unpredictable. Since they became friends at primary school, Simon learnt mentions of Joe's appearance, height, or personality were unwelcome.

Simon was the Goose to Joe's Maverick. Basing their relationship on the *Top Gun* characters was unsettling. Goose died in the film. Simon questioned if Joe would miss him if he wasn't there. Since the school year ended, he knew time was running out to make an important decision. He was certain he'd done well in the GCSEs, although it didn't give much comfort. Excellent grades would lead to more problems. Thomas Pritchard's son was set to be a barrister, no matter what Simon wanted.

'Wake up.' Joe waved a hand in front of Simon's face.

'Sorry, I was away with the fairies.'

'Good job Alex isn't around to hear you saying that.' Joe sniggered. 'He'd pound the crap out of you.'

Simon's eyes rolled upwards. 'Stop making gay jokes around Al, especially when the others are nearby.'

'It's only messing about. He's not gay, so it's not a problem. Look at the size of him. Besides, have you ever heard of gay farmers?'

Simon considered there was probably a reason for that. Homophobia made it harder for people to come out. Charlotte confided in him she liked girls as more than friends. While he told her she shouldn't feel ashamed, they were realists. They couldn't tell their father. Thomas's archaic views would lead to more violence.

After discovering Alex kissing a boy, Simon wondered if he should mention it. At the time, Alex ran away. Later, he acted as if nothing had happened. Simon wasn't as firm friends with Alex as he was with Joe. Sometimes they worried Alex felt excluded.

Why are there candles burning? Simon pointed at a circle of tea lights on the floor. 'Oh, I get it! That's why you're wearing the special occasion shirt. You're meeting a girl!'

'No, I'm not.' Joe blew out the flames.

'You light candles to sit here alone? Yeah, right.'

'I was reading. The candles give more light.'

'There's this brilliant invention called torches. Try one. What are you reading?' He leaned in to peek behind Joe's back. 'I don't see a book.'

Joe jumped aside. 'Ease up! What's with the Spanish Inquisition? Anyway, why are *you* here?'

'I thought I'd go for a walk.'

'Long way from your house, mate.'

'Sometimes I need to be as far away as possible.'

Joe's forehead wrinkled. 'Is your dad back?'

'How did you guess?' Sarcasm soaked his words.

'I hate how he treats your family.' Joe smacked a fist into his other open hand. 'Be with people who care. Mum misses you. She keeps asking when you're coming for dinner. Join us tonight.'

'Your mum makes souvlaki to die for. I'll be there.'

'Be prepared for YiaYia saying you need feeding up. All I ever hear from Gran is, "Joseph, you must eat" even when I've just had a meal. To be fair, you *are* looking skinny. What's going on?'

'Nothing. I'm fine.' Simon cleared his throat. 'So, who's the lucky girl?'

'I told you, I'm reading.'

'If that's how you want to play it.'

'Oh.'

The boys turned towards another visitor.

'Seems we've all had the same idea,' Simon said. 'What brings you here?'

'Think I've left a lipstick somewhere.' Kat scanned the mainly empty building. 'I took it from Mum's dressing table. She's going ape shit.'

'You came all this way to find a lipstick,' Simon replied.

'It's Mum's favourite shade; Rimmel's Heather Shimmer. Women should never be without their best lippie.'

Simon's mouth curled into a smile. 'You and Joe had the same idea about getting dressed up.'

'What, this old thing?' Kat brushed her hands down her velvet dress.

'I'll help you find it,' Simon said.

Kat frowned. 'Find what?'

'Your mum's lipstick; the reason you're here?'

Simon had an inkling why she was there. He didn't dare speak the truth. It would destroy his dream of being with her. He watched Joe and Kat at the holiday club, trying not to notice their shared stares and smiles. He wanted to believe his best friend wouldn't go there. Months ago, when Simon confided he liked Kat, Joe offered to help him get the girl. Unlike Joe, Simon didn't want a wingman. He hoped Kat would've seen him for who was and appreciate it. Unfortunately, she was oblivious to his attempts to get closer to her.

Dylan listened to Simon's problems. They had a strange relationship where Simon viewed the man as an older, mysterious brother. While he loved Charlotte, Simon needed a male role model. Their father ruled with dictatorship and fear. Although Dylan's secretiveness made Simon wary, he liked having someone who listened without judgement. Joe was a good friend, but most conversations descended into banter. Simon was falling apart. He worried he'd never pull himself back together.

A series of blasts came from nearby. Kat shrieked. 'What the hell is that?'

As Joe placed an arm around her, Simon headed for the window. He rubbed it with the side of his hand, removing some of the dirt.

'It's Dylan, shooting at crows in the trees,' Simon said. 'Probably trying to keep them off The Witch's vegetable patch.'

Joe and Kat joined him, looking outside.

'There's the creepy bloke who lives in the hut.' Kat shivered. 'He always runs into his shed when we appear. Hey, isn't the bloke Erin's mum was seeing called Dylan?'

'It's a popular name.' Simon moved away. 'He's hardly come from Blandford to live in a shack.'

'How do you know his name?' Joe asked.

'I must've heard The Witch saying it. Anyway, who wants chocolate?' He emptied the sweets from his rucksack onto the rug.

'I can't.' Kat patted her stomach. 'Diet.'

'You don't need to lose weight, Princess,' Simon replied. 'You're perfect as you are.'

Joe pushed the other two aside. 'Well, I'm starving.' He grabbed a Yorkie bar. 'Cheers, Si. We can always rely on you.'

Not for much longer, Simon thought.

CHAPTER 30

Sunday 22 August 2021

In The Mill's bar, Joe finished telling the story of how Simon interrupted Joe and Kat's date. It was one of many memories Joe had shared. Remembering happier times made him calmer, but the agony in his voice remained.

'Perhaps Kat would be alive if she'd got together with Simon. He was a better bloke than I ever was.' Joe downed the contents of his glass.

'Simon adored Kat,' Charlotte began. 'Sorry for being so insensitive.'

Joe shrugged. 'It is what it is.'

Charlotte continued. 'When I found a pink scarf in his bedroom, Simon was mortified. He said Kat dropped it and he'd meant to return it to her.'

'That must have been when Kat was in The Pink Posse.' Stevie snarled. 'They were a candyfloss explosion topped with sprinkles of bitchiness.'

'Kat hated being part of their gang,' Joe added. 'When we started dating, she was glad to be free of them.'

131

Erin gripped the edge of the table. 'I hated those girls. After returning here from Blandford, they saw me in town and started calling me a slut and other choice words. Do you remember The Pink Posse standing outside the school where we did the holiday club?'

'We had a lucky escape,' Stevie began. 'They wanted Kat to convince the organisers to let The Pink Posse be helpers. Of course, Kat didn't do it. She was relieved to be free of them.'

'My poor wife has had so much to deal with. Kat was a wonderful person. I should've told her.'

Elbow leaning on the table, Joe propped his chin on his hand. Erin moved a bottle of whisky aside while he looked away. Joe insisted on having a whole bottle rather than making regular trips to the bar. When the others protested, he lashed out like a tiger protecting its prey. Charlotte gave the bar steward the night off. Donna Morfett was a trusted member of staff and confidante. A generous wage encouraged Donna to keep some of Charlotte's secrets.

'Lots of married couples take each other for granted,' Stevie said.

'I bet you never make your other half feel like shit,' Joe replied. 'The good vicar never tells her husband he's a bastard.'

'Kat stayed with you because she loved you.'

Joe grimaced. 'She stuck with me because divorce is admitting defeat. She was stronger than anyone gave her credit for. Kat was the best of us, particularly for keeping our secrets.'

Erin whispered to Stevie. 'I didn't tell her any secrets, did you?'

'No.' Stevie nibbled her thumb cuticle.

Joe addressed Charlotte. 'Kat should've hooked up with your brother instead. Simon treated her like a queen, let alone our Princess.' He raised his glass. 'Here's to Kat and Simon. I hope they're happy together in heaven.'

No one joined in the toast.

'Hey,' Stevie began. 'Isn't this the theme tune from *Jonathan Creek*?' The others listened for a moment.

Charlotte ran to the bar and switched off the stereo. Returning, she shook her head. 'I should've got Donna to turn it off before she left. I'm so sorry.'

Stevie frowned. 'What's the problem?'

'It's "Danse Macabre"', Charlotte replied. 'The dance of death.'

The women looked at Joe, who was more interested in drinking.

'It's just an awkward coincidence.' Erin checked her watch. 'Time for bed. I can barely keep my eyes open. Charlotte, are you sure we'll be safe overnight?'

'I've stepped up security.' Charlotte's tone was flint sharp. 'I'm terrified. If someone's out there killing people, they're doing it on my territory.'

Stevie yawned. 'We trust you'll look after us. I'm sure the police are monitoring things.' Stevie tapped Joe's shoulder. 'Come on. Seeing as it's a twin, you can stay in my room. You need to give a statement tomorrow and pack to go home. I confess I'll feel safer having you with me. Actually, is there a room for the three of us?'

Charlotte looked up from typing on her mobile. 'There aren't any family rooms.'

'We'll be all right,' Erin said. 'I'm too knackered to drive home. Lock your doors, everyone. If we need each other, phone. Glad we got each other's numbers yesterday.'

Stevie nudged Joe, who was pouring another drink.

'Knock it on the head,' Stevie said.

'Like someone did to Kat?' Joe's red-rimmed eyes confirmed he was in hell.

Stevie placed her hands into a prayer position. 'I just want to make sure you'll be OK. Focus on leaving tomorrow. No one wants to be here any longer. No offence, Charlotte.'

'None taken.'

Joe clenched the bottle to his chest. 'I'm staying to drink to my Princess! Also, I'm not leaving tomorrow. I'm going to hunt down the animal who killed her. I'll smash his head in and shove him face first into the water.'

Stevie wrung her hands around each other. 'Joe, please.'

'I'll stay here with him,' Charlotte said. 'I will be up for a while yet. There's too much whirring around my mind.'

'Are you sure?' Erin asked. 'It's difficult for you, what with the memorial and anniversary.'

Charlotte placed an arm around Joe and drew him closer. 'We'll stick together. Simon's best friend and I have lots of catching up to do.'

Despite his drunkenness, Joe knew he needed to be more alert around a barrister. After Erin and Stevie left, Charlotte was silent. Joe wondered if she knew what Kat and Joe had done. He was convinced Kat also received a blackmail note in her invitation. When they opened the post, husband and wife avoided the issue. Later, Joe searched for her envelope. She'd hidden it well.

Was Charlotte the reason they had to stay at The Mill? It made sense. The Mill was her property. She obviously had questions for the Six about Simon's disappearance.

While pouring another drink, Charlotte stared at Joe. He looked away. If Charlotte knew what he'd done, he might as well be in the mortuary next to his wife. As he often did, Joe cast his mind back to January 2017.

CHAPTER 31

January 2017

Bottles and drinking glasses became blurred as Joe stood behind the minibar. Despite the chilly room, sweat coated his palms. The decanter slipped from his grasp. Whisky soaked through his trousers.

Kat marched into the lounge. 'You'll wake the baby! I've only just got her off to sleep.' She pulled her dressing gown tighter.

Noticing Joe staring at the floor, Kat approached the mini bar. Shards of glass glistened on the carpet.

'Get away from there.' She grabbed his elbow. 'I'm sick and tired of cleaning up after you. Why do you drink so much?'

He pushed his wife away. 'Why is our granddaughter here?'

'I'm helping out. Thalia's had hardly any sleep since the little one was born.'

'Our daughter shouldn't have had a baby at seventeen, then.' Joe kicked the glass.

Kat moved aside. 'Stop it! There's enough of a mess already. Also, we were only a year older than Thalia when we had our first child. What's the matter? You're shaking.'

'I did a bad thing.'

Joe slumped downwards. With practised movements, Kat caught him under the armpits and eased him over to the sofa. After taking her usual armchair, she waited. Joe dropped his head into his hands and cried. Kat fought the impulse to comfort him. If she did, Joe would think she accepted his drinking. She had to let him speak to know what to do next. Drunk Joe was usually more truthful. Sometimes Kat took advantage of it. When he rolled in drunk, she grilled him like a detective interrogating a criminal.

Kat didn't go to the pub with Joe anymore. Watching him getting wasted while others gave her looks of pity was embarrassing.

'Have you been gambling again?' she asked. 'I have a mind to report the pub for letting people play poker there. How much have you lost this time?'

'The car...' His breathing hitched. 'It's...'

Kat went to the bay window and pulled back a curtain. The sight of Joe's Audi made her gasp. The bonnet was crumpled like a concertina. She cast a look around the cul-de-sac, thankful for the lack of lights in the other houses. The early hours of the morning covered the shame.

'What the hell have you done?' she shouted, forgetting her sleeping granddaughter. 'The insurance will never pay out. How many times have I said to get a taxi?'

Joe twiddled the wedding band around his finger. 'I felt OK to drive. The barmaid didn't take my keys. She usually does.'

'I'm fed up of hearing about her. Once and for all, tell me. Are you having an affair?'

'No! We're friends. She listens to me.'

Kat practically fell onto the chair. 'You don't need to confide in anyone else. I'm here, waiting to listen.'

'I've let you down, Kat. Sorry I neglected you. If I say what's happened, you'll leave me.'

She clenched the arms of the chair. 'Tell me.'

'The car... I... I–'

'What?'

'I swear I didn't have much to drink tonight,' Joe began. 'The girl came from nowhere. She ran across the lane. Flipping kids were playing chicken. Remember, it was in the *Daily Echo*?'

Kat recalled commenting on how the reckless youngsters needed their heads banging together. Local kids were daring each other to run in front of cars, mainly in quiet roads and lanes.

'I must've been driving too fast,' Joe continued. 'I thought taking Butler's Lane rather than the dual carriageway would be safer.'

'So you *were* over the limit?' She did nothing to soften her scathing tone.

Joe clenched his knees. 'A shape darted across the road. I figured it was my imagination. Now I know it was the first kid running into the field on the opposite side.' He paused.

'Keep going.' Kat cranked her hand in a circle.

'At first, it seemed like I'd hit a deer. The car was driveable even though it took a whack. I parked on a grass verge as I didn't want to get close. Then I saw a girl lying on the road. There was blood. I approached. A lad, probably the one who ran first, came out of the bushes. I had to go before he could identify me.'

Joe reached for Kat. She crossed her arms.

'You left an injured kid on a deserted road and drove away? How could you?'

In that moment, Joe realised he'd lost his wife. She would stay. They were the type to be married for life, despite their misery. They would never recover from this, though.

After peeking through a gap in the curtains, Joe groaned. 'If the police see the state of my Audi, I'm done for. I can't go to prison! I'll never survive it.'

Kat assessed *their* options, because it was *them,* not only Joe. His behaviour affected the Andinos. She was an all-round fixer. As she stared at a family photo hanging above the mantelpiece, she knew what she had to do.

Joe watched from inside as she drove the Audi into the garage. After Kat returned, she grabbed Joe's elbow, forcing him back onto the sofa.

'Listen up,' she began. 'Forget all that being The Leader crap. *I'm* sorting this out. This is what will happen. We'll find out from the news what happened to the girl. It's likely it will be reported. If she's dead, I won't cover for you. I refuse to do that to her parents. If she's alive, difficult as it is, we'll try to carry on as normal. I'll get your cousin to fix the Audi. He won't ask questions.' As Joe opened his mouth, she waggled a finger. 'Shut up and listen for once. If the girl lives, you'll start sorting your shit out. The goal is for you to go to AA. I know it will only happen when you're ready. In the meantime, ease up on the boozing. You have a family to live for. I *do* love you. What I hate is what you've become.'

'I'm still your Joe.' He barely managed the sentence for weeping.

'Unfortunately, you've drowned the wonderful young man I knew in drink. Your alcoholism might have killed someone! We *can* overcome this. There are conditions. Find a pub nearer to home where you can walk, not drive. After some sleep, we'll sort out our stories about what happened. The police might come knocking on the door.'

Kat allowed Joe to hold her hands.

'How can I ever thank you enough?' he asked.

'Be the boy I once knew.'

****

Joe held up a newspaper in front of Kat.

'I'm trying to watch *Eastenders*!' She swatted the paper aside.

'The girl I hit is all right.'

Kat pressed *standby* on the remote control. The drama in her lounge became more interesting than Albert Square. Joe threw a TV guide aside to join her on the sofa. Kat read the front-page article from the newspaper while he waited.

'Did we read the same thing?' Kat asked. 'The girl has a lot of recovering to do. She might not walk again.'

'She's alive. Now we can move on.'

'How can you be pleased you've possibly paralysed someone?'

'I hate myself more every day! Even looking at our kids makes me feel guilty. If one of them had been hit by a car, I'd be devastated. I deserve to be miserable forever.'

'I'm not letting you take us down with you. We have to try to move on.' As Kat said it, she didn't believe it. Keeping the secret was hard, but she had no choice.

Joe stood. 'I'm going to the pub.'

'There's a minibar right there.' Kat pointed to the corner of the lounge.

'I need to get out.' He eased his collar away from his neck. 'It feels like I'm suffocating.'

The slam of the front door signalled another broken promise. Claiming it was for nerves, Joe was drinking more.

Kat shivered as she turned up the thermostat. It wouldn't warm her. The chill was an omen. Death's cold fingers raked over Kat's grave.

CHAPTER 32

Sunday 22 August 2021

So much for Charlotte's extra security, Joe thought. He'd left The Mill without finding a locked door or seeing a member of staff. Two murder victims and Charlotte wasn't taking anything seriously. Joe had to act instead.

The effort of walking on a bumpy country road became tiring. He needed sleep, but not before getting answers. His phone's torch struggled to display the unlit area as he marched. A deep pothole stubbed against Joe's toes. Stumbling, he threw out his arms to right his balance. Although he felt sober in mind, his body betrayed him.

Joe congratulated himself for not falling. He shoved aside the earlier horror of walking past the goat shed, where he'd paused to apologise to Alex. Joe missed his old friend and realised he had done since they last saw each other in 1992. It wasn't intentional. Different goals disbanded The Six. Joe wondered if the others were also relieved when the group finished.

Alex stayed on at school to do AS-levels. Thinking of becoming a primary school teacher, Stevie went to college. Erin did A-levels at a different college. No one blamed her for staying away from Trillhaven. Dylan's death, and finding out he'd been nearby, was a lot for her to process.

Joe re-read the message on his phone.

I know who killed Kat. We can't talk in The Mill. Meet me in Mill Lane.

The futility of trying to resuscitate Kat wracked Joe's body. Finding out who'd hurt her and taking revenge was all he could do. He would be The Leader once again. Consequences didn't matter. If he was meeting with a murderer, so be it. Joe was prepared to kill, too. With his wife gone, he'd lost everything. Even his family didn't seem enough.

When Joe received the text, shaking off Charlotte was difficult. The woman could talk. Throughout, he offered occasional nods. Despite his fresh grief, she nattered about long-gone Simon. Joe knew if he stayed with her much longer, he was likely to lose his temper. Simon was missing, probably dead by his own hand. While devastating back then, years had passed. Joe's wife had just been murdered. Charlotte should've shown some respect. It was typical behaviour from the self-centred Pritchards.

Before going to bed, Charlotte gave Joe a strange look and warned him to be careful. He thought she was referring to a killer being out there. As he continued walking, Joe remembered Charlotte was checking on something in reception when Joe received the message. For a moment, he wondered if she'd sent it. He questioned why she didn't say who the murderer was when they were alone in the bar. Why bother meeting elsewhere? Maybe it wasn't Charlotte who'd sent the text.

The mysteries surrounding being at The Mill were frustrating. Joe had obeyed by staying at the bed and breakfast. A newspaper cutting added to the note meant he had to be there. After seeing the face of the girl in print, Joe panicked. He hid the contents of his envelope from Kat while wondering what was in her post. Then he figured he had enough to contend with and didn't question her any further.

Until then, discussion of the accident was taboo in the Andinos' home. Although Kat tried to hide it, Joe knew she trawled the internet for updates on the injured girl. The last he'd heard, she needed a cane to walk and had finished her GCSEs. She was the same age as The Six when they formed.

Joe regretted the time he peeked over Kat's shoulder. On the computer screen, the girl's parents offered a reward for information revealing the driver. Press attention picked up again on the first year anniversary. Previously, Joe dared to believe he could move on. From research, Kat said the police didn't have a number plate. The only detail the girl shared was the car was black. Her boyfriend, who was also playing chicken, couldn't identify the vehicle or a shadowy man.

Escaping prosecution didn't make Joe feel lucky. Kat's death was his punishment. Someone had ripped out the heart of his family. He related to the girl's parents' need for justice. After killing Kat's murderer, he would confess to the hit-and-run. He might as well be locked up for two crimes.

The torch light wobbled along the road and into adjoining fields. When they didn't feel like battling stinging nettles through the wilderness, The Six used Mill Lane. Part of the fun came from staying upright on the bumpy surface after an evening's drinking.

Memories made Joe keep moving. Recalling the softness of Kat's hand as he grabbed it made him smile. She pushed him away, always with a wink. Kat didn't want to hurt Simon. She was blameless. Joe believed he should've been the one who died.

He struck another obstacle. Bracing his hands, he forgot again how to break a fall. On all fours, he picked up his mobile. The light still glowed. He trained it ahead, noting a pothole wasn't to blame. Snapped wire snaked across the road, wound around trees and fences. He lowered onto his backside to rub sore shins. Grit was embedded into the cuts in his palms. Kids were playing stupid games again. Didn't they ever learn?

Two bright orbs burned into Joe's eyes. His raised hand couldn't block the full beam of car headlights. Joe had expected the messenger to arrive on foot. It didn't matter. He only cared about avenging Kat and Alex's murders. As Joe tried to stand, pinpricks of pain jabbed his kneecaps.

The car's lights moved. The vehicle moved into a pulling-in space, used to let oncoming traffic through. Wondering if the driver wanted to talk inside the car, Joe hobbled forwards. Four interlinked circles came into view. The car was an Audi. The driver reversed and then moved forwards. Remembering the excitement of buying an Audi, Joe smiled.

Believing the messenger had come as far as they wanted, Joe approached. A lash against his legs struck him again. He would make a complaint to Charlotte tomorrow.

Wincing, he edged upwards and stepped over the unbroken wire. Car tyres gained traction on gravel. Someone could get hurt. Battered by injury, alcohol, and grief, Joe's movements were slow.

The car picked up speed. Wire twanged. Metal slammed. Joe rose upwards. His cheekbone smashed against the ground. He realised the girl he hit must have felt the same when Joe's car smashed into her.

Hell fire pain coursed through his leg. He groaned. The limb was bent at an unnatural angle. Previously, he'd believed his life would end because of a failing liver, not by a killer car. His weary mind teased out the truth. The driver knew Joe had been involved in a hit-and-run. After Alex and Kat, Joe was next on the list. Why was someone killing them all?

Tired of living a lie and without Kat, Joe laid on his side. The car sped towards him. He spotted something familiar. After the accident, Joe tried to make amends with Kat. He'd bought a joke sticker and put it on the windscreen of the Audi. Claiming it was tacky, Kat told him to remove it. To annoy her, he didn't. The last thing Joe saw was a sticker bearing the names *The Leader* and *Princess*

After the accident, he'd never felt the same about his Audi. He should've got rid of it. No one should be killed by their own car.

A vision of a smiling Kat entered Joe's mind. It helped to drown out the sound of his crunching bones.

CHAPTER 33

Monday 23 August 2021

'Please let Joe be safe. Amen.'

Stevie ended the prayer and checked her mobile for messages. Nothing. Joe wasn't at breakfast and his car was missing. Erin was contacting his family on social media.

Stevie recalled the changes in teenage Erin after the return from Blandford. Their past fights made Stevie cautious in accepting Erin's apologies. They fought because of their similar fiery temperaments. Through the course of the holiday club, they'd become friends and realised their similarities could be positive. Stevie looked forward to rekindling their relationship as adults.

Since discovering Alex's body, a cloud of dread loomed over Stevie. The cloud darkened when she found Kat's body. If Stevie believed in curses, she had definitely received one. While Joe might not have been in danger, the dread cloud wouldn't shift. A knock sounded. She opened the door.

A woman wearing a polo shirt embroidered with *The Mill* logo smiled. 'I'm here to clean your room, unless you want me to come back later.'

'No problem. Please go ahead.'

Making her way downstairs, Stevie remembered The Six always stayed on the ground floor. After Joe's foot crashed through a wooden step, upstairs was out of bounds. Despite knowing the current building was more solid, Stevie took careful treads downstairs.

Heat swarmed in the glassed reception area. Wiping her sweaty face, she questioned Charlotte's design choices.

'Yes, it's time. Bye.' Erin ended the call.

Stevie approached her, sitting at a table. 'Hope I didn't interrupt.'

'Not at all. I was talking to my agent. We're discussing my new book. She's been patient. I've been getting itchy feet, or fingers, I guess, for writing.'

'That's exciting.' Stevie took a seat.

'The dedication will be to The Six. It's the least I can do for Alex and Kat.'

'It's such a lovely thing to do.'

'Have you seen or heard from Joe?'

'No. How about you?'

'His phone goes to voicemail. I've messaged his children. I kept it as light as possible, offering my condolences about Kat, and asking for future updates on how Joe's doing. Telling them he's missing didn't seem right until we know more. The poor family has to deal with their mum being killed. Three of them answered. They're worried sick and said Joe should be at home rather than staying at The Mill. I agree, particularly as I suspect he's an alcoholic. Maybe I'm wrong.'

'Unfortunately, I agree. Alcohol and mourning don't mix well. Let's hope Joe isn't drink-driving.'

'Hey, Charlotte,' Erin called as the woman appeared in the reception booth. 'How was Joe after we left you two together?'

Charlotte looked up from scrutinising a wedge of papers. 'Not great. We chatted for a while. Then I went to bed. He said he was finishing his drink and then going straight to his room.'

'Why did you leave him?' Stevie stomped towards her. 'There's a murderer out there!'

Charlotte fixed the woman with a stare. 'I'm aware. Joe promised he would go to bed. The Mill offers a minding service for children, not adults.'

'I'm sorry,' Stevie replied. 'This situation is scary. We should've gone home rather than stay overnight.'

'Please ask housekeeping to check Joe Andino's room,' Charlotte said to the receptionist. Along with Stevie, she joined Erin.

'How are you, Charlotte?' Erin asked. 'It's awful we haven't acknowledged Simon's anniversary beyond the memorial.'

'Don't worry. I understand. Thinking of him and the possible reasons he's gone is tough.'

'It must be difficult for you and your mum,' Stevie added.

'Simon is still very much part of our family. I know people believe it's odd, me buying a place near where he disappeared. As a child, I was often fearful because of my father. After he died, I could do what I wanted without judgement. I bought this place because it gave The Six so much joy. Someone's ruined it with Kat's and Alex's deaths.'

'Mr Andino's belongings appear to be in his room,' the receptionist called over. 'The housekeeper says the bed hasn't been used.'

Stevie's drumming fingers gained momentum on the table. 'Where is Joe?'

Charlotte clutched her head.

'Are you OK?' Erin asked.

'I've had a migraine for days. This feels too close to what happened to Simon. Joe was his best friend and now he's also missing. No offence, having you here was a terrible idea. Simon never wanted this. It wasn't meant to be this way.'

Erin's eyelids narrowed into slits. 'What do you mean?'

Charlotte stood and straightened her jacket. 'Simon wouldn't have wanted these awful things to happen. Excuse me. I have accounts to do. Keep me updated on Joe.'

'How weird was that?' Stevie said as she watched Charlotte leave.

'She's upset,' Erin replied. 'Anniversaries can be emotional. We have to decide what to do about Joe.'

'In a sec. I need a piddle.'

'Stay classy.'

****

Stevie looked away from the mirror above the sinks. God's acceptance should've been enough. She knew there was power in accepting mistakes. God's forgiveness was a one and done thing. Self-forgiveness was a continual process.

Stevie pulled the folded paper out of her pocket. She didn't dare leave it in her room for prying eyes. Whoever had discovered the years-old article did so with purpose. When training for the clergy, she considered disclosing her past. She'd tried to tell her husband. He knew her life was complicated before they met. What she did would horrify him, though.

After entering a cubicle, Stevie put down the toilet seat to sit. The paper shook in her hand. There was no point in destroying it. There would be copies. The person who sent it was obviously smart.

Student Suicide: Man Dies After Jumping From Cliff

The headline screamed an accusation at Stevie. In the first term at university, she told a terrible lie.

From the moment she saw him in the Student Union, she wanted Eddie. The party in the pub carried on at his student house. All night Stevie tried to get his attention, without success. Seeing a chance, she followed him upstairs. As she waited outside the bathroom, Eddie and his friends laughed while snorting coke. The conversation turned to potential conquests. When Stevie's name was mentioned, she grinned. Eddie mocked "the ugly weirdo". Hysterical laughter came from the bathroom. Eddie added he'd only consider Stevie as a pity shag. Her low self-esteem grasped the nugget of hope.

Finding his nametag on a door, Stevie slipped into Eddie's room. Every second she waited, she hated her desperation. Sex wasn't a long-term solution for her poor self-image. Ultimately, it left her cold. In the moment, though, she reached a fleeting high. A lustful gaze from a boy seemed like acceptance. After, the boy usually got rid of her without so much as a kiss.

An intoxicated Eddie hardly noticed Stevie lying on his bed. He collapsed next to her with a groan. Stevie panicked as his eyes closed. There was a choice to make: stay and try, or leave and feel empty.

She made the usual advances. He pushed her away. While vomiting on the carpet, he called her a freak. She ignored the insult and decided revenge was the best way to deal with the rejection.

After removing her trousers, Stevie tore her T-shirt to expose her bra. Eddie wiped his stained mouth and asked what she was doing. She screamed for help. His housemates rushed in to find a distressed young woman. Women comforted the victim. Lads threatened violence upon their former friend. Eddie could hardly stand, let alone defend himself. Stevie begged them not to phone the police. He hadn't raped her, although sexual assault was bad enough. She covered her face as she cried, saying she couldn't talk about it.

In the following days, rumours spread across campus. People either ignored Eddie or called him names. His friends wanted nothing to do with him. Stevie became everyone's favourite victim. She realised you had to be careful what you wish for. It wasn't the type of attention she wanted.

Eddie went home in the holidays and jumped off a cliff. When she heard the news, Stevie dropped out of university. Her parents didn't ask why she'd made the decision. The police questioned her about the sexual abuse allegation. She told them it was a stupid rumour.

In The Mill toilets, Stevie scanned the article, detailing Eddie's suicide. It hadn't named her. While she could claim ignorance, her conscience knew the truth. Whoever sent the piece surely had more proof.

She had stayed at The Mill as instructed, even though she feared being next for Kat and Alex's killer. Being around Charlotte was hard, too. Making eye contact with Simon's sister demanded strength Stevie wasn't sure she possessed. Her earlier outburst at Charlotte for not looking after Joe was cringeworthy. She had to keep Charlotte onside and oblivious.

As with Eddie, Stevie wrecked Simon's life, too. She learnt how to make a damning accusation in 1992. Simon's disappearance was Stevie's fault.

CHAPTER 34

Friday 21 August 1992

Alex raised a can of lager. 'Here's to The Six for completing the holiday club.'

The others scattered around the mill, joined in the toast.

In the background, Carter the Unstoppable Sex Machine sang "The Only Living Boy in New Cross" The song spoke to Simon about being part of something while still feeling alone. Before, friendships with Joe and Alex were enough. Being in The Six had come too late for Simon. Nothing lasted forever.

Erin turned down the volume. Pushing her aside, Simon grabbed the dial and flicked it back up.

'The Witch won't like the noise,' Erin said.

'She hasn't complained so far!'

Joe approached the two. 'The Witch doesn't give us grief. Let's not make her kick off tonight.'

The building became silent.

'No point having the stereo on if I can't hear it.' Simon dropped to the floor next to Stevie. 'Erin's being the fun police,' he continued. 'Is it why you're always dressed in black, Erin? You're a prophet of doom, sitting in the corner, always thinking. What goes on in that head?'

Erin and the others frowned at each other. Over the past week, Simon's irritability had increased. Whenever they asked if he was OK, he snapped back short answers.

Stevie raised a bottle of gin to her mouth. Alex and Joe chorused and clapped. 'Chug, chug, chug!'

Accepting the challenge, she continued. Mid-drink, Simon swiped the bottle. Gin soaked Stevie's KLF T-shirt.

'Nice one, you twat!' She punched him in the arm. 'You only had to ask. Now I'll stink like a brewery.'

'Stop being such a drama queen.' He grasped the booze like a toddler caught with something they weren't allowed.

'What's bit your arse?' she asked. 'Being catty is usually my department.'

'Nothing.' He took a swig of gin.

'Stop bitching,' Alex said. 'This is supposed to be a celebration. What's the matter with everyone today? Joe's already been a complete wanker.'

Joe crumpled the can he was holding. 'I was joking, Farm Boy! Of course, you weren't going to kiss me. I freaked out when I opened my eyes and you were there.'

'I was trying to wake you up!' Muscles strained in Alex's neck.

'Maybe this will cheer you all up.' Joe rooted through a carrier bag. 'This is a good haul. Confiscating booze at the disco was a brilliant idea, Al.'

'Stupid adults believed we'd get the kids to hand it over and then we'd throw it away.'

'That was *my* idea,' Simon said. 'It's typical of you, taking over. Being a thug means no one challenges you, right?'

'How many times do I have to apologise for hitting you? If you'd stayed out of my business, it wouldn't have happened.'

'I only wanted to help the boy who was confused about his sexuality, and, come to think of it, you too.'

'It's over.' Alex reddened. 'Move on. Anyone fancy a bevvy?'

Erin took her usual corner spot. 'It's nice to see you two talking at last, even if you're still arguing.'

'Why *did* you fight?' Kat asked.

'Doesn't matter,' Alex replied. 'What music shall I put on?'

Simon placed a fingernail under the ring pull of a can. He flicked it over and over. 'Changing the subject won't change you, Al. Life's easier when you accept who you are.'

Alex barrelled at Simon. Stevie stood. Alex knocked Kat's elbow. Her eyeliner application travelled from her eyelid to her cheek.

'Stay out of my business!' Alex yelled with his face close to Simon's.

Joe rushed to stand between the two. 'Lads, be civil or piss off.'

Stevie swayed. 'Come on, Al. Let's go through the cassettes. These arguments are getting on my tits.'

'Dude,' Joe began as he joined Simon, sitting on the blanket. 'What's wrong?'

'I can't take much more.'

'Ignore Al. He gets mouthy when he's drunk.'

'He's the least of my problems. Everything's going wrong.'

'Let's go outside and chat.'

'Forget it. I'm being a miserable git.' Simon straightened. 'Who's up for tequila? I brought shot glasses.'

'No thanks.' Kat's mouth puckered. 'Tequila is gross.'

'I'm in!' Stevie took a running jump and landed with a thud on the floor.

Kat finished wiping eyeliner from her face and cleared her throat. 'I could do with a wee.' She winked at Joe.

He smiled and nodded. 'I'll keep guard.'

'For God's sake, Princess, there's nothing outside wild enough to hurt you!' Stevie said.

'I hate the dark.'

'Leave her alone,' Joe said. 'There's no lighting out there. Kat needs a look out.'

'You're such a gentleman.' Bitterness spiked Simon's words.

****

Simon stomped into the mill.

'Did you find them?' Erin asked.

He paced around the building. The throbbing bass of SL2's "On a Ragga Tip" matched his angry energy.

'Earth to Simon!' Erin called. 'Did you see Joe and Kat?'

He spun around and glared at her. 'Yes, I certainly did.'

'What's going on?'

'Stop playing the innocent. You know they're together. I expect you all do.'

Erin's eyes widened. 'Kat and Joe are a couple?'

Stevie sniggered. 'They've been at it since the holiday club started.'

'I suspected something was going on.' Alex shrugged. 'None of my business.'

'Why are you so bothered, Si?' Erin tapped her fingers against her mouth. The tapping ceased. 'Oh, I get it! You fancy Kat.'

'No, I don't.' He lowered his head.

'Don't be embarrassed.'

Simon smacked his palm against a wall. 'Stop taking the piss out of me!'

'I wasn't.' Erin retreated.

'Chill out,' Alex said. 'No need to be aggressive.'

A cackle came from Simon's mouth. 'Says you; Mr Handy-With-His-Fists.'

Alex shook his head. 'I've had enough of your shit. You've done nothing but pick fights. I'm leaving. Is anyone else coming?'

'Me,' Erin said. 'This night isn't fun anymore.'

'I'm staying,' Stevie slurred. 'Turn the music up, Si. This tune is an absolute banger.'

'Whatever's bugging you, Simon,' Erin said, 'please tell one of us. We care.'

'I'm beyond help.'

'Come on.' Alex took Erin's arm and headed for the exit. 'There's no reasoning with him tonight.'

Stevie waved. 'See you later, boring gits. We're getting wasted.' She clinked her glass of tequila with Simon's, knocked it back, and then focused on him. 'What's the matter? You look sad.'

'It's ending.'

'The holiday club?'

'Me. I'm ending. This is the end of the old me. I'm not as kind as people think.'

Stevie swatted his arm. 'Give over. You're the kindest person I've ever met.'

'I try to be nice. Sometimes I want to scream to make people see my pain. I thought I was naturally kind. Now I wonder if it's a cover for this darkness.' A tear slid down his cheek.

'Don't cry.' Stevie caught the tear with her finger and then pulled him into a hug.

After breaking away from each other, their eyes locked. They kissed. Frantic hands scrabbled. Stevie removed her top. The sound of Simon's zip was a reality check. He pushed her off and did up his trousers.

'I can't do this, Stevie.'

She latched an arm around his neck. 'It's OK. No one has to know.'

'No!' He pushed her aside. 'I need a friend, not a shag.'

'I'm fed up with boys taking advantage of me! At least *they* see it through, even if they call me names afterwards. Why doesn't anyone love me? I'm as good as the likes of Kat!'

'Of course you are. I respect you too much to let this happen.'

'Bullshit!' She forced his hand onto her breast.

'No!' He stood and backed away.

Stevie grabbed her clothing. 'Don't you dare judge me. I'm not disgusting!'

'You're lovely. I don't want to ruin things. Let's forget this happened.'

Leaning back, she gave a smile. 'Take what I'm offering. Otherwise I'll say you tried to hurt me.'

His face whitened. 'What the hell do you mean?'

'I've seen how you fellas operate. You get together, say you've slept with me, and congratulate each other. This time, the girl wins. I'll say you attacked me.'

'You can't accuse me of sexual assault!'

Stevie crossed her arms. 'Watch me. Make me feel cheap and this is what happens.'

'I don't know who *any* of you are anymore!' Simon grabbed his jacket. 'I was wrong to believe The Six could help me.'

'Take your do-gooder act somewhere else. Get out of my sight.'

Simon did. Nobody saw him again.

CHAPTER 35

Monday 23 August 2021

Stevie took a moment from packing. She assessed the room. Although it was swish and modern – better than what she could usually afford – she didn't want to be there anymore. What did high thread count linen, complimentary food baskets, and rainfall showers matter? She longed for the familiarity of Thame, her husband, the local church, and its people. The blackmailer would have to expose her secret. She would face the consequences.

Alex and Kat were dead. Joe was missing. They were all there for Simon's memorial. Was he alive? He was a decent person who unravelled before disappearing. Everyone has their breaking point. When they reached it, some seek revenge against those who caused them to break.

The thought of Simon as a killer seemed ridiculous. Yet Stevie knew how twisted a person can be, especially one in turmoil. While a childhood of neglect affected her, she didn't make excuses. The sexual assault allegation she made against Eddie led to his suicide. Self-hatred for threatening Simon with a similar allegation gnawed at her gut. He'd rejected her because he didn't want to ruin their friendship. Instead, she wrecked it.

Questions attacked Stevie's mind. If Simon was alive, what was he like as a man? Had he forgiven her? Was he taking revenge on The Six for letting him down? Trying to block scattergun questions, she clasped her head. Thinking of him as alive was nonsense. Considering Simon as Alex and Kat's murderer was even more ridiculous.

Stevie's thoughts switched to Joe. His disappearance was her main concern. After finding Kat's body, Joe understandably fell apart. As Stevie looked at her suitcase, she wondered why they had stayed at The Mill after the deaths. A stupid sense of loyalty and fear of blackmail were the answers.

She got up from the bed. Her focus shifted. The sad fact was The Six was long gone. The memorial was a nostalgic indulgence. People had died for it. While unzipping the suitcase, Stevie vowed not to be next.

A knock sounded on the door.

****

In the bathroom, Erin scooped up toiletries. Tidy packing didn't matter. For the baby's health, she needed to leave soon. Concern at twinges and occasional spotting made her get an emergency GP appointment. The doctor's eyes almost popped out of his head when he heard about what was happening at The Mill. While he understood Erin wanted to support her friends, he said she had to prioritise the baby and herself.

In their phone conversation, Gemma tried not to apply pressure, but her concern was obvious. The surrogacy was her only chance of being a mother.

Erin decided to follow Simon's example and place kindness above everything else. Being kind sometimes meant making difficult decisions. Erin chose the baby over searching for Joe.

Last time she saw him, Joe was drunk. Thoughts of his car potentially crashing into a ditch were terrifying. Thankfully, there had been no reports of local car accidents. The news should have been encouraging. Instead, the silence was unsettling.

A knock sounded on Erin's door.

****

Charlotte stared at the wall in the office. She wondered if her business would ever recover. Three deaths, all confirmed as linked to each other. Charlotte's school friend, Derek, gave more details than a sergeant should. Whoever had killed Joe did it with malice.

After finding Joe's body on her daily walk, The Witch called the police. Derek said tyre marks on Joe's body showed a car had driven over him a few times. Snapped wires, previously strung across the road, probably slowed him down before. Joe had been drinking a lot. Along with an unlit road, he didn't stand a chance of survival.

A pink tulip was discovered with Joe's body. Derek also revealed the contents of a note left alongside it.

Joe drove me to this. If a man ruins a person's life with his car, it is killing with kindness to take his life in a similar fashion.

Along with the note was a copy of a newspaper report. The hit-and-run incident caused local debates. People argued over who was to blame: the girl or the driver. Some stated the girl deserved her injuries for playing chicken. Others mounted a witch hunt for the driver, who had fled the scene. In a Facebook comment, someone threatened to run the driver over with his car and see how he liked it. Someone had done exactly that to Joe. Only hours before, he'd lost Kat. The Andino family would never be the same again.

Pink tulips were Charlotte's favourite flower; a token of Simon's caring. She never wanted to see the flower again. Bitterness visited once again. It took a seat, grabbed Charlotte's hand, and hurled her into the past.

The week before her brother disappeared, a family argument escalated. Simon punched their father. Charlotte couldn't tell who was the more surprised of the two. In his defence, Simon had to do something. Thomas's hands squeezed their mother, Beatrice's throat. She was being punished for trying to leave her husband.

Simon returned from the mill to the carnage in the Pritchards' kitchen. Charlotte was on the floor, trembling from her father's blows. The crack of Thomas's nose as Simon's fist connected was glorious. Beatrice and her children used Thomas's moment of disbelief and pain to flee. Eventually, they returned. They always did.

After hitting Thomas, Simon went to the holiday club disco. Claiming she'd be safe in a hotel room, Beatrice encouraged her children to go out. Throughout the evening, Simon danced and chatted. Underneath the performance, Charlotte noticed his wobbly grin and trembling. Simon clenched his fist, bruised from punching his father.

Her brother's actions back then still affected Charlotte. She would always be loyal to him, even when it challenged her conscience.

Bitterness left Charlotte. In its place, regret wrapped itself around her. If she'd stopped Simon from going to the mill that night, maybe his friends would still be alive.

CHAPTER 36

Monday 23 August 2021

Stevie thumped the steering wheel. After receiving the news of Joe's murder, she could only nod. Years of counselling others taught her suppressing her emotions wasn't wise.

Once again, she bashed the heel of her hand against the wheel. Another turn of the ignition offered only a crunching noise. She slammed the door behind her and kicked a tyre.

'Useless piece of crap!'

Charlotte joined her. After saying goodbye to Erin and Stevie, she was standing outside The Mill.

'What's wrong with it?' Charlotte asked.

'Do I look like a bloody mechanic?' Stevie leaned on the bonnet. 'Sorry. I'm stressed and want to go. Giving another statement about a dead friend has done me in. Now the sodding car won't start. Weird, as it was serviced last week.'

Erin got out of her car. 'What's happening?'

'My car isn't working. I'll have to call a rescue service.'

'They'll likely take ages,' Charlotte said. 'If the car needs fixing, it'll be even longer.'

Stevie glanced at The Mill and frowned. 'Sorry, I can't be here a minute longer. I'd rather not be a sitting duck for a killer.'

'Imagine how this will ruin my business.' Charlotte cleared her throat. 'The least I can do is to arrange for your car to be fixed. A member of staff will bring it to Erin's. That's where you're going, right?'

'The police asked me to stay local for a few days.' Stevie sighed. 'They might need more info. I'm not happy with how they've dealt with all this. Joe and Kat would probably still be alive if we hadn't been told to stay. At least I'll be safe at Erin's house.'

'Don't worry,' Charlotte replied. 'I'll make sure your car is sorted.'

'It's so kind of you, just like…' Stevie shook her head.

'You can say his name. Any friend of Simon's is a friend of mine. I'll phone when it's fixed.'

'Despite the circumstances, I'm glad you'll be with me,' Erin said. 'Being alone with my thoughts isn't what I need.'

Stevie watched her chewing her lip. Charlotte earlier confided how Erin almost fainted when told about Joe's death. Brave as ever, she refused medical help.

'Do you want me to drive?' Stevie hoped Erin would refuse. It had taken a lot of self-talk for Stevie to get into her own vehicle. An imagined scene of Joe's body being driven over made her shiver.

Charlotte mentioned a pink tulip left with the body and what was written in the note left with it. Because of her job, Stevie brought out people's confessional sides. She wished the murderer would confess and end her fear of being next. She took her bags from her car boot and placed them on the back seat of Erin's vehicle.

'Keep in touch.' Charlotte hugged the women.

After leaving The Mill, Stevie and Erin settled into silence. There are no comforting words when three of your friends are dead.

'Spending time with you will be nice,' Stevie offered.

'It's a shame it had to be this way. The whole thing makes me feel sick.'

'Say if you're not feeling well.'

'I have to be OK for the baby.'

'It's an amazing thing you're doing.'

Erin shrugged. 'Not really. I can have children. Gemma can't. It's a no-brainer.'

'Not many people would offer to carry a child for someone else.'

'Don't think it's been fun.' Erin pointed to her tummy. 'I'm looking forward to no longer resembling a barrage balloon.'

They joined in laughter as Erin turned on the radio. 'I loved this song, back in the day!' Erin raised the volume. The old friends sang together.

'Watch out!' Stevie smacked her palms on the dashboard.

In front of the car, a figure darted across the road. Erin swerved. Stevie shrieked. Erin slammed on the brakes. The car stopped inches from a tree.

Erin exhaled. Stevie opened her eyes.

'Are you OK?' Stevie asked. She loosened the seatbelt, tightening into Erin's precious cargo.

'I think so.'

'What on earth was he doing?' Stevie's voice trembled. 'Where's he gone?'

A knock sounded against the driver's side window. Erin looked over.

The dead had risen.

CHAPTER 37

Monday 23 August 2021

Erin fumbled for the lock. Too late. The door swung open.

'Dylan?' Erin managed as the man dragged her out of the car.

'It can't be. He's dead!' Stevie reached for her mobile.

'Throw the phone into the footwell and then get out,' the man snarled. 'Erin, get rid of your mobile, too.'

He knows her name, Stevie thought. She considered running. They were in a country lane, next to the woods. Hardly anyone took the road, which was considered more scenic than a fast route. She knew even if she escaped, the man would likely kill Erin. His hateful glare confirmed it.

Stevie studied the attacker as he whispered in Erin's ear, and she whimpered. A flicker of recognition sparked in Stevie's mind. She wondered if he was the man who lived in The Witch's shack. Dylan was never around when The Six appeared, but Stevie saw him once. On the way home, she spotted him smoking and she hid in the bushes to watch. The man threatening Erin with a knife had similar thick hair, with the same kind of height and build as the man from 1992. Back then, Dylan was a mystery the rest of The Six didn't want to solve. Whenever anyone mentioned him, Erin changed the subject.

This can't be Dylan, Stevie thought. *Why is she calling him that?*

The man instructed Stevie. 'Stop staring and get over here!'

He locked an arm around Erin's chest. His free hand held a knife to her throat.

As Stevie approached, he pushed her in front. 'Move!'

She scanned the area as she led. Shade from the trees was usually a blessed relief from the sun. Instead, she was marching into the dark pits of hell.

A dusty circle appeared in the forest. The man shoved Erin onto a log.

'Sit next to her,' the man told Stevie.

'I lost my mind, believing you were Dylan,' Erin said. 'You always were similar.' She addressed Stevie. 'This is Wily, Dylan's brother. I guess he's here for me, although it hasn't stopped him from going for the others. The sick bastard enjoys hurting people.'

The man punched her in the stomach. She gave a loud groan as she bent over.

Stevie jumped up. 'She's pregnant!'

Wily jabbed the knife towards her. 'Sit down or I'll gut you like a fish.'

While Stevie took a seat, he grabbed Erin's hair and pulled her head back.

He lowered towards her. 'I've been waiting for this moment. Did you really believe I'd let you destroy Dylan's life?'

Erin stared at him. 'You took your time.'

'Don't play games with me, bitch. You're lucky you've lived this long.'

'If this is about me, why kill my friends? They've done nothing.' Her earlier shouting became more of a whisper.

Never looking away, he sliced the air beside him. 'Move another inch on the log and I'll show you my butchery skills.'

Stevie stopped shuffling and anchored her nails into the oak.

'Why are you doing this?' Erin asked.

'Because I can and I should. It's been a pleasure ruining your life, as you did Dylan's. I heard about the memorial for the boy who killed my brother. It was the perfect opportunity to begin my plan. I gave the group "incentives" to make you stay at The Mill for the long weekend. Then, I started killing.'

'The others had nothing to do with Dylan!' Stevie cried. 'Why kill them?'

'Shut your mouth, Sister Act.'

She grabbed her white collar. 'I'm a vicar, not a nun.'

'Same old religious bullshit.' Wily poked the knife tip against Erin's face. 'Tina and Erin ruined Dylan's life by leaving him. They didn't believe he hadn't killed Nick, that brat paperboy. Of course, Dylan came to Trillhaven to get Tina back. Even though I told him not to bother, he didn't listen and died for his trouble. If it wasn't for The Six and your evenings at the mill, Dylan wouldn't have met Simon. My brother would still be alive.'

As Erin struggled, the knife nicked her skin. Beads of blood bloomed on her cheek. 'As far as killing motives go, that's pathetic.'

'Sorry, my plots aren't good enough for you, Agatha Christie.'

The knife slashed deeper into Erin's face. She howled as her flesh tore.

'Reckon you're so clever,' Wily hissed. 'Well, I'm smart, too. After paying Dylan a visit, I stuck around. Even though we had a fight about his ugly bitch landlady, it was obvious he needed me. He had too much pride to ask, so I camped out in the wilderness. I found out a lot about you kids.'

Stevie's eyes widened. 'You were spying on us?'

He laughed. 'The spooky man watched you for a few weeks. I learnt a lot, mostly boring teenage drama. I was ready to leave. Then Simon gave me a reason to stay.'

'Did you kill him?' Erin asked.

Wylie clasped his ribs as hysterics took hold. Before continuing, he took a breath. 'No, I didn't touch soppy Simon. More's the pity. I discovered many things about him, though. The boy was obsessed with Dylan. Simon murdered him.'

'What utter crap,' Erin replied. 'Simon wouldn't have hurt a fly.'

He flashed the knife in her face. She jolted back.

Wily continued. 'It all adds up. Simon disappeared the night Dylan was murdered. If that's not a sign of guilt, I don't know what is. From outside the shack, I heard the boy hero worshipping Dylan. I expect Dylan eventually told Simon to back off, and he took offence.'

'No one believes the rumours linking Simon's disappearance to Dylan's death,' Stevie said.

'Well, you should. Once, I heard Simon telling Dylan he wanted to strike out and hurt someone. Turns out it was my brother.'

'If Simon killed Dylan – which is ridiculous –,' Stevie began, 'why are you here now? Why not do something in 1992?'

'I bet he's been doing a long stretch,' Erin replied.

Wily pointed at her. 'Bingo! Unfortunately, I got banged up not long after Dylan died. Prison gave me some thinking time, and I realised Simon killed him. I considered what I'd learnt about Simon: a girly fondness for pink tulips, telling secrets to Dylan, and pretending to be kind. After my release from prison, I began *Project Killing Kindness*. Granted, it's not as fancy as Erin's book titles. It served the purpose, though. You all thought you were so caring and friendly, being in a group.

'*You* had to pay, Erin, for abandoning Dylan when he needed you. Shame your whore of a mother is dead and I didn't have the pleasure of killing her. I'm also righting the wrongs of Simon murdering Dylan. The coward boy probably topped himself, but I'll still have what's mine. Not kind to kill someone, is it? Simon took my brother. I decided to take what Simon cared about. I'm killing kindness – Simon's fake kindness – with the death of each member of The Six. In prison I made connections. I had fellas finding out where you live and work, and all your dirty little secrets. Blackmail made you all stay at The Mill. Genius.'

Erin rubbed her wound and then studied her bloodied palm. 'Alex, Kat, and Joe didn't deserve this. Killing them has solved nothing. If you want revenge, you should've killed only me.'

Wily grinned. 'Oh, I will. Both of you are about to meet your maker. Then I'm going to The Mill to finish off Charlotte.'

'No!' Stevie shouted.

'Let her go.' Erin stood. 'Take me. Stevie won't say anything.'

'No, Erin!' Stevie made her body a shield in front of her friend. 'Think about the baby.'

'How noble and kind you both are.' Wily smirked.

Stevie lowered her head and murmured.

'What's she doing?' Wily asked.

'Praying.' Erin squeezed Stevie's hand.

He sniggered. 'It won't help.'

Wily raised the knife.

Stevie closed her eyes.

Erin screamed.

Like a tree being felled, a body struck the forest ground.

FROM: Chris Palmer

SUBJECT: Checking Progress

DATE: Oct 4, 2021, 9:19 AM

TO: Rein92

I trust this email finds you well. Unfortunately, I haven't heard from you in a few weeks. Perhaps you're considering if my publishing offer is genuine. I understand you have to be cautious. What you have to share is going to blow people's minds.

Rest assured, I've kept your email address private. As agreed, I won't use your name in our emails. The publishing contract has to be in your actual name. There are ways around this to make sure you can't be traced. Don't worry. I've considered everything.

I know you were shocked when I approached you. You weren't expecting anyone to find you. When I want something, I pursue it. I think you can relate. Like you, I also value privacy.

Even though Palmer Publishing is fairly new, several agents are sending me manuscripts from bestselling authors. I want your work to be a huge part of my publishing house's success. This is a once in a lifetime opportunity to give your story twice. I believe your skills can extend to non-fiction writing, too.

In your last email, you shared your anger about how the public learnt about Killing Kindness. *View it as a bonus, rather than a problem. The police and the press knowing about the novel led me to you.*

I understand your annoyance about how the USB stick got into the wrong hands. My police contact was desperate to give me a copy of Killing Kindness. *Imagine what a corrupt police officer would do with your novel if they were offered money. Claim what's rightfully yours.*

The fame you have now isn't for being an author. Hiding must be awful for you. With my help, you'll be recognised for your writing again.

As two determined women, we can set the publishing world on fire. Your original fictionalised novel using real events, followed by the factual version, is gold.

When the book is published, the tabloids will try even harder to find you. With my connections and finances, I can guarantee you a new location and anonymity.

Don't worry about the legal stuff either. My excellent legal team has everything covered. No one will silence your voice.

If you wish to go ahead, you must deliver both parts of the book by 6 March 2022.

I know it's a quick turnaround. You've said you're a fast writer, and have finished the novel beyond the rough first draft. Your research and viewpoints from actually staying at The Mill will be added dynamite. While the deaths of members of The Six are a hot topic, we should publish as soon as possible.

As discussed, there will be collaborators in the non-fiction section. While I understand your concerns, I ask for your trust. The others' opinions will enhance your writing. They're considering writing a book without you. I confess this is my back-up project if you don't accept this contract. Do you want others telling your story?

Kind regards, Chris.

FROM: Rein92

SUBJECT: Re: Checking Progress

DATE: Oct 4, 2021, 9:31 AM

TO: Chris Palmer

I like how you won't let go of what you want. Getting a copy of my novel in such a backhand way could've been annoying. Instead, I admire your commitment.

When the press leaked extracts from Killing Kindness, *I couldn't contain my rage. No one steals what's mine. Also, it's an author's worst nightmare; people reading the first draft. The book is perfect now I've had time to work on it, not that I'd give it to the tabloids.*

I've only recently forgiven Paige for sharing my new email address with you. She says you wore her down after finding her on social media.

Well done for figuring out Paige was my mother's former best friend. People don't stay friends with my mother for long, though. Despite the media massacre, Paige believes in me and won't let me down again.

You're a clever woman, Christine, sorry, Chris. You've stated before you don't like the longer version of your name. Stop trying to pass yourself off as a man. Own being female. We can be as powerful in publishing as men. If not more so. I'm currently researching Palmer Publishing and you.

While I understand it's best to release the book while public interest is high, you can't do it without me. The threat to publish the others' versions without me is ridiculous. What they have to say is nothing in comparison to what I know.

Other publishers and agents are interested in working with me. This is a competitive market. I need the best deal. My future depends on it.

FROM: Chris Palmer

SUBJECT: Re: Checking Progress

DATE: Oct 5, 2021, 9:25 AM

TO: Rein92

It's great to hear from you. I understand why you want to consider your options. There are many sharks swimming in the publishing pool.

The internet will reveal plenty about my background. I come from a well-connected, business-focused family. This is my business, though, not my father's. I don't need a man to succeed.

Research will also show how qualified I am. I'm not playing at publishing.

With respect, you'll find it difficult to get another agent or publisher. This book contains a lot of controversial things many won't touch. People died. Families are grieving. My carefully planned strategy won't cause any legal issues.

My sources tell me Paige has approached agents on your behalf. There are snakes out there, desperate to lead the police, press, or both to you. Careful with who you trust. My discretion is guaranteed.

Even your former agent is gossiping. She told my assistant at a recent book launch she was glad to be free of your demands. Throughout the evening, she made cruel jokes about your desperation and how she enjoyed rejecting your work. Apparently you offered Killing Kindness *to her before staying at The Mill. She won't be laughing when she sees how much money we'll make. Let's show all the doubters you can fly high as an author again.*

Adding the non-fiction section gives you the chance to tell the chance to tell the truth. While it was genius to write a novel based on reality, others weren't following the same plot as you. We'll show them they were wrong.

Be in charge of your own ending.

Kind regards, Chris.

FROM: Rein92

SUBJECT: Re: Checking Progress

DATE: Oct 5, 2021, 11:33 AM

TO: Chris Palmer

That poor excuse for an agent can rot in hell for all I care. She's the has-been, not me.

Now I've finished my research on you, I can confirm we have a deal for Killing Kindness.

The novel is finished. I will now write the non-fiction section. There are conditions, though.

When the complete book is published, you must give me a new home, as promised.

We need to discuss how you'll pay my royalties. A bank account in my name makes me traceable.

When the police contact you, you won't give them any details about me. I have to stay in hiding for my protection.

The collaborators can say what they want in response to what I write. This is my *book. It's about time I told my version; fantasy and reality.*

FROM: Rein92

SUBJECT: Silence Isn't Golden

DATE: Oct 9, 2021, 7:06 AM

TO: Chris Palmer

Chris, it's been four days since I've heard from you.

Do you want my book or not?

FROM: Rein92

SUBJECT: Not a Fool

DATE: Oct 10, 2021, 6:16 AM

TO: Chris Palmer

If you're setting me up, I'm not biting. So much for you being someone I can trust.

FROM: Chris Palmer

SUBJECT: Sorry

DATE: Oct 10, 2021, 10:10 AM

TO: Rein92

Please accept my sincere apologies. I've been dealing with a family emergency. Rest assured, I still want to publish your book and am excited about it.

FROM: Rein92

SUBJECT: Re: Sorry

DATE: Oct 10, 2021, 10.15 AM

TO: Chris Palmer

I'll let it go this once. Don't mess me around again.

Let's get this book deal sorted.

FROM: Chris Palmer

SUBJECT: We Have a Deal!

DATE: Oct 11, 2021, 10:10 AM

TO: Rein92

I'm delighted you're working with Palmer Publishing.

As agreed, the novel and non-fiction section must be delivered to me no later than 6 March 2022.

It's great the novel is already written. I trust you will complete the non-fiction section in time. I'll get a contract to you in due course.

Here is how the project will work:

- *The overall book is called* Killing Kindness.

- *Part One is the novel. This includes a storyline using the notes you made when staying at The Mill bed and breakfast.*

- *Please leave the novel's ending on a cliffhanger, as we discussed. I've considered keeping the original ending with you as the only survivor. Leaving the novel open-ended, though, makes readers want to read Part Two to find out the answers to their questions.*

- *Part Two is non-fiction. This is titled* Killing Kindness*: Conversations in Killing.*

- *Unlike the novel, the non-fiction version will be chronological. Begin with the events of 1992, followed by what happened at The Mill in August 2021.*

- *Contributors will write their own extracts in the non-fiction section. These people will read the completed novel and then write their responses.*

- *Email your writing to me daily. While this isn't usual practice, it's necessary. The contributors need to react to what you write.*

- *I will choose which of the contributors are most suitable for replying to your accounts. I will act as a messenger, taking your message to the right person. The contributors understand they must always be ready to reply.*

- *I will send their replies back to you. Your truth and theirs are up for comparison. I encourage you not to engage with the contributors in depth, if at all. The narrative must keep moving.*

- *As the main author, you will receive the highest percentage of royalties. Your name alone is on the book cover. The contributors will be listed inside.*

- *All the contributors are giving their royalties to chosen charities.*

  I am excited about this book. This is the beginning of something big, Erin!

  Kind regards, Chris.

FROM: Rein92

SUBJECT: Re: We Have a Deal!

DATE: Oct 11, 2021, 10:40 AM

TO: Chris Palmer

You almost lost the deal by mentioning my name in your last email. Fortunately, I can be forgiving when I want to be. I'll let it go as you're so excited.

It's not like the details we've shared in emails can't be connected to me. The anagram of my name for email wasn't wise. Arrogance sometimes catches me out.

The contributors can do what they want with their money. I expect they're trying to look good by donating to charity. I hope you're not expecting a similar gesture from me. I need every penny I can get. On that note, I'd appreciate receiving the contract soon.

I'll start writing today. I won't lie, I've missed it.

Prepare yourself for what really happened to The Six. It will blow your mind.

PART TWO
KILLING KINDNESS:
CONVERSATIONS IN
KILLING

Introduction

Erin Sullivan

What you are about to read is the truth. I'll excuse you for doubting my ability to be honest. After all, I created fiction from real events in my novel, *Killing Kindness*.

In this part of the whole book, I'm giving only *true* accounts. Prepare to compare fiction with non-fiction. You'll be shocked at what *really* happened. Throughout, you won't be able to stop reading. I'm teasing you with crappy taglines. I hate those things. Most readers do, too. How many more times must we be told a book is breathtaking or unputdownable? We'll be the judges of that.

Titles for novels are sneaky little things. Occasionally, the title pops into the author's mind before we've written a word. Other times, it's dragged out like drawing blood with a rusty knife. *Killing Kindness* was a gift from Simon Pritchard, not that he knew it. The title is an obvious nod to the saying, *killing with kindness*. It's about overdoing kindness, often overpowering the receiver. The literal killing part of the saying was an absolute gift for my writing.

Always question the motives of those who often offer kindness. Are they wrapping you in care or slowly suffocating you? Consider Simon's kindness more deeply. People died because of it.

I wrote the first draft of the novel *before* Simon's memorial. Let that sink in. Charlotte's invitation came at the perfect time. The explosive book I'd wanted to write had arrived. *I* made it happen. Sure, not everything worked out as planned. When characters try to take over, this happens. I can adapt.

My original ending for *Killing Kindness* was more final than the cliffhanger of a body falling in the forest. Sometimes you have to let the publisher win. I agreed to leave readers wondering who died: Stevie, Wily, or me. It doesn't matter how the story ended. The news of *real* events went nationwide. Now I get to finish the story with the whole truth.

Don't believe the tabloids. There's more to "The Sadistic Summers of The Six"; the media's ridiculous term for the events of 1992 and 2021. Journalists like to dig deep. Coming up with nothing, because I won't give them the dirt, they twisted the truth.

My characters are real. Some of the plot in *Killing Kindness* isn't. It's artistic licence.

After reading fiction and fact, do not call this part-memoir. My story isn't about triumphing over adversity. It's about my skills as a writer.

Now you've finished reading the novel, here's how this second part works. I'm the main narrator, presenting what actually happened.

After writing my memories, I regularly sent them to the publisher. They were passed on to contributors; survivors or people close to those who died. This is where the discussion bit, *Conversations in Killing*, happens.

In advance, the contributors read the novel. Then people chosen by the publisher replied to my accounts in this non-fiction section.

Decide if *they* are being truthful. Why should I be the only one placed under scrutiny? No one is ever 100% honest.

Get ready to delve into August 1992 and August 2021. You'll discover more about Simon, who advocated kindness and failed. The secrets of The Six will be revealed.

Compare two eras where kindness died. You'll never consider kindness the same way again.

1992

Monday 3 August 1992

Erin

The Six. It's a basic name for a group, right? That's because it was. *Every* group of six teenagers who worked at the holiday club was called The Six. It's not as prestigious as I depicted in *Killing Kindness*. Many other versions of The Six followed. None had a summer quite like ours, though.

I didn't want to be a helper at the holiday club. We'd barely settled in at my aunt Fran's house when my mother, Tina, decided to keep me occupied over the holidays.

Fran was concerned about the fights between my cousin, Gemma, and me. I confess I started the arguments. I was agitated from sleeping on an airbed and listening to Tina's snoring every night.

The garage conversion was a health and safety hazard. Comets of black spores burst through peeling wallpaper. Mustiness ate into our clothes, making us smell like a charity shop. I still can't believe I didn't develop a chronic breathing condition. Tina never complained to her sister. I grew up with a mother who always played nice for fear of upsetting others. I decided never to be the same.

When the holiday club started, Gemma and I could finally avoid each other. The nosey brat often trailed me around the house. When I rifled through her parents' belongings, Gemma protested. We all enjoy a good snoop around. Don't deny you've peeked in someone's bathroom cabinet.

Fran was one of the holiday club's organisers. It took some persuading on Tina's part for Fran to take me on as a helper. The committee was concerned about my reputation. Most of Trillhaven knew me well, for the wrong reasons.

I liked to cause trouble, and not because of being inherently bad. Spare me the original sin crap. Marking us as sinners from birth is Stevie and her invisible friend's department. We choose to become who we are. Own your choices.

My choice was to be a modern Sherlock Holmes; reading body language, words, motivations, weaknesses, and strengths. For me, everyone is a potential character.

As a condition of staying in her home, Fran demanded good behaviour. Thankfully, Tina didn't tell Fran about me being expelled from the school in Blandford. I left that out of the novel, at the point where I first met The Six. It would've put me at a disadvantage from the start. You definitely would've thought I was a bad girl.

Tina and I needed a home after discovering the paperboy, Nick's, bloodied cap; evidence Dylan killed the child. That part of the novel is true, sort of. More on that, later.

Not long before the discovery of the cap, I was kicked out of school for dealing ecstasy in the girls' toilets. The head teacher was ecstatic at being able to get rid of me. My manipulative skills worked a treat. I made sure a teacher "caught" me dealing. Blandford and I were done.

Getting the other members of The Six to accept me was important. From the beginning, I tried to behave.

It was obvious Stevie and I weren't best friends material. Still, I needed her onside. Getting her friendship was hard work, but eventually I wore Stevie down.

Alex and I didn't have much in common. He wasn't my type and had little to offer. Now I know why, although I often wondered about his sexuality.

Joe the lad hadn't changed. Before I left for Blandford, we nearly had a thing. As fumbling hands unclasped my bra, I pushed him away. Being another notch on The Leader's bedpost wasn't for me. Besides, I preferred older boys, men, I guess.

Kat, the pathetic Princess, was a victim waiting to happen. The Pink Posse was her desperate attempt at belonging to something. When they made her a practical slave, she soon discovered how toxic they were. After joining The Six, Kat's relief was obvious.

Simon was, well, Simon. He couldn't help but be good. Kindness oozed out of him. Trying to understand Simon became my mission. Occasionally, he wobbled my defences, making me vulnerable to friendship.

Simon's kindness and the solidarity of The Six threatened to change me. My plan wouldn't allow it.

Gemma Masters

Aunt Tina convinced me to contribute to this book. If she's doing this despite fearing what might happen, so can I. While my role in Erin's novel was small, what I will reveal is huge.

Erin's snooping around our home was the least of the trouble she caused. Upsetting my family was one of her favourite pastimes. I followed Erin, not because of being clingy. After she damaged my parents' belongings, I tried to fix them. You probably think I should've let Mum and Dad know what she was doing. It wasn't that simple. I couldn't take on Erin.

At first, Erin's sneaky behaviour seemed harmless. I believed it was a mischievous game we played together. As an only child, the prospect of having a cousin living with us was exciting. I imagined a sisterly connection. How wrong I was.

Believing we were playing pranks together, I encouraged Erin. We giggled when my dad tried to shave with a razor, missing its blades. When the blades turned up, I wasn't laughing. In our house, I was the only one who had cornflakes for breakfast. Erin was lucky no one else saw the blades. *I* was lucky I spotted them on the spoon before having a mouthful. Across the dining room table, Erin raised an eyebrow at me. Aware of the painful consequences of telling, I kept quiet.

My childhood silence still bothers me. I'm sorry I didn't tell The Six Erin spied on them. After I caught her, she made me keep it a secret. I had no choice.

Reflecting on how I should've done something haunts me. Maybe if I'd told The Six about Erin's deceit, *Killing Kindness* might never have happened.

Now, nothing gives me greater pleasure than to expose the lies. Contributing to this book is where I will share the truth. Don't expect it from Erin, no matter what she says.

Tina Sullivan

Last time I checked, I'm very much alive. It's proper nasty, Erin making me dead in her book. She said years ago I'm dead to her, but it cut deep. Friends reckon it's just a story. Problem is most of the book is real life stuff.

Telling the truth here scares the shit out of me. It's got to be done, though. If I'd spoken up before, maybe none of this would've happened. I'm so sorry.

Thanks for writing my words down properly from my emails. I'm crap at writing. Erin's the author, but I ain't proud of her. How the fuck did it come to this? Sorry 'bout my potty mouth. Mum used to give me a clip round the ear for swearing. Never learnt, did I?

Erin doesn't call me *Mum*. When she called me it in the novel, I was shocked. Expect she did it to look nice and normal. When Erin was a kiddie, I tried to make her call me Mum. Little tyke wasn't having it. I should've told her off more.

Being a single parent is bloody hard. Erin's dad buggered off after finding out I was up the duff. She's never met him. Erin told people her dad was in the army fighting baddies. Dylan didn't know what hit him when he met Erin. He was an ex-soldier.

Even as a little 'un Erin's imagination was big. Her teachers loved the stories she wrote. I thought I was doing right by encouraging it. Now I know big imaginations mean big lies.

Erin, why did you make me a pissed up slut in the book? I get you're ashamed of me for not being smart. I left school before exams 'cos my mum was dying of cancer. I had to take care of my little sis, Fran. Dad was useless.

I ain't an alcoholic, either. I like going to the pub with my mates, but no more than the next person. Also, I ain't a slag. Before Dylan, I'd been single for six years.

I'm trying to get my head around Erin being pregnant. She swore she didn't want kids. As a kiddie, she pulled dolls apart and threw the bits across her bedroom. She's always been weird about babies. When I met Dylan, Erin begged me not to have any more kids. I thought she was jealous and wanted to be the only child.

God help the baby Erin's carrying if it turns out like her. It's a shitty thing for her mum to say, but you'll soon understand why I said it.

Erin

Tina, I could write an entire book on how dreadful you are as a mother. Your weakness caused me so much embarrassment. Thankfully, I had the strength and intelligence to take my own path.

Where are you now, Tina? Living in someone else's house and sponging off them, no doubt.

Reading your dictated words, full of swear words and lazy wording, makes me cringe. I did you a favour in *Killing Kindness* by making you sound more normal. My writing skills certainly didn't come from you.

As for you, Gemma; get over it. You weren't complaining as a child when you grabbed my coattails and clung on. It was embarrassing at the holiday club how you followed me everywhere. I toyed with you, trying to help you build up some resilience. Obviously I failed. Being a university lecturer doesn't mean you're savvy. Bet I can still fool you. Read on and weep, dear cousin.

Let's return to the start of the holiday club on Monday 3 August 1992. The surprise on the group's faces as I entered the team room was brilliant.

I said something similar to what's written in the novel, '"We had to return. Mum's boyfriend, Dylan, turned out to be a criminal. If he finds us, we're dead."' The others fell over themselves to be the most sympathetic. It's not often you're dealing with a girl who's escaped their mother's murdering other half.

Time makes some of the details hazy. This account is close enough to how my beginning in The Six happened.

****

After I slumped onto the stinky sofa, Kat dabbed a tissue at the tears I'd squeezed out.

'You poor thing. It sounds like you've been through hell.'

'Why wasn't Dylan convicted?' Stevie frowned. Before my arrival, I expected she'd be tricky to win over.

'There's no concrete evidence,' I replied. 'Dylan definitely killed Nick. It makes sense. Mum thinks so, too.'

See, Tina? When talking to others, I called you *Mum*. I couldn't have people thinking I'm unfeeling. That's psychopathic behaviour.

As I told the gang about Nick's murder, I missed out the discovery of Nick's cap in the garage. It was information I stored away for the future. Authors prefer to show rather than tell.

'Do you reckon Dylan will come here?' Joe asked, sitting in the chair that would later become The Leader's. 'Don't worry. I'll protect you.'

He spread his parted legs wide, the way males do, as if their balls are too big to be contained. Peacocks, the lot of them.

'Thank you,' I replied while thinking, *A short arse kid is no match for an ex-soldier*. I continued. 'Dylan would be an idiot to follow us. Mum and I know about the illegal stuff he's been doing. The last I heard, he's left Blandford. He's probably in hiding with his brother, Wily. They're as bad as each other.'

Wily was a brilliant touch; a name that sums up being devious. For a while, Wily served me well in *Killing Kindness.* More on that later.

I remember standing up to make an announcement. Before delivering the rehearsed speech, I took a deep, dramatic breath.

'Before I left for Blandford, I wasn't a nice person. I was mean to some of you.' I focused on Stevie and Kat. 'Because Mum's never around, I'm insecure. She's let me down with the constant drinking. She'd rather give a man attention than notice me.

'My aunt Fran thinks I'm a nuisance. Even my cousin, Gemma, is spiteful. All my life I've wanted to be one of the girls. When it didn't happen, I lashed out. Sorry, Stevie, for starting rumours about you sleeping around. I was jealous of your popularity. Kat, I shouldn't have started fights with The Pink Posse. I wanted to be your friend, but being rejected by that gang hurt. Hopefully, in time, you'll all forgive me. Being part of The Six could be good for me, if you'll accept me.'

And the Oscar for best performance goes to…

Nearly all of them lapped it up with hugs and comforting words. They offered tea, chocolate, and hugs; standard teenage acceptance.

My new plot had begun. The Six were the blank pages. I was both author and character. It was almost perfect. Simon and Stevie's frowns confirmed they needed more convincing. I knew I could make them believe Erin Sullivan had changed.

Stevie Young

Spoiler alert; I'm alive! It will take more than a second-rate novel to kill me off.

Thanks for the opportunity to contribute to this section. God speaks the absolute Truth, and so will I. After reading the *Killing Kindness* drivel, I've been itching to give the *true* version of events.

I'm glad Erin noticed that Simon and I didn't immediately buy the changed girl act. After Erin's performance, begging for forgiveness, I discussed it with Simon. Being wary of Erin made him feel bad. Unlike the pushover she portrayed, he questioned many things. Having a father like Thomas meant Simon took time to trust people. He didn't scatter kindness confetti.

I genuinely believe people can change for the better. No one expected I'd become a vicar, least of all me. This isn't because of a past as a promiscuous teenager who made sexual assault allegations. I'm still shaking from reading those parts. When we reach that in this book, I won't be silent.

To avoid conflict, I welcomed Erin into The Six. She didn't behave like a group member, though. Erin was often around, but on the outside, looking in. The habit of sitting in the corner of the mill watching us was odd. At the time, I thought it was because she was shy and lacked self-confidence. Now I realise we were caged mice for her to poke at and make notes on our reactions. Was she preparing the novel back in the nineties?

Also, we never called Erin The Thinker. In fact, like Simon, we didn't have a nickname for Erin. Unlike Simon, we couldn't find a friendly name to match her personality.

The others asked me to be nicer to Erin. I kept a distance because I couldn't understand her. For the sake of harmony, I tried to engage with Erin. Sometimes I thought she could be a friend, even on a basic level. I wish I'd trusted my initial instincts.

The lies Erin created about me in the novel are ridiculous! I wore bright colours because of liking them, not out of a need to be noticed. Back then, I was introverted and still am. I was called The Clown, more on account of my clothes than humour. It was only around familiar people that I was comfortable enough to make jokes.

While I loved dance music, I wouldn't have dreamt of going to a rave or taking drugs. The consequences of doing something illegal terrified me. My paranoia at being caught underage drinking in the mill amused the others.

My parents weren't neglectful hippies only interested in protests and sharing a bong. It's a teenage rite of passage to think your parents are embarrassing, but I never spoke about them in a negative way to Erin.

I remember her taking the mickey when The Six chatted about families. Erin said my parents cared more about hugging trees and scrounging benefits than me. I'm afraid to say I retaliated. I shouted my parents were loving people and she had no right to say such lies.

Mum was a social worker and Dad was an accountant. They were hardly loafing around, sponging off the dole. Not so much as a cigarette appeared in our house. I've never smoked either. Sorry to disappoint those who enjoyed the scenes where a vicar-in-the-making behaves badly. I get on my husband's nerves, trying to make him quit smoking.

Coasting through exams without revising would've been amazing. Unfortunately, *Erin* did that, not me. Our year group was jealous when we heard she received brilliant results. Erin's clever, scarily clever.

I worked my backside off to get qualifications. I'm dyslexic, not stupid. When I was younger, getting a diagnosis was difficult, let alone support. Since then, I've developed lots of coping methods. My husband is checking my writing before I submit it for this book.

I'd like my bishop to know I was never a troublemaker. I don't have any wrongdoings to confess.

I never pushed a child's face into the apple bobbing bucket at the holiday club. Would it surprise you to learn Erin was the culprit? She claimed it was an accident because of her leaning over. Everyone believed it. While Simon and I were almost certain of what we'd seen, we didn't want to think Erin was so spiteful. We let it pass.

Finally, I didn't tell the head teacher to stick the school up his arse on the last day. Erin said it to *her* head teacher in Blandford, after being expelled for drug dealing. Gemma trembled as she begged me not to share the secret. Until now, I haven't.

Believing she wanted to be a better person, I gave Erin a chance.

Hindsight is a terrifying thing.

Wednesday 5 August 1992

Erin

The Six's first time at the mill was pretty much as I depicted in *Killing Kindness*. Joe and Kat had a secret relationship. Simon pretended it wasn't happening. I tried to get him to confide his real feelings for Kat to me. As ever, he was guarded. Instead, I engineered it for Simon to turn up in places where Kat and Joe went for privacy. Somehow they kept their relationship secret until the last night.

After the events of the summer of 2021, the Andino family gathered ranks. In various newspapers, they shared how horrified they were at how I portrayed Joe and Kat. I did them a favour. My fictional aggressive Leader and pampered Princess were far more interesting than the real-life versions.

The Andinos aren't squeaky clean. Media whores will cash in on anything. The money-grabbing Greeks saw an opportunity and took it. So did I.

Working out who are the good and bad guys is never easy.

Thalia Andino

I'm Joe and Kat's daughter. Contributing to this book is the least I can do for my parents. I'll try to be calm when writing my responses. As a fiery woman, it isn't easy! Erin won't have the satisfaction of winding me up, though.

None of my family has been paid for press interviews. Every penny has gone to an eating disorders charity. The Andinos won't profit from tragedy, unlike Erin. We've closed ranks. It'll take more than a failed author to break us.

After the courtroom drama, most people know who Vinnie Scott is. For those who don't, he was Erin's private investigator. When the evidence of how he played me was covered in court, I could've died of shame. Thankfully, my loved ones know I was the victim.

Vinnie and I "met" outside the family restaurant. Now I know the bastard was keeping tabs on us. As we chatted, he hooked me in. Considering the losers I'd dated before, I should've seen the red flags.

Vinnie and I carried on seeing each other. I believed we were in a relationship, although he never made it online official. Come to think of it, he wasn't on any social media. Everyone is on at least one platform. I could kick myself at not figuring out how shady he was. He claimed to be a security guard with changing working hours. I'm cringing at my stupidity in believing so much bullshit.

After Vinnie got all the info he needed from me, he disappeared. I spent ages wondering what I'd done wrong. When I saw him in court, I dug my nails into the seat to keep from scratching his eyes out.

My mum, Kat, shared lots of her memories with me. Erin's snobbery is showing in how she depicted Mum as a spoiled Princess who hated her council estate background. She loved the community and we often visited friends there. Mum wasn't clamouring to get out. Moving into the Andino family home was the best option because it's huge.

I'll also clear up some stuff about The Pink Posse. After a few weeks, Mum left the gang. The girls shoplifted, dabbled in drugs, and slept around. It wasn't Mum's scene. She told those bitches to do one well before joining The Six.

Mum wasn't a thief, even as a teenager. When she found out my brother stole from a toy shop, Michael was forced to confess to the manager. The bloke was satisfied with an apology, but Mum insisted Michael did jobs at the shop as a punishment. As with most issues, we discussed what my brother had done at dinner. Mum gave a long lecture on honesty. Poor Michael didn't look up from the table the whole time.

Thanks for giving me a voice in this book. The love I have for my parents will whitewash Erin's lies.

Erin

What a touching last line, Thalia. Did you trawl through Instagram for an inspirational quote? Will you add those words to a photo of you in an outfit barely covering your boobs and backside? Here's some advice: if you don't want to keep attracting losers like Vinnie, stop showing off the goods.

I won't waste any more page space responding to Thalia. All I'll say is parents often hide their pasts from their children. Kat didn't tell her daughter everything.

Teenage Kat *was* a diva worthy of the name *Princess*. No one can dispute it. She constantly complained when shuffling in the dirt through the secret entrance to the mill. Playing a damsel in distress suited her. Joe always leapt to be her hero, and Simon charged in as her knight. Kat was a tease who enjoyed having two boys vying for her attention.

After Joe and Alex bigged-up the mill, I couldn't wait to see it. The old building sounded like a perfect spooky venue to fuel my imagination. It was also small enough to observe The Six.

In *Killing Kindness*, I offered a mill far more impressive than reality. Authors use settings to create an atmosphere and drive the plot. My writing skills worked overtime to make the mill inviting.

A freight train of disappointment crashed into my expectations when I saw the building. It was a crumbling ruin, stinking of rats' pee, and full of litter. Despite the scorching summer, concrete floors and bare brick made it an icebox. Boarded windows meant we always used torches, even in the daytime. It was a shithole, but I've learnt to be flexible. I turned it into a place to watch and learn. The nostalgic writing in *Killing Kindness* is real. I came to love the place where my future career took shape.

When I began writing the first draft of *Killing Kindness*, something was missing. Yes, I had a menacing mill, but characters also give life to a novel.

Stephen King nailed writing about a group of teenagers' horrific summer. I needed someone mysterious and menacing in my novel. Stephen King had Pennywise. I claimed The Witch.

Brenda Bartlett AKA The Witch

Erin can't say a witch owning the mill was her idea. Here I am.

I thought being called The Witch was over years ago. When I read Erin's portrayal of me, I laughed at first. That woman certainly has a vivid imagination.

Sorry to disappoint you, Erin. My name is Brenda. I'm an old woman who likes Sudoku, romance novels, and a Horlicks before bed. Hardly witchy behaviour, is it?

In 1992, I wasn't keen on those youngsters being in my mill. I didn't want to turf them out at night, though. Teenagers can be mouthy sometimes. Also, I didn't leave a note giving them permission to use the building.

Every morning, Dylan checked the building for damage and littering. He refused to tell the group to get out when they were there, claiming it wasn't his job. Now I know why he avoided The Six. To their credit, they never left any mess. I let them have some fun, hoping when the summer was over, they'd move on.

Erin's description of Alex, a burly lad, as being afraid of me was hilarious. I'm five foot one with as much clout as a wet lettuce. I stopped laughing when I reached the part in the novel about what later happened to Alex. I expect we'll cover it later.

As for my gingerbread house, it was a mistake. I told the decorators to use a tasteful shade of terracotta. I shouldn't have left them to choose the colour or work unsupervised.

When I returned from doing the Tesco shop, I nearly had a fit. My cottage was gingerbread. I knew the brats who called me The Witch would link it to "Hansel and Gretel". The colour stayed for a few weeks while the decorators had other jobs to finish.

I wasn't the only one who was teased. Bert up the road was named The Magician on account of his long white beard. Everyone called Marge from the post office Hobbit because of her being petite with enormous feet. Small villages are quiet places where bored children create fantasies. Unfortunately, some people never grow out of making up stories. I'm looking at you, Erin.

Erin

The Witch's real name is Brenda! She should thank me for making her more interesting. This is why telling the truth isn't always wise. I'm disappointed The Witch is a plain old woman. Of course, I knew she wasn't an actual witch. Back then, though, she had an air of mystery.

They say never to meet your heroes. I'd also add, never engage with people you've turned into characters.

In my account of Wednesday 5 August 1992, I covered seeking The Six's friendship after a terrible time in Blandford. I didn't need them. Empathy and affection are weaknesses.

Writing a fictional scene of how I clasped Simon's hand as we entered the mill made me queasy. It was worth the discomfort to gain readers' sympathy. How could you not pity the girl who told Simon, "'It's not the dark that's scary. I'm afraid I've blown it with everyone.'"?

I needed you to believe Simon and I were connecting. If the kind boy likes the naughty girl, she's redeemed. The fact is, throughout the holiday club I hardly spoke to Simon. His constant do-gooding felt like holy water singeing my sinful skin.

I certainly never asked for Simon's help to fit into The Six. Being just another member of the group wasn't part of the plan.

In the chapter where The Six first went to the mill, I described Tina and Dylan's relationship. Writing this was cathartic. Their connection was a bomb, ready to explode. Afterwards, I picked up the pieces and made it into something new.

Dylan and Tina should never have got together. I have no regrets, though. The moment I met Dylan, I thought I'd found the answer. After his death, I realised I was asking the wrong question.

Tina

Writing 'bout Dylan is hard. Stupid me tried to forget about him. As if I can ever do that! After he died, the papers were on my case to do interviews. I told them to piss off. Sorry, I'm swearing again. Oh well. As my old dad used to say, "Take me as you find me or not at all".

I didn't know Dylan followed us to Trillhaven. When I later heard he made friends with another boy, I puked my guts up. Nick's murder was enough of a shocker. Finding out Dylan and Simon knew each other nearly tipped me over the edge.

If Simon killed Dylan, I reckon it was self-defence. When he was angry, Dylan could be scary. Once, he smacked a fella in the chops for trying it on with me. To be fair, the handsy prick deserved it.

It weren't all bad with Dylan. What he did to Nick was horrible, but I have to tell the truth.

I didn't meet Dylan in a pub, as Erin wrote. At the bookies where I worked, Dylan got chatting with my mate, who worked there, too. Dylan and I flirted and then he asked me out for a drink. He was staying with my friend and her hubby in Trillhaven for a few days.

Our relationship was hard and fast. We both loved heavy metal and rock music. Perhaps Erin felt left out. My head was turned. Maybe I didn't give her much attention. With Erin, though, you always have to be noticing her. She wore me out.

I'd never felt that way about a bloke before. When men hit on me in the bookies, I'd tell 'em to bugger off. Dylan seemed different. He didn't look down on me 'cos I wasn't as clever as him. Not many people know he came from a middle class family, not the rough lot Erin wrote about.

When Erin met Dylan, she waited on him hand and foot, getting him beers and crisps. Usually she mouthed off if I asked her to do anything for me. I was worried she'd kick off when Dylan said 'bout moving together to Blandford. She'd been playing up something terrible at home and in school. Instead, she surprised me by being excited at moving. Erin was always full of surprises.

Blandford was supposed to be a new start. It all went to shit. Erin got in even more trouble. She was suspended a few times for smoking in the bogs, mouthing at teachers, and scrapping. It became worse when she took against the head girl. Dylan told Erin to show the girl the kind of person Erin really is. I think Dylan meant he saw good in Erin and she should be more like that. As always, she did what she wanted.

One day, the head girl was on her bike going down the steep hill into town. Her brakes didn't work. She smashed into parked cars and broke both her arms. A lad told the police he'd spotted Erin near the girl's bike in the school bike shed. The police couldn't prove Erin was involved. The lad later said he wasn't sure anymore he'd seen her. Shitty for a mum to say, but I expect Erin threatened him. He wouldn't have been the first.

Blandford wasn't working out. Dylan had become a miserable bastard, constantly worrying about his handyman business. He hardly had any jobs and my wages from the supermarket only covered the rent. We started arguing. Erin always took Dylan's side 'cos for her the sun shone out of his arse. Until Nick came along, Erin thought she was Dylan's favourite.

Poor Nick. I can't stop feeling guilty about his death and wondering if I could've stopped it from happening. Simon might still be around, too, if I'd said or done something.

Erin

Tina, you don't know half of what really happened. Brace yourself.

Friday 14 August 1992

Erin

I spiced up the chapter where Charlotte and Simon had a heart-to-heart. Listening to their chats could be dull. Charlotte was so clingy I almost pitied Simon for being related to her.

The primary school where the holiday club took place was a great spying ground. Multiple buildings, recesses, and rooms offered places for me to hide. I have no regrets about listening to the Pritchards discussing their violent father. If you talk where others are likely to hear, that's your problem.

When Charlotte came to the team room for Simon, I regularly followed them. Sitting in the disgusting place The Six had as a base was depressing. The adults took over the staffroom with comfortable seats, space, and lots of refreshments. Having to go there to beg for teabags and whatever was left in the biscuit tin pissed me off. The adult helpers were lazy housewives enjoying an extended coffee morning. They gossiped in the staffroom while The Six did all the work.

Fran was the worst; thinking she was the queen bee. Spitting in her tea before I handed it over was always fun. Making drinks wasn't part of my job. Fran tried to show people she could control me. She was proud of taming wild Erin Sullivan, as if it could ever happen. Confession time: I once put laxatives in Fran's tea. It kept her on the toilet and away from me.

Let's return to the Pritchard children and the chat about their bullying daddy. Back in my day, many parents gave their children a few taps to keep them in line. Tina said if my dad had been there to smack me when I misbehaved, I would've turned out differently. We'll never know. He probably ran away in horror at the thought of a future with Tina.

I remember gripping the edge of the youth club wall to look around the corner as poor little rich kids, Simon and Charlotte, moaned about their dad. The man was rolling in money. What did they have to complain about? The Pritchards' house was practically a mansion. Out of curiosity, I went there once. Standing outside, I imagined living there and having Charlotte's huge wardrobe of clothes. Then I got over it. Who the hell would want to be her?

The details I added in Simon and Charlotte's discussion were taken from previous conversations I'd overheard. Charlotte's desire to become a barrister was amusing, although she certainly had enough chatter for it. It's clichéd to follow Daddy's footsteps, desperate for his approval. To his credit, Simon had the balls to fight against it.

I confess I added other parts that didn't happen in the novel. Charlotte wasn't upset about a lack of friends. I wanted to portray the young girl as a sympathetic character. After meeting again as adults, I wish I hadn't. She thinks she's so superior with her fancy job and owning The Mill.

Because I'm supposed to be honest in this section of the book, I can confirm Charlotte *did* have friends. They were a bunch of nerds obsessed with books and computer games. I love reading. To prepare for writing my own, I grew up devouring books, but never role played. Charlotte's crew of fantasy freaks created worlds where elves and goblins do weird stuff. In my novels, the characters and settings are so brilliantly written they could be real. Oh, it *is* real, isn't it? Ladies and gentlemen, I give you *Killing Kindness.*

I only listened to some of Simon and Charlotte's chat on Friday 14 August 1992. Nothing was new: Charlotte was needy, their father had been lashing out again, and Simon dished out crappy advice. Faced with the threat of dying of boredom, I left.

Later, I saw Charlotte following Simon to our team room. Knowing better than to enter, she waited outside for him to return. I swear it was an excuse to see Joe. Despite her current sexual persuasion, teenage Charlotte had the hots for him.

I wonder what she made of Joe at Simon's memorial. Perhaps she didn't notice Joe at all. She was in her element, acting the sisterly version of a merry widow. Charlotte's still latching on to her brother and trying to be part of The Six.

Get over it, Charlotte. Simon's gone. The Six isn't the same, particularly as most of its members are dead.

Charlotte Pritchard

I'll never fail to be amazed and sickened by how Erin bounces back. Even this legally questionable book has happened. While I could contest it, I'd rather be my brother's advocate. In court, I'd enjoy pulling Erin's words to pieces. Instead, I'll do it here. Unlike Erin, I tell the whole truth and nothing but the truth.

For some reason, likely homophobia, Erin can't accept I'm gay. My wife, Harriet, was in hysterics when she read the part about my alleged teenage crush on Joe. At that age, I knew I was a lesbian and had no problem with it, other than not telling my prejudiced father.

My "favourite" line from Erin's novel, portraying me as obsessed with Joe is, "Eventually, he'd work his way around most of the girls. When Charlotte was older, Joe would see she was a potential girlfriend and not only his best friend's sister." My self-esteem wasn't so low I would've waited for a boy to shag around until he got to me. Also, let me repeat, *I am gay*.

When we discovered her name in *Killing Kindness*, Harriet's laughter turned to concern. With her P.I. buddy, Vinnie's help, Erin did her homework. I've stepped up security measures and we've moved home. Erin's probably too busy keeping her own life private to find us, anyway.

Erin's ridiculous version of Friday 14 August 1992 must be addressed. I went to The Six's team room to find Simon so we could leave together. On that day, it wasn't Stevie who called me a stalker and shouted to go away. *Erin* blasted the Ugly Kid Joe song. From the tuckshop, we often heard it playing. She enjoyed sharing how much she hated everything about everyone. Why on earth didn't we see the signs?

All the children dreaded going to an activity Erin led. Unfortunately, we didn't know in advance who would be in charge. Erin was reckless with safety and spiteful.

Once, I saw her slap an already distressed girl. Erin said if I grassed she'd tell the organisers I did it. The terrified girl Erin hit agreed to confirm I was the attacker. Erin understood which buttons to press. I stayed silent because I didn't want Simon to think violence ran in the family.

Simon and I *did* chat about Thomas – our poor excuse for a father – behind the youth centre building. The night before, Thomas had beaten Mum more brutally than ever. Simon had stayed over at Joe's house. When I returned from the shops, Mum was bawling on the stairs. I won't describe her state, as it could be triggering.

I told Simon privately what happened, sparing Mum overhearing and feeling the shame that was never hers to carry.

Thankfully, Thomas went back to London, where he was spending more of his time. We suspected he had a mistress. None of us, including Mum, cared because it kept him away. Now I worry about the mistress and hope he didn't hurt her as well. Erin would likely state my mum should've left her husband. *No one* gets to judge our situation.

Eventually, I fought back against Thomas. Despite missing my brother, I gained strength enough for us both.

I became a barrister because of valuing justice, not to annoy Thomas. Perhaps I wouldn't have considered doing it if he wasn't in the role, too. Maybe this influenced me, in part, but only because I wanted to do it better.

Thomas took bribes and regularly bent the law. He refused to pay for my education, so I had a few part-time jobs and took out loans. When I began my career, I celebrated my success, knowing I owed that bastard nothing.

Mum and I didn't go to Thomas's funeral. The extended family was outraged until I showed them a file I'd kept on his crimes and abuse.

On Friday 14 August 1992, Simon and I discussed how to support Mum. We didn't concentrate on my loneliness. Simon never offered an ominous message about how The Six was disintegrating. Being with them made him feel safe and wanted. It's obvious why Erin cast fictional Simon as falling apart. She needed a villain in the making for Dylan's death.

Erin, you claim to focus on reality, and yet you've written bitter fiction. I guess you live in a fantasy world because your own life is lacking. You really are The Thinker, trapped in an imaginary world. What a pathetic existence.

Monday 17 August 1992

Erin

In *Killing Kindness,* I introduced The Six in the team room, chatting and laughing. Domestic settings are perfect for making the reader feel safe and cosy. Then BAM! A dramatic scene follows, shocking the reader.

Stevie will probably have plenty to say about how I cast her as my rival. I couldn't have The Six living in harmony; in fiction or real life. This isn't The Secret Seven.

Stevie's already moaned about how I misrepresented her. With that coloured hair and neon clothing, she resembled a *Drag Race* reject, let alone a clown. That girl was so desperate for attention.

Stevie

If the best Erin can do is make snide comments about my hair, I wouldn't bother replying. Yes, I had some awful hairstyles and outfits. Didn't everyone in their younger years? My husband and I giggle when looking through old photos. The eighties and nineties have a lot to answer for regarding my styling choices. Despite being introverted, I embraced being called The Clown.

Erin was unreadable, always in black clothing. It would've been cool in a goth way, except she hated goth music. Whenever Simon played anything remotely dark, she turned it off. We never knew her musical tastes or interests, apart from being difficult. Erin was a closed book who would later open up, steal our lives, and claim them in print.

Erin neglected to mention Kat and I were friends long before the holiday club. We didn't grudgingly become friends. Kat and I met as toddlers, living on the same council estate. Our mums were best friends and Kat was like a sister to me. Unlike Erin's version, we called Kat *Princess* with affection, and she loved it. After 1992, we had regular phone chats, emails, and occasional visits.

Despite my concerns, I tried to be friendly with Erin. As the three females of The Six, Kat wanted us to have each other's backs. The Pink Posse was a difficult experience, but she was still open to friendship.

Erin refused every invitation we made to come to our houses. I suspect it's because a council estate was below her, even though she was living in a garage conversion.

Whenever we went to the mill, Kat and I tried to start conversations with Erin. She usually rolled her eyes, said she needed space to think, or walked away. I'm not sure what sort of deep discussion she expected from teenagers. Whatever we said wasn't good enough. The Thinker believed she was above us all. Erin spent most of the time guarding the stereo and changing the songs we'd chosen to play. I guess she's always needed to be in control.

In the chapter from Monday 17 August 1992, apparently I said Simon was going to snap. There's the drama llama author appearing again. Although it's years ago, I'm certain I didn't say or even think Simon was reaching a breaking point. He certainly wasn't ready to turn into The Hulk because Alex left him to do morning registration alone. Almost everything in the chapter is a lie, particularly the "fight" between Alex and Simon.

Erin

In *Killing Kindness,* what I shared about the conversation between Simon and a sexually confused boy is true. The lad was worried his dad would be angry if he found out.

For once, I wasn't purposefully spying. In an opposite room, I was tidying up after a needlework session. I remember visualising sticking needles into voodoo dolls of the lazy kids who'd left the mess.

When I heard crying, I chose to ignore it. Emotional outbursts were common in a place full of kids. If I checked on the upset child, it would mean extra work. Besides, I've never been the comforting type. I only started listening when I heard Simon's voice.

Of course, good old dependable Simon had a key to the room no one else could use. My annoyance rose as I lingered by the admin office. I'd been denied a private space, perfect for thinking and planning. I was considering how to steal the key from Simon when the boy he was helping dropped a bombshell. Simon offered advice and ticked off a politically correct list regarding homosexuality.

Further up the corridor, Alex appeared, shouting goodbye to someone. As well as being a big lad, he had the mouth of a town crier. I expect farmers need to be loud to call in their animals, or something of the like.

I slipped into a room next to Simon's and kept the door open a little. The sound of shuffling outside encouraged me to take a peek. Alex was being an eavesdropper, too. See? I'm not the only naughty one.

Tim Richards

I'm not sure what my role is now. In my heart and head, I'll always be Alex's partner.

At first, I refused to be involved in this book. The rage and pain inside me are relentless. My counsellor thinks writing could help me let it out. Not everyone gets to give their side of the story, particularly where someone like Erin's concerned. Here, I will speak on Alex's behalf.

After receiving the invitation to Simon's memorial, Alex told me about the holiday club. Memories flooded in. Some cut deep. Others made him smile with fondness for The Six.

The events of Monday 17 August 1992 proved difficult for Alex. Not for the reasons Erin made up. This is how Alex said it happened. I believe him over a fantasist.

****

Although it was the first time he didn't help Simon with registration, Alex felt guilty. He'd got caught up chatting and lost track of time. My Alex always was a chatterbox.

He searched the corridor, ready to apologise to Simon. Ahead, Alex spotted Erin darting into a room. As usual, she was avoiding people. The Six often gave her space, hoping for a better mood when she returned.

Alex considered asking Erin if she'd seen Simon. Before he could, Simon's voice carried from the admin office. The sound of a distressed child made Alex alert. Even with an open door, he didn't want anyone questioning why Simon was alone with a boy.

Alex looked over at the room where Erin hid. She would've been able to hear the upset kid. Typically, she put herself first. Alex often wondered why she worked at the holiday club and figured it must have been for the money. Oh, how wrong he was. How wrong we all were.

Alex didn't eavesdrop on Simon's conversation with the kid, as depicted in *Killing Kindness*. As Alex entered the room, Simon was comforting the boy. This is more or less how Alex said it went.

****

'Please don't feel ashamed,' Simon said to the youngster. 'Do you mind if I tell Alex?'

The boy hesitated before giving a slow nod.

Simon addressed Alex. 'One of his mates called him a poof. He's struggling with his sexuality and reckons this could be a phase.'

The reality of the boy's struggle hit Alex hard. Until then, he hadn't discussed homosexuality – in general or his own – with anyone.

'It might be a phase,' Alex said to the boy, 'and it's OK. You're young and there's time to figure out who you are. There's a chance you *are* gay.'

Alex noticed the youngster recoil at the word *gay*.

As Alex continued, he realised his advice was for himself, too. 'Labels don't define us. You're so brave for starting this conversation. It must've taken a lot of courage.'

Alex said he would remember the boy's grateful smile forever. It opened a dam Alex had tried to keep closed for years.

Simon added, 'We'll ask an adult supervisor to talk about this with you some more, OK?'

The boy was accepting. Alex and Simon shut the door and chatted in the corridor. Erin must have heard them. As ever, she lied in her account of their conversation. This is what actually happened.

'I'm proud of you,' Simon said.

Alex blushed. 'Don't know why.'

'Are you gay?'

The question was too abrupt, too soon. Alex tried to accept who he was and was preparing to tell a trusted few. He didn't have a boyfriend, let alone kiss a male student in the school changing rooms. Really, Erin? The gay clichés are so disappointing.

'I can't do this right now.' Alex turned away.

Simon grabbed his shoulder, probably to offer comfort. A distressed Alex pushed him off harder than intended. As you'll have seen from media photos, Alex was stocky, even then. As Simon lost his footing, Erin darted out of her spying den.

'You hit him!' she shouted, while pulling Simon up from the floor.

'I didn't!' Alex cried. 'It was an accident.'

'A likely story.' Erin's tone was citrus sharp.

A now standing Simon frowned. 'Al didn't hit me. I fell over.'

'I'm so sorry, Si.' Alex's voice wobbled as he fought against tears.

He never braced to put the boot into Simon while the boy was on the floor. There were no punches, blood, or threats.

Alex found Erin's frown at Simon and Alex shaking hands and apologising to each other chilling. She tried to create a rift between the lads. When it didn't work, she made it happen in her novel.

Using someone's sexuality struggle for kicks is disgusting. I'll never forgive Erin, least of all for that.

Wednesday 19 August 1992

Erin

When I read *The Great Gatsby*, *Animal Farm*, and *The Lord of the Flies,* I admired the authors' use of symbolism.

I'd love to claim pink tulips in the holiday club's group kindness activity were a symbol I created. Simon *did* bring a bunch of pink tulips for his group's display. Later, in my writing, the flowers represented more than he intended.

I hated every second of Kindness Day. Fran came up with the idea after watching do-gooder Simon in action. I let my group get on with it. When I was given the eager-to-please children, I groaned. Then I realised I was onto a winner. It meant no work for me.

They produced an attractive banner, but their dance routine was painful to watch. None of them had any rhythm. To this day, I feel like stabbing someone whenever Mariah Carey's "Anytime You Need a Friend" comes on the radio. As my group practised their performance, I pretended to be interested. Fran often looked over, trying to glare through an overgrown fringe. I played nice. Much as I hated living in her former garage, I needed somewhere to live. Getting kicked out of the holiday club would've ruined my fun, too.

Simon and Alex weren't baiting each other as we prepared kindness contributions in the hall. There was a disappointing lack of rivalry.

Yes, I also made up the earlier fight where Simon pushed Alex to come out. Don't expect an apology. People should thank me for making Alex and Simon more interesting. Their fictional fighting worked well against the kindness parade. The gays love a parade, right? Despite what's been said, I'm not homophobic. I portrayed Alex as mentally tortured because it suited the plot. A sexuality struggle gave his one-dimensional Farm Boy character depth.

Kindness Day preparation was incredibly boring. Alex didn't call Simon's pink tulips poofy. Simon never made threats of smothering Alex with kindness. The real events are friendly, nice, and unbearably dull.

Focus instead on the pink tulips and their echoes from 1992 to 2021. Flowers aren't always delicate and pretty. They're also linked to death. Go and look at a grave.

Tim

Erin making fictional Simon say, "'Perhaps I should smother *you* with kindness'" to Alex is disgusting and amateur. Call yourself an author?

Sorry, I can't write anymore. I'm not giving that woman the satisfaction of feeding on my emotions.

Charlotte

Have you read any of Erin's books? If so, you have my sympathy. She spewed them out every couple of months. I'm no writer, but I'm sure time it takes time to get a novel into shape. While some authors write fast and produce great books, it's not the case for Erin. That said, *Killing Kindness* is better written than Erin's other novels. Maybe stealing from real life helped. It isn't a writing method I'd promote, though.

Erin's portrayal of Simon as an emerging villain is ridiculous. I'm surprised she didn't have him twiddling a moustache, pantomime style. If anyone was a baddie back then, it was Erin.

Unfortunately, I was in Erin's group for Kindness Day. I begged Fran to let me join another team, but she refused. Sometimes I wonder why she didn't stand up to Erin. Then I realise Fran had to live with the girl. Can you imagine trying to sleep, knowing Erin's in your house?

In the hall, Erin goaded other groups by bitching about their kindness contributions. Alex and Simon ignored her and didn't argue about Alex's chosen kindness statement or pink tulips. It was all Erin; so much for her being honest in this section of the book.

Erin called the pink tulips poofy, laughing as she mentioned smothering Alex with kindness. An adult supervisor took Erin aside. While clenching her fists, she glared at the woman. Then suddenly, Erin plastered a smile on her face and claimed it was only a bit of fun.

Here's the kicker; Erin chose *Killing with Kindness* as her slogan, not Alex. Again, she's neglected to share something important. Throughout, she commented on how kindness can be powerful and deadly. All of us in her group were uncomfortable, but didn't dare disagree. When Fran joined us, we could've kissed her feet. Erin was oblivious. She was busy splashing blood red paint around the word, *Killing* on our banner.

Erin's novel is only being published because this non-fiction part gives others a voice. Before, no publishers would touch *Killing Kindness*. The press got their wrists slapped for printing extracts. Erin, I know you "leaked" your own novel. Desperate much?

Erin

Charlotte, jealousy is a bad look. You can't bear for your brother to be out of the limelight. Simon and his disappearance are so 1992. Stop milking it.

I will be famous again for the right reasons; my books. For old times' sake, I'll send you a signed copy of this book.

Thursday 20 August 1992

Erin

The first time Dylan and Simon met was a nasty surprise. Until then, I didn't know Dylan followed Tina and me to Trillhaven. The defeatist part of me thought he'd stay in Blandford. There were a lot of dangers that could've kept him away. Whenever he phoned at Fran's house, Tina threatened to tell the police. I knew she was too gutless to do it.

Of course, Dylan figured Tina would escape to her sister's house. I wondered if he'd be brave enough to approach us. Unfortunately, he became too close to Simon in the process.

The second night at the mill, I got the rest of The Six drunk. Alcohol wasn't part of every evening. Try doing a holiday club, full of screaming kids, with a hangover. That night, I brought along my uncle's potent homemade gin. While the others glugged, fooled by the fruity taste, I took smaller sips.

Simon was soon wasted as his tolerance for booze was low. Joe offered to walk him home. Thankfully, Simon was too proud to accept the offer. When I followed him, I became curious. His usual route wasn't in the direction of The Witch's house. Sorry, I refuse to name her Brenda. Life never fails to disappoint me.

Watching Simon fall over a tree root, I moved into the shadows. His drunken behaviour was getting on my nerves. Light spilling from an open door stopped me from leaving.

The Six thought from its small size the hut was for storage. The shack contained something far more interesting than tools. Dylan appeared. Rage fizzed in my blood. He was in Trillhaven and hadn't told me.

My annoyance shifted to Tina. We had to leave Dylan, but she'd been overly dramatic about him allegedly murdering a paperboy. Fran acted as gatekeeper when Dylan phoned, thinking he was just a stubborn ex. Tina hadn't mentioned Nick's death. We agreed my aunt wouldn't offer us a home if she knew a suspected criminal was on our tail.

All the hurt disappeared as light spilling from Dylan's new home shone upon him. There he was; my bright and shining star. Along with the moths heading for the light, I edged closer to Dylan.

After pulling Simon up to stand, Dylan placed an arm around the boy and led him inside. As was often the way with Dylan, I was left outside alone.

Crouched underneath an open window, I listened to their conversation. I learnt Dylan planned to prove his innocence and make us a family again. He was playing a long game by keeping a distance. Later, he wanted to approach me first. I allowed hope to enter my heart.

After Simon left, I took a breath before opening the shack door. Dylan's face switched from shock to happiness. Finally, we were reunited.

Despite his confusion, Dylan agreed not to tell Simon about all our meetings. Those moments were for us, nobody else.

When I looked at Simon's smugly happy face, I had to stop myself from shouting he didn't own Dylan. Simon probably thought having a secret was cool. Knowing what it was made me powerful. Every time Dylan and Simon met, I eavesdropped and learnt more.

In the novel, I gave Simon an aggressive edge. The truth is disappointing. He didn't vent his frustration on Dylan's furniture on Thursday 20 August, while stating,"'This anger is scary."'

Simon didn't have darker emotions. Even when discussing his father with Dylan, he talked about the abuse as a fact of his life. As Dylan's sympathetic voice travelled through the wooden walls, I tried to catch it. Kindness should have been *my* reward for all *I* had endured.

Dylan was a gentle soul and not just the gruff man I portrayed. My vengeful pain jabbed at the keyboard when writing *Killing Kindness*. If Dylan had realised what was right under his nose, he'd be a hero; alive and dead.

At one of our secret meetings, I asked Dylan why he spent time with Simon. Dylan claimed the boy reminded him of himself. For years, Dylan's father physically abused his wife and son. Eventually, Dylan stood up to him and moved out with his mum. I was pleased he'd shared this with me. He'd never revealed his troubled past to Tina.

With each meeting, we confided more in each other. Dylan wanted to stop drifting and make a home. I was ready to offer comfort when he began talking about Simon's bravery. A long speech about the horrors of "brave" Simon's life tested my patience.

I reached a snapping point when Dylan added he should've been more honest with Tina. Not once did he mention *my* loyalty. I felt betrayed and later took revenge by creating an evil man who deserved death in *Killing Kindness*.

In the novel's chapter dated Thursday 20 August 1992, Dylan says to Simon,   "'… don't ignore your anger. Use it. Look out for number one. Make those who've hurt you realise the damage they've done.'"

As a final act of kindness, I let Dylan be my mouthpiece. Those are *my* words. This is how I live.

Charlotte

As a barrister, I'm grateful for the many things I've learnt. One is keeping calm when the person you're prosecuting is despicable. Erin's lies about Simon won't break me.

Here's something to make Erin rage. I knew Simon and Dylan were meeting each other. Even better, I met Dylan. In a time before everyone had mobile phones, I had to find Simon because there was a family emergency. He'd told me he'd be at the shack. When we met, Dylan was friendly, polite, and funny. I could see why Simon enjoyed his company.

I've examined the evidence around the Blandford paperboy's murder. Nothing indicates Dylan was the killer. Simon told me about the crime. Initially, I was concerned about him being around a suspected murderer. At our first meeting, I asked Dylan about it. Simon was embarrassed by my forthright questioning, whereas Dylan didn't flinch. He described his friendship with Nick with what I believe was total honesty. Dylan pleaded with us to accept he didn't kill the boy. Previously, I'd never seen a man cry. Thomas wasn't the weeping type. He made others cry, particularly his wife and children.

Dylan's sadness increased as he shared the pain of Tina and Erin leaving. I admired his faithfulness in living in a crappy hut. He planned to give Tina space before showing her evidence of his innocence. No matter how much I asked, he refused to reveal what the proof he had was. The conversation focused on him creating a family again with Tina. I pitied him for having Erin as a potential step-daughter.

Dylan told Simon and me that Erin also came to the shack. He saw it as his duty to keep an eye on her. When talking about her bad behaviour, Dylan put it down to low self-esteem. As a favour to him, Simon and I tried to be nice to Erin. Aware of her neediness, Dylan wanted us to be more accepting.

It gives me great pleasure to share how Dylan said when Erin stared at him he shivered. Despite that, he defended her. When she arrived at Simon's memorial, I remembered Dylan's plea to be kind to her. I wish I'd trusted my instincts rather than misguided advice from a long-dead man.

Erin's fixation with making my brother a baddie is hilarious. If he stood on an ant by accident, Simon felt guilty. Erin casting him as a tortured soul, getting into fights, and having evil thoughts is unbelievable.

The final "thought" she fictionally planted in Simon's mind from Thursday 20 August 1992 is absurd. *"Perhaps I need to show them who is boss. Kindness is to my advantage. They'll never expect lovely, kind Simon to take charge. What a shock it will be when I do! Tomorrow will be the perfect ending for the summer of The Six."*

Simon swishes his cape and raises an eyebrow, ready to commit dastardly deeds upon The Six. The villain plots against his former friends, preparing to kill them one-by-one. What complete and utter nonsense. There was no revenge to be had.

Give up writing, Erin. This isn't foreshadowing. It's a smack in the face with a fist full of obviousness.

Erin

Charlotte, I'll keep this short. Dylan loved me. You know nothing about it. He put up with Simon because Dylan was too kind for his own good.

Holding onto a long-gone brother and trying to defend him is pathetic. Get over it.

Friday 21 August 1992

Erin

The last day of the holiday club was difficult enough without the evening disco. Excitement at what was to come made me jumpy. Stevie asked if I was on something. As if I'd waste drugs on "entertainment" from the local DJ. He covered all Trillhaven's birthday parties when we were younger and was still playing the same songs in 1992.

To liven things up, I spiked the punch bowl. Laughing at hyperactive kids whizzing around on my uncle's gin helped to pass the time. Fran ordered me to leave the refreshments table. She didn't dare make an accusation. The little snitch, Gemma, probably told Mummy everything. I didn't care. Family wasn't important. Only one particular person deserved my affection.

Initially, the rest of The Six hadn't planned to go to the mill after the disco. Alex had to be up early to do whatever farmers do. Joe was going on holiday. Simon's family were doing posh people's stuff. It didn't take much to convince The Six to a final session at the mill, though. As I thanked them for a summer I'd never forget, I choked on false tears. My fake sadness expressed regrets about being separated in September. I had to lay it on thick.

The mission to play nice at the holiday club hadn't gone as well as I'd hoped. Being surrounded by whining kids all day and pathetic teenagers at night tested my patience. I knew The Six hadn't always seen me at my best. Friday 21 August 1992 was the final chance to fool them.

Our last evening at the mill was more peaceful and friendly than depicted in *Killing Kindness*. As if I'd write the true version! My goal is to entertain readers, not send them to sleep. I spared you a snooze fest of Stevie and Kat filling in a "Does he really love you?" magazine quiz, Joe bragging about how much he could drink, and Alex sharing farm tales.

Surprisingly, the most interesting study was Simon. He seemed to be more on edge than I was, and not because of the tequila I'd slipped into their drinks. His constant watch checking and fidgeting showed he was running on adrenaline. Despite how much I asked, Simon wouldn't share his thoughts.

Alex and Simon didn't have another argument that evening, resulting in Alex leaving. As you now know, they never fought anyway. Since their chat with a sexually confused boy, I'd tried to drive a wedge between Simon and Alex. I gossiped to one about the other, stating something nasty had been said. Neither took the bait.

All night, Alex dished out praise like Pollyanna on uppers. It seemed he was making a positive memory for his friends. Good job, considering what happened years later.

Stevie

Finally, there's some truth from Erin. Simon and Alex *were* friendly on the Friday night. Their friendship had strengthened throughout the holiday club. Sometimes, in a trio of best friends, one gets left out. Joe, Alex, and Simon made sure it never happened.

The stereo played our favourite songs in the mill. All of us, apart from Erin, sang along to Carter the Unstoppable Sex Machine. "The Only Living Boy in New Cross" was part of our summer soundtrack. I can still sing it word-for-word. The lyrics *are* sad in places, I'll give Erin that. The desperate feeling of being lost is any teenager's issue. In *Killing Kindness*, Erin claiming Simon was considering ending his life as he listened to the song is sickening. She has no right to claim anyone's thoughts. She's taken enough.

Erin showed her homophobia in the novel. The fixation on Alex's sexuality is disgusting. On our last evening, Joe didn't wake up to find Alex's face near his. Joe never accused Alex of trying to kiss him. While Joe believed he was God's gift to girls, he knew it didn't extend to the same sex. Besides, he was too busy laughing to sleep. What teenager would have a kip while their mates are singing, dancing, and chatting?

Although Erin kept the cans of lager coming, we weren't drunk. She kept trying to push the booze on us while having little herself. Now I know it's because she added tequila. Simon was sober. He said he had a headache and drinking wouldn't help. We hadn't gathered a stash of alcohol from the kids at the disco, either. An inch of cooking sherry a boy stole from his mum's baking cupboard wasn't going to offer much fun.

While we're on the subject of alcohol, Simon didn't grab a bottle of gin from me and spill it on my T-shirt. Erin desperately wants to portray Simon as confrontational. We never fell out, least of all over something so silly. The only spirit I can stomach is the Holy Spirit. I've never coped with anything stronger than beer. No gin was consumed. If I spilled something on myself, I wouldn't have had a hissy fit. I've always been a clumsy eater. Dad used to say there was more dinner on my clothes than in my stomach.

236

Despite your efforts to ruin our memories, Erin, The Six had a great time together. I think you use spite and lies to cover your sadness. After forgiving what you'd done to us in the past, we welcomed you into the group. Maybe you're nasty because it hurt to see what you don't deserve.

It didn't have to end this way. You could've had a *real* story of friendship to write about. It's not for you, though. Crime sells, right?

Tim

Something big happened that night, which I'm proud of on Alex's behalf. Erin doesn't know about it. She can't claim this.

As they went outside for air, Alex resolved to tell his secret. He expected Simon would be kind, and he was. Alex told him he was gay.

When Alex shared with me the relief of coming out, he became sad. It wasn't because of a past fear of disclosing his sexuality. Unlike what Erin wrote, Alex was well and truly out as an adult.

Simon, the first person he confided in, took Alex's confession with him. After the disappearance, Alex had never felt so alone. He'd lost his best friend and confidant.

Erin

I suppose I should cover the revealing of Kat and Joe's teenage romance. It was only because of a potential love triangle forming with Simon that I took an interest.

Joe and Kat were hardly discreet. Their jumping apart and wiping away lipstick whenever someone appeared was so obvious.

Eventually, Kat confided in Stevie about her feelings for Joe. Probably because I was a fellow girl, they discussed it in front of me. To have heard drama queen Kat, you would've imagined it was like *Romeo and Juliet*. There were no barriers to Joe and Kat being together. So what if Joe's best friend, Simon, had a crush on Kat? No one wins in matters of the heart. I should know.

Another day of Princess swooning over The Leader wasn't going to happen on my watch. I made a boy at the holiday club give Simon a note telling him about Kat and Joe's relationship. It added how they'd been laughing at Simon for liking Kat.

After receiving the information, Simon did nothing. Watching him pretending it wasn't happening made me want to scream. This is why I gave Simon a juicier story in *Killing Kindness*. In the novel, when he found Joe and Kat kissing outside the mill, it was dynamite.

Once again, the truth is boring. In a comical chain like a Benny Hill sketch, I followed Simon, who followed Joe and Kat. Joe didn't play hard man, telling Simon he would have to deal with the relationship. Simon never hit Joe or said their friendship was over. As usual, Simon was terribly polite about it.

Nice guys always finish last. They also disappear.

Thalia

At my parents' wedding anniversary party, they read out letters written to each other. Focus on my mum's words rather than Erin's spite.

Kat Andino

Joe Andino was a boy you couldn't fail to notice. He knew it, too. When he discovered the opposite sex, Joe became a bit of a player. I swore, despite his good looks, I'd never fall for the swagger and patter.

Some of the best relationships are built from friendship. Joe and I were friends long before we got together. In primary school, he defended me against the nasty kids in the sandpit.

Joe teased me when I went through a phase of making everyone use my full name, Katrina. He said I'd always be *Princess* to him. After that, I became known as *Princess* to just about everyone.

When we were sixteen, we worked the summer at a local holiday club. I'm sure many of you went there. Being surrounded by noisy children is hardly the most romantic of settings, but it was the making of us. We often escaped to be alone and talk about our lives and futures. Joe became a sensitive young man and our Leader.

Although we were part of a group called The Six, Joe and I were often The Two. Why did we keep it a secret? There were a few reasons. I needed to know I wasn't another conquest for The Leader. Joe cringes whenever I teasingly use that nickname. He was a natural leader of the group, but never in an aggressive way.

As teenagers, we thought we had to be careful about having a relationship because of Simon. He was Joe's best friend and – I'm cringing as I say this – he had a crush on me. I'd known about it for a while, choosing to ignore it to spare Simon's embarrassment. For me, he could only ever be a friend; the very best of them.

At the end of the holiday club, Joe and I became official. The Six were going on to different things. The Two vowed to stick together. We declared our love for each other. I'm aware sixteen-year-olds all fancy someone different at least eight times a month. Joe and I were for keeps, though.

Outside the mill where we used to meet up, Simon found Joe and me kissing behind a tree. We were planning to tell him, but Simon found us first. Joe was devastated at the thought of losing his dear friend and begged for forgiveness.

It took Simon a while to stop laughing. Then he said he used to fancy me but was long over it. After witnessing my Princess strops and noticing me getting closer to Joe, Simon figured he and I were better off as friends. The effort of all those secret meetings was for nothing! Simon confessed, along with Alex, they'd been laughing at us, waiting for us to confess.

I reeled off a list of girls who would've jumped at the opportunity to be with Simon. He was well-liked and many girls had their eye on him. Simon couldn't see it. We never got a chance to see him have his own romance. Our friend disappeared that night. You all know the story.

Although he's not here, Simon is still a part of our lives. One of our children is proud to have *Simon* as his middle name. I thank Simon for his kindness and friendship. I wish he could've seen how far Joe and I have come.

Thank you, Joe, for always giving me gentleness and love. May we have many more wonderful years together.

Thalia

My mum's letter shows how much my parents loved each other and exposes the lies Erin told in her novel. While I have the chance, I'll clear up other crap in *Killing Kindness*.

I can't imagine Dad ever calling Mum a "prick tease" for not letting him feel her up. Even though they were teenagers then, it's icky reading about them getting it on. Dad was always a gentleman. His family insisted on it. Mum and Dad married young and had babies soon after. It was all proper, as a traditional Greek family expects. Yes, I know I'm an unmarried single mother. Times have changed.

As Mum's letter she shared at the anniversary said, Simon didn't lose his temper when he found my parents together. He certainly didn't bash Dad across the head with a branch or end their friendship. They all parted as friends. Unfortunately, that night they went their separate ways permanently.

Erin

Enough of this teen dream romance nonsense. Let's move on to something far more interesting.

I always viewed Simon and Stevie as my enemies. Being members of The Six, we kept things civil. Occasional lapses showed they didn't fully believe I'd changed for the better. Their questioning looks and whispers grated on me. While I enjoyed being a puzzle others struggled to solve, I wouldn't tolerate Simon and Stevie's judgement. It's why I gave a different version of Friday 21 August. You're better off reading my entry in *Killing Kindness* than knowing the reality, but this is where I'm supposed to write the truth.

Simon returned to the mill, laughing at catching Kat and Joe having a snog. I was confused by Stevie and Alex thinking it was funny too. I asked Simon if he was trying to cover being upset. He said his crush on Kat was over ages ago. My cousin Gemma later paid for giving me outdated information.

Limbs twitching with anger, I paced the mill as Simon, Alex, and Stevie discussed Joe and Kat's "lovely" relationship. I faked illness and Alex insisted on walking me home, as he was ready to leave.

Halfway up Mill Lane, I suddenly remembered I'd left my bag at the mill. Relying on boys not paying attention to details, I hoped Alex wouldn't remember I hadn't brought a bag. After offering to go back to the mill with me to get it, I convinced him I'd be safe. Alex went home.

I had to hear what Simon and Stevie were saying. Maybe they were discussing me. I wish what I saw and heard was as I wrote in *Killing Kindness*. Let Stevie tell you what happened. If these contributors must be in *my* book, put them to work.

I didn't stick around for long. I had other places to be and a better person to be with.

Stevie

Of course, Erin won't share what really happened between Simon and me. While reading her disgusting chapter, I couldn't stop trembling.

My church is aware of the allegations Erin made about me and knows they're false. She could've ruined me, not only personally, but as a vicar, too. Thankfully, my congregation believed me when extracts of the novel appeared in the newspapers. My husband wants to consult with a solicitor. For now, I'll give the whole truth here, something you'll never get from Erin.

On Friday 21 August 1992, Simon and I were the last ones at the mill. The heaviness of a vanishing summer weighed upon us. The next month, I was beginning studies on a path to becoming a primary school teacher. I had lots of doubts, though. It's baffling how kids are expected to choose GCSE subjects so young. How can teenagers be certain of their later careers?

As we laid on a blanket against the chill of the concrete floor, Simon was silent. Previously, we'd been in confessional moods, sharing our concerns about getting older. We certainly weren't necking shots. Despite Erin spiking the others' drinks, Simon had none, and I wasn't in a boozing mood.

I'll start by addressing Erin's fictional Simon saying, "'Sometimes I want to scream to make people see my pain. I thought I was naturally kind. Now I wonder if it's a cover for this darkness.'"

Erin's displaying her own messed up personality here, without the kindness part. What Simon actually said was along the lines of, "'The future worries me. I'm making plans that might upset my family. It's strange putting myself first for once.'"

I said it's OK to look after your own needs. After his disappearance, I wrestled with guilt, hoping I hadn't given Simon "permission" to do something terrible to himself. Eventually, I accepted I don't have the power to control others' lives. This is a lesson Erin never learnt.

Simon and I *did* share a kiss. It was an awkward moment following a peck on his cheek, thanking him for listening to my problems. We *both* then kissed on the lips. Unlike Erin's depiction, I'm not a predator. There was no fumbling or clothing being removed. Reading the novel's description made me more embarrassed for Erin than myself. It's worse than trashy erotica.

The *real* kiss ended quickly. Simon and I pulled apart and laughed. We took the mickey out of each other at how rubbish it felt. I didn't try to force Simon to have sex with me to compete with Kat, or for any other reason. Also, I wasn't going to lose my virginity on a filthy floor with a friend. Yes, I was a virgin, not the school bike; another of Erin's lies.

Most importantly, Simon never turned me down because I didn't try it on with him. I certainly didn't make sexual assault allegations. As part of my work, I counsel rape victims. The courage it takes to make their attackers face justice is astounding. Erin created a character of me who could have set those victims backwards in their bravery.

That evening, Simon and I left the mill separately, as close friends, nothing else. The kiss was already a funny distant memory. When we said goodbye, it felt final. Little did I know my instincts were right. I wish I'd hugged Simon tighter and not let him leave.

Brenda

Thank you for letting me tell the truth before Erin starts lying again. It's important people know my part around what happened to Dylan and Simon. The fact of the matter is I was on holiday in Torquay with the Women's Institute.

Although it would've been terrifying to witness the events of Friday 21 August 1992, in some ways I wish I'd been there. Simon and Dylan might still be here. I'm not sure how I could've intervened, though.

What kind of monster looks out the window at a dead body and then watches a boy going into the river to kill himself? Certainly not me. It sounds more like something Erin's characters do. I suppose she had to make the novel's version of me witness a boy's suicide. *Erin* is the witch. She loves nasty tricks and manipulation.

Another thing to clear up is a man called Wily never came to my home. There wasn't a fight after he tried to sexually assault me. With Dylan as the rescuer, I expect Erin wanted to portray him as a violent vigilante. If a man attacked me, even Dylan's brother, I wouldn't keep it quiet. I'm not scared of the police. I have nothing to hide. There aren't any skeletons in my cupboard or a cauldron bubbling over the fire.

Also, I'd never employ a handyman to live on my grounds without checking his background. Dylan was honest about how he was questioned but not charged with the paperboy's death. I believed in his innocence.

Dylan was a gentle soul who never smiled after snapping the neck of an injured chicken that had strayed from the coop. Why on earth did Erin create such a sick thing? It didn't happen. Dylan loved animals and adored my goats.

When I returned home the day after his death, I wondered if it was the wrong house. Cordons covered the area. When someone said Dylan was dead, I couldn't speak. Discovering Simon was likely dead, too, nearly finished me off. Opposite to Erin's version, Simon and I never met, although I knew he visited Dylan. Unlike some villagers, I don't judge other people.

Because the police were gathering evidence, I stayed a few nights with my son. Sorry to disappoint you, Erin. I'm not a sad, lonely, old spinster. I have three children and lots of grandchildren; happiness you don't deserve. When I found out about your pregnancy, my blood ran cold.

Erin

Brenda, I gave your dull life some meaning by casting you as The Witch. Where's the thanks? Considering you weren't there on Friday 21 August 1992, it's best to let the expert do the writing.

I'll share what *really* happened. Of course, I can't remember every word spoken. This account is close enough.

Readers, you may need to take a seat before reading what's coming.

****

After witnessing Stevie and Simon's embarrassing kiss, I prepared to see Dylan. As Stevie pedalled off on her bike, I lingered in the dark. When Simon headed for the shack, my plans were threatened. The boy stole my rightful time with the man I loved.

A few days before, Dylan and I shared a kiss. As I cried while spinning a story about Tina's nastiness, he offered comfort. Within his hug, I searched for more. To this day, I can feel those lips skirting mine. I swear tortured passion flashed in Dylan's eyes as he stepped aside and apologised.

That Friday, I watched Simon enter the shack. Hiding behind the tree where Kat and Joe got it on left me hoping for something similar with Dylan. Despite his protests, he needed to understand us being together wasn't wrong.

After a while, I crept towards my usual spot underneath an open window. Even gnats swarming in the warm night couldn't keep me away. I listened to Simon and Dylan's conversation. If only I hadn't. But then, this book wouldn't exist.

'Are you all right?' Dylan asked Simon.

The kettle rumbled as it finished boiling. Never a good sign. Endless cups of tea always led to long chats.

'I'm ready to go,' Simon replied. 'Tonight is the only chance. My father's making us go to London for the weekend. He's up to something.'

'Are you absolutely sure you want to do this?' Dylan's tone was tinged with concern.

'I have no choice. Can you get my rucksack, please?'

I heard plodding footsteps and shuffling.

'It's pretty heavy,' Dylan said. 'Barely fit under the bed. Can you carry this stuff?'

'I'm stronger than I look.'

'You *are* strong.' I could hear the smile in Dylan's voice. 'I'm proud of you.'

To stifle a scream, I chewed my knuckles. Dylan's pride should've been for me, not a poor little rich kid.

'Is your friend prepared for me turning up?' Simon stumbled over the words.

'Everything's sorted. In a bit, I'll phone for a taxi. It's on me.'

Coins chinked against a hard surface. 'Let me pay. I've been saving and nicking cash from Mum's pot. I feel shit about doing it.'

'Considering how your bastard father treats you all, I reckon she'll understand.'

'What if he searches for me?'

'He doesn't know you and I are friends. Concentrate on having a better life.'

Deep sobs came from the pathetic Simon. I checked my watch, wondering if the blubbing would ever end.

'Leaving Mum and Charlotte doesn't seem right. Dad might hurt them more without me there.'

'You can't be a punch bag anymore. I'll keep an eye on things. Remember, you go first and then eventually Charlotte and your mum will follow. Trust me.'

'Thanks so much. I'd never have done this without you.'

'We'll stay in contact. I'm always here for you.'

Dylan never promised to always be there for me. He was supposed to reunite with me after I proved his innocence.

Prepare yourself. This one's a belter of a devious plot. I planned to tell the police *Tina* hid the cap in the garage. After discovering the item, her fingerprints were on it. Mine definitely weren't. Tina didn't hide her dislike of Nick. Her friends and colleagues at the supermarket often heard grumbles about "that bloody boy". Yes, I was prepared to frame my mother for a boy's murder. So what?

As Dylan got closer to Simon, I realised sharing my plans for Dylan and me to be together was important. I should've told him sooner how I'd saved him from prison by making Tina keep quiet about the cap. Infatuation muddled my thinking. While I was lovesick, Dylan was busy protecting Simon. The kind lad always won. No more.

The door of the hut slammed against the outer wall. The frown on Dylan's face was like an arrow of disapproval. Against its piercing, I continued. Until then, I'd hidden my anger from him. Simon glared at me while reclining in a chair with his feet up, staking a claim. *I* belonged with Dylan, no one else.

'How dare you take over?' I screamed at my rival.

Even Dylan's touch on my shoulder couldn't silence the rage monster. I shrugged him off to grab Simon's rucksack and threw it outside.

'Go on, piss off!'

I didn't realise I was outside, lunging at Simon, until an arm locked around my waist. Dylan holding me should've been comforting. Instead, the pain of unrequited love made me sink my nails into his arm.

'Erin, calm down.' Dylan inspected the bloodied crescents in his skin. 'I'm worried you'll have another breakdown.'

'That was *our* secret. How could you tell Simon about my suicide attempt?'

'He hasn't. Sorry you went through that. Look, I'm not staying. You can chat alone.'

Simon dared to give *me* permission to speak to *my* man. Fury propelled my legs as I ran. With the added weight of a bag on his back, Simon fell. The turtle lying on his shell was grounded.

I reached into my pocket. Reason disappeared as a threat approached. I span around, plunging the knife into flesh. The blade went into Dylan's heart. Wincing against his own injuries, Simon knelt beside Dylan.

'Don't touch him.' I held up the weapon. 'He's mine, not yours.'

Simon raised his hands in surrender. 'I'm checking he's OK. Surely you don't want him to die?'

I considered the question. In an ideal world, Dylan was with me. The harsh truth was he wanted Tina. Sob stories like Nick and Simon were always more important than me. A living Dylan wouldn't make my fantasy a reality. Dead Dylan would be mine forever as a set of memories and what-ifs that came true.

I pushed Simon aside and lowered my ear to Dylan's face. With the rattling last breath, I placed my mouth over his. Air into my lungs made Dylan part of me forever.

'He's dead,' I said.

Simon doubled over, splashing vomit on the ground. Later, I was grateful for the further evidence of him being there. Newspapers still use it as proof Simon murdered Dylan, regretted what he did, and disappeared.

Simon focused on the knife in my hand. 'I promise not to say anything.'

'That's a lie. Why should you get to start over when I've never had the opportunity? Since I returned to Trillhaven, Stevie and you constantly bitch about me. The Six weren't very welcoming either.'

'You never bothered getting involved. We're all concerned about you.'

'Why does everyone say I'm the problem? Your tiny brains can't understand me. Besides, it's your fault Dylan's dead.'

'You killed him!'

'Oh, shut up. People like you make me sick, fooling others into believing you're kind. You're as selfish as the rest of us. Abandoning your family is a perfect example.'

'It's not for long. I'm doing this because I care about them.'

'Prove it.'

'What do you mean?'

The moon's glow flickered upon the water; a flashing welcome sign.

'Walk into the river and drown yourself.'

Simon's eyes widened. 'You're joking, right?'

'I'm deadly serious. Here's a good reason for you to end your life. If you refuse, I'll do it for you. Later, I'll complete the set by killing Charlotte and then your mother.'

'Why are you doing this?'

'Because you saw me kill someone. Because I can.'

'Please, don't hurt my family.'

'Do as I say and I won't. Leave the bag by the water's edge. It will look like you were running away and then changed your mind.'

Dylan's blood stained the canvas as I rubbed the knife on the rucksack; "evidence" of Simon's crime. No way was he going to be sainted after death. It was bad enough it happened in life.

'Why won't *you* kill me, rather than making threats?'

I almost admired Simon's bravery.

'It's more exciting watching you battle with whether or not to kill yourself. It's your turn to suffer. You claim to be kind. Keeping Dylan from me was cruel.'

Simon's shoulders slumped. He shuffled forwards. Sharp steel tickling the back of his neck kept him moving.

At the riverbank, we paused for my next instruction. 'Put rocks in your pockets to weigh you down. Virginia Woolf and you will soon have something in common.'

As Simon added the dead weights, he said, 'You haven't won.'

My laugh was gloriously shrill. 'I already have.'

Simon took a watery path to his end. A cloud covered the moon as only the top of his head became visible. When the light reappeared, Simon was gone.

There was a reason for the novel being called *Killing Kindness*. Dylan and Simon's interpretations of kindness didn't work for me, so I killed them.

2021

Erin

Does the horror of knowing I'm a murderer make you want to stop reading? Or is the promise of more revelations to come too irresistible? You've already turned the page to learn more. Humans are such immoral creatures.

Maybe you're wondering how I can confess to murder without fear. For the rest of my life, I'll be in hiding. When I agreed for *Killing Kindness* to be published, along with this factual section, I knew of the risks. The police will step up their pursuit of me. The only statement I'm making is in this book.

Before launching into what happened at The Mill in 2021, I'll give some background. I sent the "invites" to stay at the bed and breakfast.

For a while, particularly in lockdowns and isolation, I'd researched and plotted a novel based on The Six's summer of 1992. Charlotte's invitation to Simon's memorial came at the perfect time. Meeting up with the group would bring life to my characters and advance the novel's plot. I planned to observe while making things happen. Old habits really do die hard.

Before the memorial, I'd finished the first draft of *Killing Kindness*. Of course, the 1992 chapters had already happened, with fictional parts added.

The 2021 chapters were roughly written, with the intention of adding more details as I spent time with the others and events happened.

Originally, I was going to change everyone's names in the final draft. Yes, I know people still could've recognised themselves, but good luck proving it and suing me. As the publication of this book shows, anything is possible. The publisher insisted on using real names, obviously to hook readers. Remember, actual people died, not characters.

As for the cliffhanger… See what I did there? Originally, I wrote a different ending. Wily killed Stevie by slashing her throat. I rammed into Wily, making him fall. I grabbed the knife and plunged it into his heart, as I did with his brother; not that I'd admit to killing Dylan in the novel. The original ending of *Killing Kindness* made me a hero. After what happened in 2021, the publisher decided against it, saying it was stretching readers' imaginations too far.

Killing Kindness wasn't only a way for me to confront the past. I needed it to be a hit. Before Simon's memorial, I was looking for new representation.

My previous agent is a dried up hag who couldn't spot a bestseller if it smacked her in the mouth. A small circle of authors worship her. In return, she gets them the best deals. Because I refused to play the brown-nosing game, she gave me the boot. The bitch's lack of support meant I had to sell my holiday villa to cover my bills and to pay for the others' food and board at The Mill. Vinnie had to be paid for the P.I. work, too. Long before August 2021, Vinnie was following The Six, bringing me nuggets of solid gold information.

Not everyone had blackmail incentives to make them attend. Which two people had deadly secrets, giving them no choice but to be there? Read on.

As ever, I relied on secrecy. Sending the invitations from me wouldn't guarantee the others taking up the offer. As Stevie's loved to state so far, I wasn't a fun-loving, friendly member of the gang. I took a risk by hoping the power of nostalgia would reunite old friends. The past pulled them back together until they fell apart.

Friday 20 August 2021

Charlotte

Here's the *real* invitation I sent for Simon's memorial, not Erin's version.

An Invitation

You are invited to a celebration of our beloved

Simon Pritchard's life.

Since he went missing in 1992, we've never lost hope of being reunited with our son and brother, however that may be.

For now, we want to celebrate the sixteen years we had with Simon.

This isn't a wake. While Simon's missing, we have hope.

We urge you to come prepared for a celebration, not mourning.

Bring your photographs, memories, and love for Simon.

Buffet and drinks provided.

Date: Friday 20 August 2021

Time: 2pm

Location: The Mill Bed and Breakfast, Trillhaven, Dorset.

RSVP: Charlotte Pritchard, cpritchd@gmail.com

While my legal team deals with it, I won't comment on Erin's confession of killing my brother. Rest assured, she won't get away with it.

Erin

I did get away with it, didn't I? I would love to have seen your face when you read how I made your brother kill himself.

Charlotte

Now I know Erin got her P.I. friend, Vinnie, to pay cash for the group's rooms at The Mill. If I'd been there, I would've questioned it. The guilt isn't mine to carry, though. It's Erin's alone. I've come to accept Simon's memorial was a lovely event and not just a sick person's reason to kill people.

Throughout staying at the bed and breakfast, Erin was never far from her phone. When I commented on it, she claimed to like making notes on people because everyone had the potential to become a character. I thought she was an odd, intense author, not much changed from the damaged girl. I wish I'd known the truth.

The memorial was a happy occasion, not miserable, with my mum sobbing throughout. We'd waited for years to celebrate Simon's life. Only after Thomas's death could we go ahead. I'm sure you'll understand why.

Erin's nerve in coming to the memorial is astounding. It's not unheard of for criminals to be obsessed with their crime, though. She must have loved seeing the impact upon people of what she made Simon do.

No one found it weird, as Erin stated that I purchased the mill. Also, I didn't buy it to take "revenge" on my brothers' friends for his disappearance. Erin really ramped up my potential evil, didn't she?

Brenda and I agreed The Mill would become a space of light and positivity. Many of The Mill's guests comment on how welcoming it feels. The dark and damaged shell of 1992 is gone. Brenda and I worked together, getting gardeners to tidy the land near the building, while leaving nature to roam freely beyond the premises.

Erin's also wrong in saying Mum didn't support me buying of The Mill. Mum owns half the property, bought with some of Thomas's life insurance.

The former mill brought such happiness to Simon and his friends. It's hard under the circumstances, but we refuse to view this as only a place of death. The Mill is full of love for Simon and those who would later die there, too.

Erin

Charlotte is right. I *did* enjoy being at the memorial, knowing it was a result of what I did to Simon. The power I had at sixteen is incredible. I made someone take their own life.

Anyone is capable of murder. Spare me the claims that you'd never kill anyone. We all have a killing instinct. Most won't act upon it. For others, an extreme circumstance triggers a murdering impulse. A loved one's life is under threat. An attacker must be stopped before they hurt you. Or you might kill because you want to. Murder is entertaining. Judging me? What are you currently reading about?

My part in Dylan and Simon's deaths was inevitable. I'll spare you an account of a murderer in the making. I hate true crime books trying to explain why someone becomes a killer. Not everyone has motives or a hard luck story. Sometimes it's simply because of circumstances and a desire to kill.

I was such a threat Simon knew he had to obey. It's not suicide; a personal act from one's own decision. I murdered Simon without lifting a finger. Consider for a moment the genius of my teenage self.

Writing about how I killed Simon was better than sex. Unleashing the secret bettered any orgasm. This isn't an exaggeration. I've had a lot of men. Nothing and no one is more thrilling than killing. Murder is most seductive.

While Simon's memorial accelerated the plot for *Killing Kindness*, it was tedious. One more testimony to his kindness risked my public face disappearing. Funerals and memorials attract hypocrites.

When I'm gone, don't bother hiding your rage. Shout at my coffin all the names you can think of. At least my funeral will be more fun than a sob fest of fake praise. Why do we elevate the dead to sainthood? Corpses don't care. Imagine how cleansing telling the dirty, gritty truth about the dead is. But you won't. Convention won't allow it. Damn the rules. Simon was a pathetic, boring boy who deserved to die for stealing the man I loved.

I arrived early for the memorial. Before checking in, I took a walk around the area. I didn't have a nap because of pregnancy tiredness. It takes more than extra weight to steal my energy.

Looking at The Witch's house from the river's edge was such a thrill. As I pictured the silhouette of a boy fading into the water, the grin wouldn't leave my face.

I headed for the shack, surprised to find it still standing. Brenda must be the nostalgic kind. I needed the closeness with Dylan, too, although he's always with me. Whenever I need courage, I think of him. He's the god I worship. I remember his kindness, helping me through difficult times. Dylan's death wasn't in vain. He dominates my dreams and motivates my desires. Everything is for him.

Outside the shack, I placed a hand on the earth. Once it was stained with Dylan's blood. On my desk is a jar containing some mud. After Simon sank into the river, I turned back to my other victim. I placed a kiss on Dylan's mouth before scooping bloodied earth into a tissue. Now, when I touch the jar, Dylan is with me. I wish I could've dug deeper where his blood must be in the Earth's core. No matter. Dylan is still my everything.

Tina

I swear I didn't know Erin killed Dylan and Simon. I'd never keep something so bad to myself. Even though she's my daughter, I'd have grassed her up to the police in a heartbeat.

When I read what Erin did, I told the publisher to do one. I don't want anything to do with that woman. The publisher said I should keep going 'cos here's where I get to tell the truth. Guess I have to then, don't I? My money from this is going to help abused kiddies. I ain't taking a penny from this shit show.

I was wronged by Erin, too. She killed the fella I loved. What a twat I was for leaving Dylan 'cos I thought he killed Nick. Thinking 'bout it, Dylan was a decent fella. He cared about me and I repaid him by calling him a murderer. Honest, I didn't know he came to Trillhaven to be with me. Things might have been different if I'd known.

I'm not scared of Erin no more. I hope when the coppers find her, they lock her up and throw away the key.

Vinnie Scott

My solicitor advised against contributing to this book, but I've got nothing to lose. Maybe I'll like myself a little more from setting some wrongs right.

I'll always regret meeting Erin. Her agent employed me as a crime consultant for authors. What a joke. I'm definitely an expert in crime now.

Erin contacted me to help with a crime novel she was writing. I took the job because of the money. As a gambling man, I'm not often on the winning side of a risk. If someone was willing to pay for my services, I'd take it.

Don't be fooled into believing private investigation is the same as fiction. We don't try to solve crimes ahead of the police. That means extra unpaid work. Standard jobs involved searching for missing people, exposing fraud, and catching out adulterers. I spent hours in a car reeking of fast food and cigarettes, waiting for something to happen.

As a ladies' man, Erin turned my head. You've seen photos online and in the newspapers, right? Those cat green eyes and knife sharp cheekbones should've been a danger sign. Erin turned out to be another unsuccessful gamble.

We soon began sleeping together. Despite Erin's bizarre behaviour, I was hooked. From minute-to-minute, I never knew what her mood would be. The mornings I woke up to a smiling woman never made me feel comfortable. Erin smiles at the prospect of causing damage.

Her jealousy resulted in cutting up my clothes, smashing my car, and gouging nails into my back. Misguided sympathy made me return. I accepted the bullshit of a woman claiming to have been abused by her mother and misunderstood. I tried to save someone who didn't need rescuing.

When Erin finished the P.I. novel, I expected her to move on. I didn't mind. As far as I was concerned, we were only having sex, nothing more. Now I know she brands you with a scarlet letter. Erin stakes a claim, ruining you for anyone else.

Erin's agent refused to foot the bill when Erin kept me on for future novels. The last few books hadn't done well. As Erin told me in detail how she'd strangle her agent, a vengeful stranger appeared. Still, I let my dick rule my mind. Questioning Erin's motives meant hearing chilling answers.

When she shared some of her ideas for *Killing Kindness,* the plot sounded clever. Basing a story on real life seemed inspired. Erin promised not to use her old friends' names and said she'd avoid anything libellous.

When she employed me to investigate the lives of The Six, I questioned why the information was important. Even though I needed the money, my concerns increased. I owed a lot of cash to ruffians who remove kneecaps as punishment. Erin claimed she only wanted to make the story authentic, and she missed her friends. After telling her to get on social media like everyone else, Erin laughed that I'd underestimated her.

She demanded every detail, particularly The Six's secrets. I pushed it aside, figuring she had an obsessive personality. I learnt not to annoy Erin. Once we argued after she used another man's name during sex. I asked who he was. Erin giggled and then placed a finger on her lips.

I couldn't figure out why a group of teenagers was important to Erin until she mentioned Dylan's death and Simon's disappearance. I accepted her version of how one of The Six might have been responsible. Trailing those people was my way of bringing someone to justice. The buzz of playing storybook P.I., solving a crime with a beautiful woman on my arm, was a thrill.

Only an idiot forgets Erin deals in fiction. I was just a character she manipulated. I could never match up to a man she said I resembled. The man whose name Erin called out when we were in bed was, of course, Dylan.

Erin

The group's conversation after Simon's memorial was tedious. The version I gave in *Killing Kindness* was far more interesting. Life is too short to chat about the weather, a child's achievements, or holiday plans. I'm a woman of words who'd rather not waste them on pointless chatter. For writing material, though, small talk is a necessary evil. If you seem attentive, big talk eventually happens; exposing what's below the surface.

As the others chatted, I pretended to be happy at The Six-minus-one being reunited. The two who received my threats to expose their secrets tried to act normal. Widened eyes and darting heads betrayed their attempts. They assessed everyone, probably trying to work out who sent invitations with added blackmail.

As we drank in the bar, I observed the group. Social media is useful, but can't replace seeing people in the flesh. In the novel, I stated we'd all gone our separate ways. It created the tension of almost strangers meeting again, lugging their baggage of lies and motives. The truth is, we all followed each other online and kept in contact. To appear friendly, I occasionally commented and cooed over their photos. Please, someone, tell me why pictures of your dinner are of interest to anyone.

With each pint, Alex became more animated. True to the butch gay stereotype, his muscular arms were thicker than my thighs. A plaid short-sleeved shirt and jeans showed he was still dressing like Farm Boy.

Stevie had muted her colours and personality. She claims to be an introvert to seem shy and harmless. Younger Stevie was a loudmouth, screaming for attention in neon clothes and clown wig hair. Seeing her dressed in black at the memorial was surprising, considering it wasn't a funeral, although I knew better.

Kat and Joe's public displays of affection were sickeningly sweet. Not even a crowbar could prise them apart. My quip about Kat missing Joe while she went to the toilet didn't go down well. Making the adult versions argue in *Killing Kindness* lit a fire under their arses. I swore if another person mentioned how in love the Andinos still were, I'd lose it. Did they expect a medal for staying married?

Charlotte swanned around The Mill, asserting her ownership. She did me a favour by mentioning the strange man who'd paid for our rooms. The gang grilled each other, figuring one of us did it and was being silently humble.

Joe's comments about how I must be raking it in pissed me off. If you start writing with the aim of getting rich, disappointment soon heads your way. For every bestselling author, there are a million struggling writers. Each book places you back on a hamster wheel of finding ideas, fighting imposter syndrome, seeking publication, and then begging people to buy your book.

When your work is rejected, your confidence plummets. After a period of misery, you vow to write again. Another rejection. Past successes are no longer inspiring. They're a mockery of what you once were and fear you'll never be again.

Your agent drops you. The bills are mounting. Words won't come. Then you have a great idea. If imagination is failing you, why not use real life? You reflect on a summer where the events are so thrilling no one would believe it; perfect for fiction. You travel back to 1992 and also use the present day to write a new novel.

At the memorial, I resolved to be friendly. Despite my efforts, I couldn't quite nail it as a teenager. Adult Erin is more accomplished. She entices men, writes beautifully, and can fool anyone.

My pregnancy was a bonus. A pregnant woman is a delicate flower holding a precious bundle. A surrogate is on the same level as angels for goodness. Complaining about the burden of extra weight made the others pity me. The pregnancy never bothered me. I've been weight training for years. While my body could take it, my mind occasionally flipped out at the thought of carrying a child for my cousin, Gemma. As ever, I did what was needed to get results.

Stevie

God bless her – because no one else will – Erin is such a liar. I was dressed in black for the memorial due to wearing my clerical shirt with the white collar. Everyone already knew I'm a vicar. There was no revelation of a naughty teen turned into a vicar, as stated in the novel.

Also, I don't have an eyebrow piercing and my mouth isn't that potty. Taking Sunday services soon breaks you of the swearing habit. The only time I've sworn in church was in training. I blurted out some unbiblical words when a baby slipped out of my hands and into the baptismal font. The parents were soaked. The vicar took over and I hid in the vestry. Afterwards, I kept a tighter grip on wriggling infants and engaged my brain before my mouth. I'm puzzling over why Erin portrayed me as a rebellious vicar. Sorry to disappoint, the edgiest I get is playing classic rock while doing the housework.

Erin's issues with me began because she feared Simon and I might not buy the changed girl act. We figured something was up, but tried to give her a chance. You'd think I would've learnt to trust my instincts when I saw Erin at the memorial. Despite what some believe, vicars aren't obliged to see the good in everyone. The good I see is God. Sometimes, it's reflected in others. Good as a human virtue is a woolly concept. Whatever good is, Erin doesn't have an ounce of it.

My husband has asked me to add I wasn't on the phone with him while driving to the memorial. He thinks it's ridiculous how Erin made him someone who constantly checks on me. He isn't the mithering type and understands with my job I could be anywhere at any moment. Erin *is* correct about my hubby never throwing away empty toilet roll tubes and leaving his clothes on the floor. Men, eh?

I nearly peed my pants laughing when I read of how I've apparently written my own eulogy. If I wrote the address for my funeral, I certainly wouldn't give a list of my "misdemeanours", as Erin called them. Besides, when will I get the time to write my eulogy? I'm too busy doing everyone else's. Let someone else do mine when I've snuffed it.

Thalia

At least Erin's confessed my parents were happy and not fighting. I may not have been at The Mill, but I know they never put each other down. Like most married couples, they had disagreements, but soon sorted it out without falling out like in *Killing Kindness*.

I'm what's considered plus size and couldn't give a shit about it. I've inherited the curvy Greek woman's shape and celebrate it. My Instagram tribe understands the beauty of the bigger woman. After having a baby, some of the weight stuck. Mum's influence made me accept who I am.

She wasn't overweight. Erin's fat phobia is showing. For the memorial, Mum wore a trouser suit, not a smock top she kept pulling down to cover her stomach. There's no shame in being a larger lady. I embrace it. For the sake of the truth, though, Mum was a size 12 and wasn't wearing "baggy tents" or unable to look people in the eye.

Erin used an eating disorder for entertainment. In her teens, Mum had bulimia. The Pink Posse taught her dodgy lessons about bingeing and vomiting. When she joined The Six and started dating Dad, it stopped.

Unfortunately, after having babies, Mum began restricting food. She felt powerless against pregnancy body changes. While she loved having us, the battle with controlling her body was terrifying.

With the last pregnancy, Mum sought help for anorexia. Counselling – which wasn't kept a secret, as claimed in the novel – became part of her recovery. Eventually, she led a local eating disorders group, along with the therapist.

Mum found getting older liberating. She no longer competed with other women or earlier versions of herself. At last, she was comfortable in her skin.

Erin's writing shows she was threatened by Mum's confidence. It's probably why Erin tried to reduce her to nothing. Erin didn't succeed. While she lives in the hearts and minds of her family, Mum is everything.

Erin

After listening to old stories for hours at the memorial, I took a break. Everyone gives you grief for smoking when pregnant. Without a nicotine fix, I wouldn't have made it through the rest of the evening. The group niceness was doing me in.

As I walked, my feet and heart headed for Dylan's shack. Leaning against the hut, I lowered to the ground, sending silent words of forgiveness to Dylan. I wasn't seeking forgiveness for killing him. It had to happen. I wanted him to forgive me for my part in people calling him a murderer. If I'd told Dylan this back then, I'd have lost him. Dylan's been dead for years. It's time to confess.

Living in Blandford hadn't turned out how I'd hoped. I thought I could change – at least on the surface – and be accepted. The problem with being the new girl in a school is friendships are solid. Most of the pupils had known each other since primary school. They refused to invest in someone who might leave, not that I had any intention of going anywhere. If Dylan lived in Blandford, it was where I'd stay.

I'm cringing at how I wanted to fit in, trying to hide my reputation. I joined clubs, sat with losers at lunch, and started conversations. No one cared, so I went back to being the real me.

Causing trouble was fun. Tina was a ball of nerves, waiting for another call about something bad I'd done. Being placed on suspension meant I could be with Dylan. Because he couldn't get any jobs, he was often at home. While Tina worked at the supermarket, Dylan and I bonded over crime books, bad TV, and music. It was perfect until Nick appeared.

Dylan made no secret of wanting to be a father. Thankfully, Tina wasn't keen. I'm glad a kid never joined the household. Its safety wouldn't have been guaranteed. You can imagine how Nick playing at being Dylan's "son" affected me.

Unable to get between Nick's and Dylan's friendship, I sought comfort in sex. While boys avoided me at school, they couldn't get enough in private. Sex made me feel alive. I took what I needed and left them wanting more. It seemed to work until that day in May 1992.

May 1992

Wesley gave a cruel grin. 'You're the town bike and probably riddled with STDs.'

Until then, no one had refused my advances. For weeks, Wesley was my sexual conquest project. Pretending to be there to buy ecstasy, I paid regular visits to his home.

Boys don't often mean what they say. Men tell lies, too. I undid the buttons of my shirt.

'Let's make this our little secret,' I said.

Wesley grabbed my arms and shunted me towards the front door. 'I've got a girlfriend. Why would I want a skank like you?'

I was fed up with being second best. Every night, I heard through paper-thin walls Tina and Dylan having sex. As my mother enjoyed what was my right, I gouged the wallpaper. Music blared through my headphones while I imagined Tina's body slashed into fleshy ribbons.

Wesley's rejection fired my fury. I tore my shirt, roughed my hair, and smudged mascara down my cheeks.

'Fine.' I can give cruel grins, too. 'I'll cry rape.'

Wesley pulled my hand off the door handle. A window was open nearby. The street busied with neighbours returning from work.

'I'll scream.'

Wesley clamped a hand over my mouth and whispered into my ear. 'Don't mess with me, whore. I know people who can end your life like that.' He clicked his fingers.

Wesley's family's criminal behaviour and network were infamous. Rumours circulated about a man who'd tried it on with Wesley's girlfriend and then went missing.

Wesley seized my throat and squeezed. After he let go, I ran outside. Humiliation tingled inside me, to my fingertips. I wanted to hurt someone, to transfer the pain. Stomping towards home, I hoped Tina was there as a potential victim.

The familiar flicking of playing cards hitting bicycle spokes changed everything.

'Are you OK?' Nick slowed his pedalling. 'Looks like you've been in a fight.'

An annoying eleven-year-old was of no use to me. I wished him gone. Unfortunately, irritating people stick like glue.

'I've finished my paper round,' he said. 'Just off to meet Dylan.'

Nick spent more time at our place than his own. His dad came over a few nights ago. Suspicion was in his eyes as he assessed Dylan. Granted, a man being around a boy might seem dodgy. Dylan cracked open beers and the men bonded. Nick's dad left happy his child shared an interest with Dylan in tinkering and fixing objects.

Nick always rode his bike while standing because it was too small. As a surprise, Dylan was doing up an old bicycle for him. Dylan and the boy connected in a way I never could.

'Hey, want to see a cool thing I discovered in the woods?' I asked Nick.

'It will be dark soon and Dylan's expecting me.'

'He's out on a job. By the time we're done here, he'll be home. I haven't shown anyone else. You love discovering new things because you're so clever.'

The child smiled as he bit the baited hook.

We headed into woods. With each step, I made a plan. The thrill of having a purpose gave energy to my strides. After struggling to pedal over fallen twigs, Nick walked beside me.

At a clearing, I paused. I'd recently discovered it after trying to find somewhere private to think. We were alone.

'Where is it?' Nick asked.

'Where's what?' I sat on a log.

'The surprise.'

My hands scrabbled behind me. 'Look over there, through the gap in those trees. Concentrate, as it'll appear at any minute.'

Nick turned to look. 'What?'

'It's coming.'

A thick branch thudded into Nick's skull. Remind you of anything? Cast your mind back to fictional Simon, hitting Joe with a branch for having a secret relationship with Kat. No experience is wasted for an author.

The force of the impact made me giddy. I righted my balance so as not to join Nick on the ground. Blood leeched from his head, staining his cap.

Finally, I'd done it. I had committed murder. Don't psychoanalyse me. Tina won't get any credit by blaming her crap parenting. No one moulded me. *I* created this glorious monster.

Fantasies of murder filled my mind long before killing Nick. The excitement of making it a reality soon dulled, though. No one would ever know I had killed someone. It wouldn't be recognised. I needed my comforter.

I washed my hands in a puddle formed from a recent storm. Blood spatter soon disappeared. A jacket in my bag covered flecks of evidence on my shirt. Then I headed for the nearest phone box.

After the call connected, my words tumbled out. 'I can't take it anymore. Everyone hates me. I'm going to end it.'

You may think it wrong to fake suicidal feelings. Do I seem like the kind of person who cares? I needed Dylan there, close to the scene I'd created. The thought of the man I loved being near the boy I'd killed was irresistible.

After making me promise to wait at the edge of the woods, Dylan soon arrived on his motorbike. Joy bubbled in my blood as his hands held mine; those that had killed the child who had come between us. I kissed Dylan. Despite moving away, I swear he enjoyed it. Our passion startled him.

Dylan promised to keep my "suicidal feelings" a secret. Later, he also promised never to tell anyone I was in the area where Nick died. Unfortunately, this meant Dylan didn't have any witnesses to his whereabouts and he became a suspect. Tina gave him a false alibi after much "persuasion" from me.

Although the police never charged Dylan, the locals gave guilty verdicts. *Paedo* and *Child Killer* were spray painted on our property. Dylan became a recluse and emotionally shut off from everyone, including me. I needed a plan.

It was a risk to let Tina "find" Nick's blood stained cap. When we were tidying the garage, *I* pulled out the filing cabinet to reveal the hidden hat and let Tina pick it up. I made threats to make her do what I wanted. Tina is so predictable. I knew she'd want to go back to Trillhaven, and I'd get her away from Dylan.

Because of my past behaviour, I expected returning to be tricky. A challenge always excites me. Tina believed Dylan had gone into hiding because we knew of his "guilt". Coming out of this stupid woman's womb is a constant embarrassment.

Later, I sent a letter to Dylan, revealing we were in Trillhaven. I offered to help him make up with Tina. Dylan had nothing left in Blandford. The Witch had put up an advert in the post office for a job, with the offer of accommodation.

Dylan trusted me and moved. Whenever we met, I promised I was working on Tina. His joyful expectancy hurt my heart. The excitement should have been for being with me, which was what I'd planned, not with my ugly mother. Still, I believed in love, hopeful Dylan would eventually view me as a woman.

It was going well until Simon claimed Dylan. Once again, I competed for his attention. No matter. I'd erased Nick. Getting rid of Simon proved to be easy, too.

Tina

If you know where Erin is for God's sake tell the police. She needs locking up.

Friday 20 August 2021

Erin

It's time to explain what *really* happened to Alex. Despite what's been said, I'm not homophobic. Being gay was the only interesting thing about Alex. After Simon's memorial, Alex shared endless photos of a recent holiday with his partner, Tim. Hiding my boredom became a mammoth effort.

Yes, I lied in *Killing Kindness*. What a surprise. Alex didn't hide his sexuality. In fact, he was so out he screamed it from the rooftops. I swore if there was another mention of Tim, I'd leap over the table and strangle Alex.

Cleverer readers may have figured out I didn't blackmail Alex, threatening to reveal his sexuality unless he stayed at The Mill. He wasn't one of the two members of The Six with a juicy secret.

I added a few lines to Alex's invitation, stating Joe was having serious troubles and too ashamed to ask for help. Alex and Joe had continued their friendship. Social media showed times spent together at football matches and family gatherings. If your best friend is in trouble, you try to help. Of course, I'm guessing. I don't have a best friend. No pity. It's for the best I don't let anyone get close.

Here's how it went the night Alex died.

****

I claimed tiredness and appeared to head upstairs. Unnoticed, I slipped outside. As I took cover under the trees on the outskirts of The Mill, I typed a message to Alex.

Joe has a major problem. I'm worried about him, but can't talk about it in front of the others. Please come to the bridge to discuss it. A concerned friend.

Alex might have worked out the message came from me, considering I was no longer in the bar. Charlotte was also a possibility as she moved around throughout the evening. Stevie popped to the toilets when I'd left, making her another option.

Prepared to destroy any links with me, I'd bought a stash of sim cards to use for such messages. Nowadays, my actions are better planned than they were with the deaths of Nick, Dylan, and Simon. A novel needing its structure to be followed in real life requires a plan. Some writers fly by the seat of their pants. Pantsers are amateurs, waiting for a muse who doesn't exist to take over. *No one* controls me.

From behind Dylan's shack, I watched Alex key in the code to the gate at the edge of The Mill's land. Using the light from a mobile phone, his strides became more purposeful. He wasn't wobbling with drunkenness as described in *Killing Kindness*. A man of Alex's size can handle his drink and he was only tipsy. Apart from Joe and me, all of them had been drinking since the afternoon. The baby thing could be a burden, but avoiding alcohol was useful. A clear head helped me to move things along.

For dramatic effect, I approached Alex from the other side of the bridge. I'd turned off my torch for the big reveal. A cloud moved away from the moon, ready to highlight my arrival. Alex spoiled it.

'I knew it was you.'

'Why?' I tried to temper my indignant tone and failed.

'After you left, I received the text. I can't think of anyone else who'd be a "concerned friend" here.'

'What about Charlotte or Stevie?' Teenage huffiness crept into my voice. I wanted to be the only one with all the knowledge. Characters aren't supposed to write the story.

'I just knew it was you.'

I opened my bag and pulled out a hipflask. 'Fancy a drink?'

'You shouldn't be drinking in your condition.'

If another person told me what to do with *my* body, I was going to stab them in the eye.

'Donna filled it up for me at the bar. The whisky's for you. What I'm going to say about Joe is difficult.'

I knew Alex would be polite. While he drank, I focused on his Adam's apple, taking in the potion.

'It's weird being here,' I said.

'Certainly is.' Alex leaned on the railing, looking into the water. 'I'm surprised you chose to meet here, seeing as it's where Simon... well... you know.'

Indeed I do, I thought. *I know exactly what happened.*

'We should follow Charlotte's lead and remember this as a place where we had great times.' I relied once again on the pull of nostalgia. 'The mill was another member of The Six; always there with us.'

Alex gulped more whisky and then held up the flask. 'Sorry, do you want some?' A slow tongue stretched out the words.

I patted my stomach. 'Pregnant.'

'Forgot.' Alex's hand slipped as he tried to grip the railing. 'Must be pissed. Oh well. It's not every day you're with old friends.'

What a joy it was to watch him drink more booze mixed with a sedative.

'Let's take a stroll while we discuss Joe.' I placed an arm around Alex's waist. The man had some heft. I'm strong, but with the extra weight of pregnancy and holding a torch, I needed to move him away before he passed out.

Alex tripped over his foot and clumsily righted his balance. 'Woah! Drunk. Better walk it off. Don't wanna upset Charlotte by getting rat-arsed at her brother's memorial.'

Despite Alex's dragging feet, we picked up the pace. Thankfully, the destination wasn't far.

'How come you know what's happening with Joe?' Alex's eyebrows met in the middle. 'You're not close.'

'Kat told me. It's best we all help him, though, particularly you.'

'Didn't like you much when we were younger. Didn't say anything 'cos of The Six.'

I ground my teeth together before speaking. 'I'm different now.'

'Admit it,' Alex drawled. 'You could be a bitch sometimes. The kids at the holiday club were shit scared. One said you were scarier than the child catcher in... what is it? The film with the car in it.' He scratched his head. 'I know! *Chitty Chitty Bang Bang*.'

My cheeks ached from a stretched smile. 'Children exaggerate. Look, we're here.'

Alex slumped against the goat shed door. Although the corrugated iron walls were still standing, I feared for them against his bulk. The gods of bad deeds smiled on me when I found the building earlier. Dylan spent hours there tending to The Witch's goats. Sometimes, we met there.

'Why are we here?' Alex swayed as he moved away from the wall. 'Oh, yeah. Joe. Whassa matter?'

'Come inside. It's going to rain.'

Weather expert farmer Alex was too far gone to notice the clear night sky. He advanced into the darkness. After taking a few steps, he yelped before face planting onto the concrete. He groaned as blood trickled from his nose, and then rolled over to lie on his back.

'Tired,' he began. 'Need to sleep.'

It took a lot of effort for me to be patient. In an abandoned armchair, I watched my victim give in to the sedative. Alex's breaths became shallow. Although I'd used it in a novel, I've never sedated someone. Vinnie hooked me up with a woman who can provide any drug you want. I told him I wasn't sleeping well and needed something stronger than a GP's prescription. For a P.I., Vinnie is far too trusting.

I knelt over Alex. Quietness made me lean in to check he was breathing. For sheer spite, I jabbed at his cheek. Alex mumbled.

Wearing canvas gloves not only helps to avoid detection. They are a useful smothering tool, too. As my hands clamped over his nose and mouth, Alex gasped for air. Sedative-sodden limbs flailed. Finally, Farm Boy gave up and rested forever.

For the final effect, I etched lines down Alex's wrists. Of course, I'd brought a scalpel with me. I didn't place him in a wardrobe. While I'm proud of my physical strength, lugging Alex would've been impossible. Having him literally coming out of the closest in *Killing Kindness* was pure genius. In reality, Alex died on a filthy, cold floor. I placed a pink tulip in his hand and left a note nearby.

I can't deal with it anymore. I'm a burden. It's kinder to everyone if I go. My death is killing with kindness, for me and others.

The note was vague enough to hint Alex had a secret, which led him to kill himself. Suicide has appeared a lot in my life. I faked suicidal feelings to make Dylan my rescuer after I killed Nick. I made Simon take his own life. For the sake of completeness, Alex's death had to initially appear to be suicide, too. Also, the others would've gone home if they thought a serial killer had started a spree. Sure, the medical examiner would spot Alex had suffocated, but there was time before that discovery.

You're probably wondering why I murdered Alex. As always, my answer is because I can.

Alex died three times: in my research, in *Killing Kindness*, and for real. I killed the kindness that came from The Six-minus-one reconnecting. Alex was so sickeningly nice. Not anymore. Kindness killed.

Tim, I'll offer some comfort. Alex said your name before he died. Now, who says I can't be kind?

Tim

I put off reading Erin's "true" account of Alex's death for as long as possible. The publisher said I didn't have to read it or respond. I must, for Alex.

Alex was my world. We'd been together for years, lived on the farm, and were planning our wedding. He wasn't the stupid Farm Boy from *Killing Kindness*. Alex was a smart businessman who produced crops for major suppliers and reared sheep. I'm certainly not a *Lady Chatterley's Lover* type. The idea of me as a farmhand is comedy gold. One splash of mud and I'm running for the hills, or rather back inside where it's clean and warm.

Here's what Erin didn't share. I'm an author who writes horror and has a successful career. I'm not saying Erin hasn't mentioned my job because of jealousy, but… Actually, I will.

In the writing community, Erin's well-known for befriending authors and then ghosting them, writing spiteful social media posts, and trying to turn writers against each other. I know your real identity, *BookBitch*. The one star reviews for all my books are hilarious.

I didn't leave Alex after issuing an ultimatum, as Erin wrote. We were way beyond revealing our sexualities.

When Alex told his parents he was gay on his eighteenth birthday, his mum was accepting, saying she'd had suspicions. His dad struggled with the farm not having an heir. Eventually, he accepted Alex's happiness was more important.

Everyone knew we were gay, including the locals. Many of them are friends. This is not the 1800s where "the gays" are likely to be hit by God's lightning bolt if they enter a church. Despite my grief, I howled with laughter at Erin describing Alex sitting through anti-homosexuality sermons. Alex and his family only went to church for weddings, christenings, and funerals. The Burtons' farm was their religion.

I can deal with Erin casting out Alex for fancying the same sex. I've dealt with bigotry most of my life. To portray him as suicidal, though, is unforgiveable. Alex went to the memorial the happiest I'd ever seen. In a few months, we were getting married and our businesses were doing well. While farmers are statistically high in suicide statistics, Alex wasn't at risk. He would've said if he was feeling suicidal. We discussed all our worries and concerns.

After a difficult year, with barren crops and sickly sheep, Alex's father killed himself. Alex took the death as a warning to look after his mental health. For Erin to have written Alex's death as suicide is distasteful to the memory of his father, people who *have* taken their lives, and those left behind.

Learning Erin offered her body to grow a living thing is hard to consider. A killer giving life! She stole the most precious existence; my beloved Alex.

One day, Erin, I'll also take from you what you value.

Brenda

I'm confused about why Erin described me as being in the background of Alex's death. The biggest shock I had that night was winning a bottle of cava in the raffle at bingo.

I certainly didn't see Alex standing on the bridge, waiting for Erin. As I've said before, I hardly saw The Six when they were kids. They visited the mill in the evenings when I was usually reading or catching up on *Emmerdale*. I wouldn't recognise the grown-up group now, not even with my glasses on.

I'm not the people-hating old hag Erin created. Thanks to being older, I get the odd chin hair, which is as far as The Witch thing goes. I wear cardigans I've knitted, for goodness' sake! I ask you; would a witch wear an Aran cardie?

It's worth adding I inherited the mill from my parents. I didn't want it to go to ruin and wasn't reluctant to part with it, as Erin stated. I tried many times to sell it. Potential buyers always backed down after learning about what happened to Dylan and Simon.

When Charlotte made an offer, I gratefully accepted. The money's helped. More than that, I like Charlotte. Occasionally, we have a drink together, although it will be a while before I return. The Mill attracts people bothering the dead and reporters trying to make more news.

Rest assured, if I'd seen Alex and Erin, I would've told the police. I'm not a backward country woman who doesn't trust the authorities. My son is in the police. He's determined to help find and arrest Erin. I'm cheering him on.

Saturday 21 August 2021

Erin

After breakfast, at my suggestion, we decided to look for Alex. Someone had to discover his body. Watching the others' reactions to the murder scene also promised to be a thrill.

Joe didn't lead us on the walk. Overgrown stinging nettles hanging over the pathway were of the past. I figured reminiscing at how The Six walked in line, friends together, would make the reader comfortable, only to hit you with the whammy of a corpse.

I wouldn't have followed The Leader again if my life depended on it. In 1992, everyone doing what Joe wanted ticked me off. Kat and Stevie obeying a boy was disappointing. A few times, I tried to push Joe aside, saying females can also lead. Believing I was trying to be funny, the others laughed. As always, I was deadly serious.

While trying to find Alex, we approached Dylan's shack. I paused, gave a loud exhale, and dabbed my dry eyes. The group surrounded me, concerned about the baby's health. I wanted the thing gone from me and soon. After reassuring them I was fine, we carried on.

As we neared the goat shed, my pulse throbbed in my ears. I reminded myself to note every reaction from my companions. It was happening; an actual discovery of a murder. I'd moved on from imagination.

Figuring she's a vicar who's no stranger to death, I let Stevie go in first. OK, I needed to see her suffering. The howling like an injured wolf was wonderfully unexpected. Perhaps it's harder when someone you care for is dead, or maybe Stevie's still a drama queen.

Stevie

I cried out because my friend was dead. It's what normal people do, not that Erin would know. I loathe how she drank in my grief and stored it in her head to use in the novel.

Alex's body didn't fall out of a wardrobe and onto me. There wasn't a note about coming out of the closet, either. Erin's writing is incredibly tacky.

While it's acceptable in the circumstances, I didn't sit on the floor, hugging myself and talking gibberish. I went into vicar mode and worked alongside Kat to take action. She showed strength gained from being in recovery from an eating disorder. Despite the circumstances, I was proud of her.

Worried the upset might lead to premature labour, Kat took Erin outside. While Kat called the emergency services, Joe and I stayed in the shed. We couldn't leave our friend alone, even in death.

As I stood near Alex, I became confused. The real note indicated suicide. The pink tulip seemed out of place. At that point, I hadn't remembered Simon's tulips in the holiday club's kindness parade.

I recall Erin returning to the shed and saying, "'Alex is holding one of Simon's pink tulips.'" Back then, it didn't register. In hindsight, well, how obvious could Erin be? Joe and I practically had to push her outside. I thought she was staring because she was in shock. Really, the murderer was enjoying looking at her crime scene.

Erin

After the police had done their thing, we went to the bar. Although I was tired after the previous evening's activities, I wasn't going to miss witnessing the others' grief.

Thankfully, they decided to stay until at least the next day. It made sense, as the police needed to finish taking statements. That saved me from having to do something risky to make the group continue their "holiday" at The Mill.

As we sat together, I looked at the remnants of The Six and ran through my death tally.

Simon: Tick.

Alex: Tick.

Kat, Joe, and Stevie: To be completed.

Stevie

Sorry, not sorry Erin didn't get to cross me off the list.

As usual, she lied about what happened when we were in the bar. We stayed together because no one wanted to be alone. When people experience a shared trauma, they want to share their common feelings. Of course, Erin doesn't count. Heartless robots don't have emotions.

Charlotte

Joining the group in the bar wasn't a business move to calm distressed customers. Alex was Simon's friend and someone who'd always been nice to me. A death happening on the same day as Simon's memorial was dreadful.

My legal mind considered a link between Alex's death and Simon's disappearance. Remember, at this stage I didn't know my brother was dead. I briefly wondered if Alex had taken his own life because of Simon's anniversary. It didn't seem right. Alex and Simon were close, but why would Alex feel suicidal about the disappearance after so long?

The mood hanging over us all was understandably subdued. Against this, Erin was wired, chatting like a speed junkie and cracking jokes. Now I know she was high on murder and buzzing off our grief. At the time, I thought her behaviour was due to delayed shock.

Erin's portrayal of me as the hotel owner, plotting against the people who might have made her brother disappear, is pathetic. Agatha Christie can rest easy in her grave. Erin Sullivan's writing skills leave a lot to be desired. Her depiction of an old gang gathered together by the victim's vengeful sister is hilariously awful. Remember, I invited them to the memorial, not to stay at my bed and breakfast. That's all Erin's work.

I must add, in Joe's defence, he was sober. Even when the others turned to alcohol after seeing Alex's body, Joe didn't touch a drop. He said drinking wouldn't end well for him. Kat squeezed his hand.

Joe didn't drink the previous day, either. I recognised the signs of a recovering alcoholic. There were no drunken scenes or demanding his car keys to drive home. Joe was sad and quiet, obviously devastated by Alex's death. Kat drew him close and never let go. I've never seen a more loving couple, something Erin will never experience.

Erin

When planning the novel, I chose an alternative set of characters. Allowing the real The Six fame seemed wrong. Then I realised I'm a skilled writer who can make others whatever I want them to be. Using people I knew meant I understood how they speak and act. As the author puppeteer, I made my characters more interesting than the real-life versions.

I decided to give Kat a different personality and background from her loveable Princess image. Her niceness made my mouth and cheeks hurt with all the fake smiling I returned.

Joe and Kat's daughter, Thalia, has covered how Kat wasn't the fat blimp I portrayed. So what? The previous bag of bones got some meat on her body, if only fictionally. Vinnie's research uncovered the eating disorder, although I had suspicions when we were younger.

Kat received counselling and ran a recovery group. You've probably guessed she didn't steal money from her employer to pay for therapy. Her boring existence needed spicing up.

Kat *was* one of the two recipients of my blackmail notes, included with the instruction to stay at The Mill. The threat wasn't aimed specifically at her. Marriage binds two people together, making them guilty by association.

Thalia

After reading the chapter where Mum apparently laid next to my sleeping drunk Dad, I cried. I shouldn't feed Erin's ego with sharing my pain, but readers deserve the truth.

Mum's eating disorder wasn't a silly little thing as Erin portrayed. At one point, Mum was hospitalised due to being dangerously thin. Dad visited her on his own. He didn't want Mum upset and spared us from seeing her in a hospital bed. He's always been a leader, but never the dictator Leader Erin portrayed. Dad always led with kindness.

After coming home, Mum gradually gained weight and picked up her life. Running the recovery group gave her a purpose. Mum and Dad were as strong as Greek gods. She was a warrior, with her partner as armour.

While I never believed it, I asked the publisher to check Erin's accusation of Mum stealing. I wanted it in writing. Anyone who still has doubts can read the letter from Mum's workplace. Of course, she never nicked money or set up a private bank account. Mum was a manager in the job centre, not working in a newsagent. She helped people earn money rather than her stealing it.

Dad *was* an alcoholic who'd given up drinking years ago. As part of going to Alcoholics Anonymous, he accepted he was an addict who didn't have to fuel the addiction. After a series of drink-related embarrassments, the thought of returning to the lifestyle terrified him. Mum wouldn't have been lying next to a pissed-up man at The Mill. I may not have been there, but I trust Dad didn't drink. Thank you, Charlotte, for confirming it.

Dad turned away from alcohol because it nearly destroyed his family. I guess boozing ultimately led to his death, although it wasn't his fault. Mum and Dad received the two blackmail notes Erin wrote, demanding they stay at The Mill for four days. I found the envelopes and their contents hidden in a clothes drawer.

I wish I'd never made my parents keep the secret we shared. Maybe things would be different.

Erin

Thalia, if you think portraying your parents as a fat thief and a bitter alcoholic is terrible, what's coming next will shock you.

The Andinos should be grateful I didn't describe Kat's murder in the novel. Instead, they mounted a media campaign, smearing my name. I have no qualms about being portrayed as a murderer. *No one* questions my talent as an author.

When Michael Andino gave an interview saying my books were only good for toilet paper, I wished I'd added gruesome details of how Kat died. Now I will.

Read it and weep, Michael, Thalia, and everyone else.

****

While the group was sad about Alex's "suicide", Charlotte pulled the mood further down by mentioning it was the anniversary of Simon's disappearance. As if I'd forget. It was the day I lost Dylan. OK, I killed him.

We stayed in the bar. The mourners didn't want to be alone with their grief. The thrill of murdering Alex wore off. When I considered my next plan, adrenaline replaced the boredom. Kat asked what was making me fidgety. I mentioned a weak bladder and we shared pregnancy stories.

Finally, Joe and Kat went to bed. I soon followed. Stevie and Charlotte stayed in the bar, having their own memorial for Simon.

In my room, I waited for Kat and Joe to settle. When I arrived at The Mill, I requested a room next to the Andinos, claiming to need supportive friends nearby. Research of The Mill's website confirmed our rooms had a joining door. Kat and Joe joked about someone sleepwalking and unlocking it. Joe said he hoped it wouldn't be him as he slept in the nude. I laughed along, aware of the fright I'd give them later.

Through the walls, I heard the couple moving around and muffled conversation. I spent the waiting time redrafting *Killing Kindness* while preparing to create the next major plot point.

In the early hours of the morning, silence was my cue to begin. Charlotte confirmed earlier – after a seemingly innocent question from me – there weren't any cameras in or outside the building. This woman is a barrister! I'm not complaining. Her lack of security was to my advantage. Instead of a night receptionist, guests had to use a phone for assistance.

Although everything was closed, I used the stairs at the back of the building and then the fire escape to exit. Earlier, I'd checked it wasn't alarmed.

I headed for a place where The Six cooled off in the sticky summer of 1992. Choosing the area as a murder scene was risky, but the stream was only open to guests. I relied on the staff living off site, and Charlotte being asleep in her cottage nearby.

The stream was made accessible, with recesses dug into the bank and steps leading to the water. It was a perfect place to picnic, socialise, or kill. A little way upstream, I stood under a tree while sending a text to Kat.

I'm spotting blood and worried about the baby. I went for a walk by the stream as I couldn't sleep. I'm scared to move. I need you. xx

Kat soon replied.

Don't worry. Probably normal pregnancy stuff. I'll wake Joe and then we'll be there. Where exactly are you? xx

Of course, she wanted to bring Joe. Those two were hard to prise apart.

Please come alone. I've got blood on me. So embarrassing. I'm by the tree we used to sit under. xx

Kat's reply raised a smile.

I understand. I'll be on my own. Be there in a few minutes. xx

Kat didn't ask why my messages came from an unknown number. I was aware the police would work out who the sender was, considering I was Kat's only pregnant friend at The Mill. Once my work was done, I'd be as far away as possible.

As the water flowed, I concentrated on the plan flooding my mind. My courage didn't disappear. I was checking all the details. Yes, I'd had experience of killing in real life and in my novels, but I wasn't an expert. Lessons on how to murder aren't readily available.

Kat scrambled down the steps. Lights left on outside The Mill guided her towards me. I slumped to the ground and began fake crying.

Kat kneeled beside me. 'Are you still bleeding?' Her eyes trained towards my crotch.

I crossed my legs tighter, grateful for wearing black.

'Don't be embarrassed,' Kat began. 'Pregnancy strips a woman of her dignity until you no longer care.'

After not receiving a reply, Kat clutched my arm. 'Are you OK? Talk to me, Erin.'

The sight of her wedding ring boosted my confidence. Witnessing the widower Joe's suffering would be such a treat.

I pretended to slip while trying to stand. Kat threw out her arms to catch me. She never saw it coming. The rock pounded into the back of her head. Kat's body slammed into the stream. Clasping slippery pebbles, she tried to stand. Ragged breaths came from her mouth. I tugged her hair, making her look at me.

'Why?' Kat managed to ask, despite an obviously broken nose.

'Because I can.'

I let go of her hair. Kat clawed at the mud. Fingertips sunk into mush. Blood swirled in the water.

I grabbed her T-shirt and dragged my victim further in. It only takes a few inches of water, a foot on a busted skull, and a person lying face down to cause drowning.

Afterwards, I placed a pink silk tulip in Kat's hand. I took her phone and then checked the scene for any mistakes. There were none. I'd created something perfect.

Once more, I killed kindness. Kat was being kinder to her mind and body by recovering from an eating disorder. No more Princess and one less member of The Six, too.

That night I slept like the dead, or what I'm guessing it's like to be deceased. I'm the killer. No one's ever going to get rid of me.

Sunday 22 August 2021

Erin

At breakfast I put up with Stevie wittering on about vicar stuff. I refused to offer praise. What does she expect for doing her job; a damehood? Thankfully, Joe arrived and interrupted the bragging.

Already upset about Alex, Joe now had Kat's disappearance to contend with. I suggested she'd gone for a walk. Joe seemed happy with that and polished off a full English breakfast. He wasn't hungover or aggressive, as depicted in *Killing Kindness*. Again, I injected some life into these tiresome people.

Stevie didn't shock our fellow diners by talking about her sex life and us being bitchy to each other in our youth. She should thank me for making her more interesting. Stevie *did* make a joke about having a female vicar in my next book. There is, Stevie. It's you.

Joe's concerns for Kat soon resurfaced. He'd seen a troubling post on her Facebook account. You've probably guessed it didn't state, "Today's top dieting tip: drown your appetite with water. Kill your hunger with kindness", as was in the novel. The wording complimented the death in *Killing Kindness*.

Here's what I really posted from Kat's phone after her death.

Being back with old friends feels like I'm drowning in love.

Joe was worried Kat felt overwhelmed by reuniting with The Six. He wondered if memories of developing an eating disorder in her teens made her vulnerable. Oh, Joe, you had far more to be concerned about than your wife throwing up.

After asserting Kat was fine and having some time out, I proposed having a picnic by the stream to remember Alex. It was one of his favourite places. In the novel, Stevie made the suggestion, taking the attention away from me.

I intended *Killing Kindness* to be released after actual events. My killing role was supposed to be secret. Things went wrong. Throughout the book, I cast myself as an innocent character. Some readers are amateur detectives. They claim on social media to have worked out the twist in my novels within the first few chapters. They can't. I'm a far better author than that. Everyone's a smart arse when reading thriller and crime fiction.

Concerned about Kat's wellbeing, Joe was reluctant to have a picnic. Stevie, God bless her, suggested Kat's "drowning in love" comment was happiness at being together again. After leaving a voicemail for Kat, Joe agreed. He was certain she'd join us soon. How right he was.

Unlike the novel, we didn't have any alcohol. I needed Joe sober to note his genuine reactions. Still, I couldn't resist characterising him as the distraught drunk in *Killing Kindness*. The alcoholism was a gift.

I guzzled lemonade and complained about pregnancy overheating. The baby earned its keep. People couldn't be kind enough to me. I gazed at the water and said I'd love to paddle, but the effort was too much. I prompted Stevie to enjoy it on my behalf. Sometimes, she can be an obedient puppy.

I watched Stevie moving upstream. Joe tried phoning Kat.

Then the shouting started.

Stevie

Rather than the lies Erin's produced, here's what really happened.

Erin kept telling me to go for a paddle. I couldn't figure out why she wouldn't get off her backside and go in. At that stage, she wasn't heavily pregnant. To shut her up and because I needed to cool off, I went in, like the proverbial lamb set for slaughter, except the death wasn't mine.

The water offered relief from my heat rash. As I moved along the stream, I didn't ponder on being an "Uber Vicar" or issues with the Church. Erin has claimed others' lives, but she'll never own my thoughts.

Much to my regret, I didn't have any suspicions about Alex's death. Difficult as it was, I genuinely believed it to be suicide. It's strange how Erin portrayed me as having a feeling something evil surrounded us. Maybe she *does* want a vicar protagonist in one of her novels. She's not having me. I'm in charge of my story.

There wasn't any daydreaming on my part or taking photos of a trio of birds on a tree. There weren't any there. Erin, lay off the rubbish symbolism. See no evil, hear no evil, and speak no evil, right? From wise monkeys to birds.

There weren't any crows cawing a warning. There was no hair resembling seaweed curling around my feet. I saw a body long before reaching it. My heart dropped as I considered if it was another suicide. I didn't think it was one of my friends, though. While devastated by Alex's death, no one seemed to be in crisis.

I called to Joe and Erin for help. Now, I wish I hadn't. I might have spared Joe the horror. There were head wounds. Unlike Erin, I'm not offering any details. A tattoo didn't identify the body. Kat was needle phobic and had never been inked.

When Erin and Joe joined me, I found the courage to turn over the body. Joe let out a sound unlike anything I've ever heard or can describe. His dead wife held a pink tulip, the same as Alex.

It took all my strength to wrench Joe away from trying to resuscitate Kat. The hatred in his eyes for denying him the chance was understandable, but she was beyond saving.

Erin darted up the bank. Obviously, she pretended to be sick and soon returned. She couldn't miss out on seeing the responses to her handiwork.

Joe wasn't difficult, least of all with the paramedics and the police. Shock made him mostly silent. I promised to look after him. I'm sorry I failed the Andino family. I was in my room, taking a moment. While I was praying, Erin was plying Joe with alcohol.

Erin

After getting Joe back on the booze wagon, I left him with Charlotte, saying I needed to freshen up.

Charlotte made herself look like a killer. Vengeful sister seeks answers about her brother's disappearance. She plans a memorial long after he's gone. Brother's old friends come to her bed and breakfast after receiving invitations. Old friends die.

I looked at the two pink tulips earmarked for Joe and Stevie. I gripped the stems, remembering the flowers Simon used in the holiday club's kindness parade. With the hall empty while everyone changed into costumes, I worked unnoticed. Simon's pathetic display of his kindness had made me angry.

Pink tulip petals were scattered on the floor. It wasn't enough. They still looked pretty. Ripping Simon's group banner solved the problem. I can still picture his face when he later saw the destruction.

In my room at The Mill, I stroked the silk tulips and reflected on progressing from teenage tantrums. I killed according to a plot, not lashing out as I'd done with Nick, Simon, and Dylan. Now, I was murdering with great skill.

I am a killer, not a giver of life. My hands touched a taut stomach, a product of hours spent in the home gym. I picked up the pregnancy belly from the bed and tied the fastenings.

No, I wasn't pregnant. Never have been, never will. The thought of something leeching *my* energy and stealing *my* nutrients is gross. It was a brilliant idea, though.

A pregnant woman is viewed as soft, delicate, and in need. I learnt how to wear the bump and researched everything about pregnancy. You'd be amazed what you can buy and learn from the internet.

In preparation, the months before I was at The Mill, I wore baggy tops when I went out, with a little padding. The Covid lockdowns and restrictions meant I hardly saw my neighbours. Many of us were isolated, which was perfect for my pretend pregnancy. No one asked questions.

While "pregnancy" could be a chore, it did have some bonuses. People on public transport always offered their seat. Women empathised. Men rushed to protect me. Add being a surrogate and you're a paragon of kindness.

By the way, I haven't seen my cousin, Gemma, in years. I'd rather kill myself than carry a child for her.

No one suspects a pregnant woman is capable of murder. I bet you didn't when reading *Killing Kindness*. I told you I was good at this writing business.

Gemma

At last I can comment on Erin making up the surrogacy story! My family has had nothing to do with Tina or Erin since we evicted them.

It began when I was having a bath. Erin pounded on the door, demanding to have a shower. I promised not to be too long. The door lock was already loose; one of many jobs Dad promised to do at some point. A small kick helped Erin force her way in. No one was there to hear me yelling as she pushed me under the water. I have no doubts she tried to kill me.

Since Dylan's death, Erin's moods had darkened. If anyone so much as looked at her, she growled like a disturbed bear. Tina passed it off as grief. Mum knew better and tried to keep Erin away from me. Unfortunately, that day Mum popped out to get milk. She thought Erin was out.

Mum returned and heard my screams. In the bathroom, she saw Erin's hands locked around my throat. I scrabbled to hold on to the sides of the bath. Mum hauled Erin off and she darted out of the house.

When Tina came back, she was devastated at what her daughter had done. I think Tina wanted us to rescue her from Erin. What could we do? It was too far gone by then. They had to go.

When Erin showed up, acting as if nothing had happened, Tina was packing. We heard her sobbing from the kitchen, where I cowered with my parents. Erin burst into the room and threatened to kill us in our beds. For a while after she left, I slept with a cricket bat next to my bed.

If the fate of the human race depended on it, I'd never use Erin as a surrogate. Can you imagine what she'd produce? For the record, I have three children, something Erin will never experience. Who would want to have kids with her? I hope Erin and the strap-on belly are happy together.

I'm not a frightened little girl anymore. I refuse to be scared of Erin any longer.

Erin

Gemma, aren't you brave, knowing I can't come near you? Don't get complacent. I have my ways. Dust off the cricket bat.

I never wanted children, which suits me fine. Faking a pregnancy is easy. Stealing a child and pretending to be a mother wasn't going to happen. Let's just say, after I escaped from The Mill, the fake baby wasn't going to make it.

Where was I before my bratty cousin started whinging? Oh yes, the aftermath of Kat's death.

Joe was sozzled. Stevie finally left her room and told me off for giving him the first drink. I said I wasn't aware he was an alcoholic and bawled at two of my friends being dead. Stevie soon apologised.

Rather than the mouthy version I depicted in *Killing Kindness*, Joe was a quiet drunk. With Kat's absence, he faded. What is it with couples who fall to pieces when their partner dies? We aren't made in twos. Being alone is better, anyway.

The police once again advised us to stick around, even after taking statements. They thought it best for us to stay together before they returned to investigate further. Making us sitting ducks for murder – apart from me – showed the police did a terrible job. Not that I'm complaining. No one could leave.

As we chatted about Alex and Kat, when I dared to say the word *murder*, Joe gasped. Charlotte agreed with my theory, although she was more subtle. The pink tulips became a solid link. With the others fearing a killer, my work was in full swing.

For sport, I listed possible motives. Stevie lacked the imagination to think of any. Joe couldn't face a discussion of his drowned wife's bashed in head. Charlotte proved to be most disappointing. Committing murders under the nose of a barrister was a huge risk. She didn't notice the clues. As punishment, I cast Charlotte as a potential villain seeking misguided revenge on her brother's behalf.

Stevie tried to cut off Joe's boozing. He still managed to sneak in drinks, with a little help from me. Of course, I knew he was an alcoholic. I needed a drunken Joe for the next stage.

Vinnie

From keeping tabs on Joe, he seemed to be a nice bloke. In fact, all of Erin's "friends" were decent. Eventually, I questioned why she needed dirt on them. Erin raged at me for not providing any damning info about Stevie and Alex.

Private detecting for Erin was easy money at first. She obviously hadn't given me the full story of why I was following the gang. Honestly, I thought she was jealous and wanted proof she'd achieved more than her old friends. After reading bad reviews of her books or finding out author rivals had bestsellers, Erin lost it.

Eventually, I decided to keep our relationship professional. It was just sex, anyway. We certainly weren't romantically involved. Erin doesn't do love, unless you're a dead man called Dylan.

Getting involved with Thalia happened by accident. I confess I was in the restaurant, run by Joe's brother, to watch Kat and Joe. The wider family met weekly. Their loud conversation provided information as I sat at a table.

Thalia caught my eye. Despite a liking for the ladies, I've never taken the honey trap route. As I stood outside, having a smoke between courses, Thalia appeared. Focused on looking down at her mobile, she smacked straight into me. The contents of her bag scattered across the pavement. She blushed as I helped to pick things up. Fellas, you won't believe what women have in their handbags.

Thalia moaned about her crap day getting even worse and begged for a cigarette. She said no one in her family smoked, so she hid the habit. As we chatted, I liked the funny, engaging woman.

Although Thalia's younger than me, we went on several dates afterwards. She'd had enough of immature boys. The last one got her pregnant and did a runner. I swear I didn't stay with her to get more info on her parents. Genuinely, I fell in love.

Unfortunately, Erin found out about the relationship. That woman didn't need a P.I. She showed me pictures from Thalia's Instagram account. Erin demanded I said she was more attractive than Thalia. Erin couldn't accept I'd chosen someone else. There is no contest. Unlike Erin, Thalia is also beautiful on the inside.

Thalia, I promise my feelings were real. Telling Erin your secret is the worst thing I've ever done. How could I know it would lead to all this?

Thalia

Vinnie, I don't believe a word you've written. Blood is on your hands as well as Erin's. I hope you rot in the prison cell.

On a date with Vinnie, I had too much prosecco. As the child of an alcoholic, I should've known better than to drown my sorrows. My daughter's father refused to pay child maintenance and was spreading nasty rumours about me around Trillhaven. Compared to my ex, Vinnie seemed to be a prince. I trusted him as I shared what happened to Dad in 2017.

Thanks for letting me tell the real story behind the secret Erin used to make my parents go to The Mill. This isn't easy to write, but I must. January 2017 was a difficult time.

January 2017

Mum and I were in our PJs, laughing at a comedy film. After having a baby and being a single parent, I continued living in the family home. I wasn't visiting, as Erin suggested.

Dad never bitched about me having a baby, either. Being a young mother wasn't ideal, but my parents were accepting and doted on their granddaughter. They supported me becoming a teacher. Whenever Mum could, she looked after my daughter while I studied.

When Dad came home that night in 2017, he entered the lounge and paced in front of the fire. Unlike in *Killing Kindness*, he didn't head for the minibar. There is no such thing in our house. Erin lapped up the alcoholic thing.

Mum and I gave each other questioning looks at my silent dad, still wearing a coat and shoes. I switched off the TV. The conversation went something like this.

'What's wrong?' I asked. 'Slow down. You're making me dizzy.'

'Why didn't I leave the keys at the pub and get a taxi?'

Let's get this straight. A barmaid working at Dad's local, who usually took his car keys, didn't exist. Dad never had an affair. Yes, I would say that, but I'm one hundred percent certain. He worshipped Mum.

As she did with her children, Mum removed Dad's outer clothing. Then she led him to the sofa.

'What's the matter, love?' She clasped his trembling hands.

'Honestly, I only had a few drinks. I shouldn't have gone alone.'

Usually, they socialised together. Dad drank less with Mum nearby. That evening, she had a cold and didn't feel well enough to go out. He'd popped to the pub on the way back from work. The business wasn't doing well. Unfortunately, stress is a boozing trigger.

'I've… had… an accident.' Dad stumbled over the words. 'The car is a wreck.'

Mum checked him over for injuries. Although in obvious shock, physically he was fine.

I looked out the window. A small dent was visible in the car bonnet; nothing unfixable. It certainly hadn't crumpled like the concertina Erin described. Aware Dad would be embarrassed if the neighbours saw any damage, I moved the Audi into the garage. Dad was a proud man who tried to stop drinking. Sadly, he didn't always succeed.

'I promise, Kat, I'm not drunk.' The pleading tone was hard to hear. 'I only had two pints.'

'You shouldn't be drinking on those tablets.' She used her soft, lullaby voice, reminding me of the safety only a mum can give.

Dad thumped his fists against his head and wailed. 'What an idiot! How could I forget?'

He'd been prescribed antibiotics for a chest infection. Sometimes they caused drowsiness. Booze on top probably affected his driving ability.

'How did you damage the car?' I asked, while not wanting to know the answer. Sometimes, facing the ugly truth is the only way to fix a mistake.

'Kids were playing chicken across Butler's Lane. Remember, it was in the *Daily Echo* how it's become a fad? If only I'd stuck to the main road rather than taking the quicker route.'

'Those little buggers are asking to be killed,' Mum began. Her face turned white. 'Oh, Joe…'

'No, I didn't kill anyone! Hitting them is bad enough. The first kid who darted across, I saw from a distance. To begin with, I thought it was a shadow from the trees. Then another ran too. I braked and the Audi slid on the ice. I tried to right the steering so as not to hit the girl and crashed into a tree.'

'Is she hurt?' I asked, while sending up a silent prayer.

'She seemed more stunned than anything else. After helping her stand, I asked if she was OK. She shivered, but that was probably because it's freezing out there. What is it with youngsters refusing to wear coats? Her only injury appeared to be a sore hip after sliding. Black ice is treacherous. I told her to wait while I got a blanket, first aid kit, and my mobile.'

'You did right, Dad.'

He continued. 'When I returned, a boy was there, shouting I'd hurt his sister. She kept saying the car didn't touch her while the lad called me all kinds of names. I said playing dangerous games, particularly on a frosty night, was reckless. I asked for their parents' details and added I'd phone for an ambulance, just in case. The boy panicked, saying to forget it, and the girl was fine. He was obviously worried about getting into trouble.'

Mum slapped her knee. 'If one of our lot had done that they'd be grounded for the rest of their lives.'

'The girl was apologetic.' Dad lowered his chin. 'She begged me not to call the police and promised they wouldn't tell anyone what happened. While I should've been relieved, it felt like I was being blamed. I *was* at fault, though. Driving after drinking is wrong. Those bloody tablets!'

Mum held him as he cried. Someone had to take charge. For once, it was me.

'Dad, listen,' I began. 'How did it end with those kids?'

He looked up. 'Before leaving, they apologised.'

'No harm done then, apart from the car, which can be fixed.'

'Don't you see? I'm still partly responsible. I can't do this anymore. Living with the consequences of my drinking is unbearable. I'm ready, Princess.'

Mum stroked her thumbs across the tear tracks on his cheeks. I turned away from their intimate moment.

'Are you sure?'

Mum had a right to be doubtful. Many promises made in the past were easily broken. Dad was resolute, though.

The next day, he joined Alcoholics Anonymous. Until Mum's death, he was sober. Despite the awful circumstances, I'm positive he wouldn't have started drinking again if Erin hadn't provided it. It's the least of the terrible things she's done, but such a violation of my dad's success.

****

To be clear, the girl wasn't injured. She was with her brother, not a boyfriend. Dad didn't leave anyone for dead. He would've chosen prison over causing anyone pain. Mum didn't act like a Mafia wife, instructing her shady husband on how to conceal a crime.

If we're guilty of anything, it's for not reporting the incident. That's on me. I begged my parents not to get the police involved. While I believed Dad's version of events, I worried about how people would react if they found out he was an alcoholic.

Addiction isn't an individual problem. It affects loved ones, too. At the height of Dad's drinking, we worked as a family team to cover it up. Excuses included him feeling unwell, tired, or he was celebrating.

Once again, I covered for Dad, afraid of him being arrested for drink-driving. Now, I wish we'd reported it. Life would be different if I hadn't taken over. I'd never have told Vinnie, ironically, when I was drunk. Erin wouldn't have had a secret to use for blackmail. She forced my parents to stay at The Mill, based on a mistake. I found the blackmail notes and will now share them.

To Dad, Erin wrote:

Joe, it's within your interests to stay at The Mill, unless you want everyone, including the police, to know your drink-driving secret.

The girl may have survived, but will your marriage and failing business after you're arrested? She was playing chicken. Make sure you're not a coward, too. Be a man and face up to your mistakes.

Join old friends at The Mill and keep your secret.

Erin's note for Mum stated:

The love of a wife for her husband is often unconditional. You've proved this by keeping Joe's drink-driving secret.

You call yourself a mother and then put your husband before your children. Other people's children could've been hurt by Joe's reckless driving. You kept it hidden because you thought you'd lose him to prison or further into the bottom of a bottle.

You will *stay at The Mill to keep protecting Joe. If you don't obey, his crime will be revealed to the police, your friends, and anyone else who will listen.*

Sunday 22 August 2021

Erin

Joe's driving incident was hardly the crime of the century. It was something to work with, though. Fear of Joe's drinking problem being exposed made Kat and Joe stay at The Mill.

Credit to Thalia for sleeping with Vinnie. Their pillow talk was helpful. He thinks I don't know how close they were. It suited me how Vinnie got his information. As the relationship progressed, I had to force it out of him. When I offered more money, his loyalty to Thalia ended.

On 22 August 2021, Joe, Stevie, and I went to bed at the same time. Overcome by grief and booze, Joe needed help getting up the stairs. I'd continued pouring nips of vodka into the soft drinks Stevie bought.

In my room, I typed some more of the novel, using recent events. I waited a while for the bar to close and the staff to leave.

Throughout, I heard Joe moving around next door, in between sobbing. Stevie had offered to stay with him. Thankfully, he preferred being alone. I don't care what she says. Stevie's always fancied Joe and probably had her eye on the widower's bed. His wife's heart had only stopped beating a few hours ago.

Finally, The Mill settled. I grabbed the car keys and a rucksack before taking the back stairs. What I'd planned was the riskiest thing yet. Not only had I stolen Joe's keys when he'd put them on a table, I was going to drive his car. It had to be the Audi; the source of a secret.

Without the encumbrance of a pregnancy bump, I dashed across the car park. In the dark, I knew no one would see I'd suddenly become slimmer. As the unlocking bleep sounded, I knelt down. It stayed dark except for the lights always on outside the building. Headlights initially off, I slowly drove away.

As part of checking the area when I arrived, I walked down Mill Lane, a narrow country road. Most drivers use main roads to reach The Mill. Locals are aware of where the potholes are. Google Maps proved useful for my research.

I parked in a field, skirting alongside the lane. From the rucksack I unspooled the wire, stretching it at different points across the lane and securing each side on fences and trees. This was my most detailed death scene yet. The first draft of *Killing Kindness* needed a lot of research. I leave nothing to chance in writing or murder. I knew which wire to use and had tested how to make it stay in place until impact.

Traps set, I sent Joe a text.

I know who killed Kat. We can't talk in The Mill. The killer might see us. Meet me in Mill Lane.

While waiting, I turned on the radio and soon switched it off. Joe's edgier teenage tastes had downgraded to a commercial pop station. Instead, I created my own musical background, drumming my fingers on the steering wheel. The beat stopped as a shadowy figure appeared.

Joe stumbled on the uneven surface, unbalanced from a hit of alcohol he hadn't felt in a while. Lampposts on the other side of the field helped me to see.

Joe hit a wire and landed on his knees. He knelt on the ground, looking up, as if in prayer. What is it with members of The Six and this God thing? He's done none of them any favours.

I hoped Joe would stand up and be a man. As I opened the window, the sound of gravel grasped by his uncertain hands was pleasing. After rising by slow degrees, he stood. I trained the headlights upon him, enjoying the dizzying effect.

Despite being knocked over by two more wires and slipping over several potholes, Joe never gave up. I almost admired him. Love makes people determined, I guess. Joe needed answers for why his Princess died. I was ready to give them.

I've wondered how racing drivers feel, fuelled by the exhilaration of speed while keeping control. Now I know. The speeding weapon slammed into Joe. Like a damaged bird, his body rose and then fell. The *thunk* of hitting the ground was so satisfying.

Excitement made me deviate from the plan. One strike was supposed to be enough. After getting out of the vehicle, I checked on Joe. On his back, he groaned like a wounded animal. When he realised I was both driver and murderer, his face was a picture.

'Why?' he asked.

'Because I can. Kat, too.'

Joe slumped. His ready defeat was disappointing. I expected him to fight until the end. Where was The Leader who always knew best? I decided to finish it. Call it a mercy killing. With Kat gone, Joe had nothing left. If I had a family like the Andinos, I wouldn't bother trying to survive either.

The sound of bones shattering under car wheels is quite something. I admit I'm having trouble finding suitable descriptive words. If I did, I wouldn't share them, anyway. Those beautiful noises, caused by my brilliance, are all mine.

Business finished, I threw a pink tulip on Joe's corpse. Then I added a note. This time, the message didn't come from the dead.

Joe drove me to this. An alcoholic shouldn't be drink-driving. Ask his daughter, Thalia, why they covered it up.

This is killing with kindness. Drunks are potential killers. It's kinder and safer for everyone if Joe is dead.

Of course, I don't give a shit about road safety. I didn't leave a newspaper report of Joe's prang, as mentioned in the novel, either. There wasn't one. A dint in a car bonnet and two kids who kept quiet about playing chicken aren't newsworthy.

I wish there was a girl who'd been injured and possibly paralysed by Joe's recklessness. It's far more interesting than the truth. Still, the contents of the note meant people would talk about Joe's drinking after his death. Thalia would have a lot of explaining to do, too. It was extra revenge for stealing Vinnie's attention when he should've been working for me.

I phoned Vinnie's "colleague" who took the Audi to burn it out. Vinnie refused to do it. He wouldn't be part of anything beyond getting info on The Six and helping me seemingly have a little revenge. In his defence, he didn't know about my plans, mainly because I couldn't trust him not to squeal. Look how right I was.

I'd explained to Vinnie that Alex's and Kat's deaths were suicides, one influenced by the other. Vinnie questioned everything. After Kat's death, he tried to quit. I pulled another weapon from my arsenal.

Previously, Vinnie mentioned his elderly blind mother was in a residential home. When I took on his services for *Killing Kindness,* I realised no matter how much money was involved, he wouldn't get involved with murder. I had a bargaining chip to use with the gambler, though. When I said I'd met his friendly mother, who believed I was the perfect girlfriend for her Vincent, he was furious. He soon backed off when I explained no matter where she was, I'd find and kill his mother if he didn't do as I said. Vinnie never doubted me. We carried on.

Joe was dead, and once again, I'd killed kindness. Joe wanted revenge for his wife's death. Instead, he joined her in death.

Vinnie

I swear I didn't know what Erin was doing. She says I want no part of murder. Go near my mother and she'll see how wrong she is.

Erin

Good luck doing it from a prison cell, Vincent.

Monday 23 August 2021

Erin

Stevie and Charlotte were panicking at Joe's absence. Throughout breakfast they discussed theories and concerns: Joe had gone for a drive, he'd killed himself, or a killer had targeted him (true). After checking The Mill and the immediate areas around it, they figured he must have headed home.

Finally, as per my plan, I convinced Stevie we should go home and let the police find Joe. After they said the word, *suspicious*, when talking about Kat's and Alex's deaths, Stevie became twitchy. She couldn't get to her room fast enough to pack and pray. Whenever she mentioned religious stuff, I held my tongue. Invisible friends are for children. Stevie likely became a vicar for the attention. I bet she laps it up, reading from a storybook full of judgement to a congregation.

By now, you've probably realised my hatred for Stevie runs deep. It's why she was last on my murder list. Watching her suffer in response to her friends' deaths was wonderful. Outside her room, I listened as she asked God why Alex and Kat died. I had to go before she heard me laughing.

In my room, I started packing. Vinnie sent a message confirming he was in place. He added a threat to hunt me down if anything happened to his mum. What a good son Vincent is. I have no more desire to be near his pathetic mother than I do to hurt her. Sometimes people in your team need an incentive to work harder. Finding others' weaknesses makes me stronger. Love for someone else is usually the best target. Mummy's boy, Vinnie, would've done almost anything to keep her safe.

On the last day at The Mill, an email from my agent threatened to disturb my buoyant mood. She'd already dropped me and wanted to give a final twist of the knife. Certain the money hungry cow couldn't resist, I'd sent her a synopsis of *Killing Kindness* minus the truthful parts of my murders. Her email stated she wouldn't represent me again if her career depended on it. She called my idea to fictionalise reality, ghastly. At that point, I hadn't revealed how real it was. I was hardly going to confess to murders before I'd finished. The proposed plot alone was a guaranteed hit. My former agent has lost her touch, churning out the same commercial crap.

After reading the rejection, I threw a vase against the wall. Then I hurled a bronze ornament at the mirror. Glass and porcelain crunched under my shoes as I ground them into the carpet. I remembered the sound of Joe's breaking bones and the tension lifted. Charlotte would see I'd lost my temper, but I'd be long gone by then. Her opinion didn't bother me, anyway.

Women always let me down. Men are often disappointing, but women are envious bitches. Tina, Gemma, Fran, Charlotte, and Stevie all tried to ruin my life. I needed to show them they hadn't succeeded, particularly Stevie. Writing about how a man killed himself after she made an allegation against him was an absolute pleasure.

Stevie

I've been working on building the emotional strength to address what Erin wrote about me and a student called Eddie. After reading the chapter where I felt guilty about driving a man to suicide, I wondered if I'd be able to contribute here. I can and I will.

My church believes me and is aware of what Erin's capable of saying and doing. This is my chance to let readers know the truth which is rather boring but, most importantly, isn't criminal.

Erin didn't add a blackmail note to my invitation to stay at The Mill. She had nothing to blackmail me with, certainly not making sexual assault allegations against Simon and "Eddie". We now know it's what *she* tried to do to a guy called Wesley before killing Nick, the paperboy. Erin was willing to make a sexual assault accusation against someone for her own needs. Writing my character as someone similar makes my skin crawl.

My time at university was uneventful. I was a typical student; drinking, studying, and socialising. I went to a few parties, but none where I met "Eddie". Also, I've never been anyone's "pity shag" as Erin put it, and I didn't make advances on "Eddie". Are we clear yet "Eddie" doesn't exist?

There weren't any seductive moves from me, no knock back from "Eddie", no being called a freak, no tearing of my own clothes, and no cries of assault. No boys were harmed in the making of my degree. Sorry. Humour sometimes makes it easier to deal with how Erin used sexual assault and suicide for entertainment.

Simon didn't kill himself because I said I'd tell people he'd assaulted me. We parted that night as the close friends we'd always been. I wish I'd stayed with him, but you can't live your life on what-ifs.

Sickening as it is, Erin wanted Simon to pay for "stealing" her precious Dylan. I'm glad she didn't finish me off, too. I'm not done with Erin yet.

Erin

Where were we before the mad vicar interrupted? Monday 23 August 2021; the final reckoning.

Leaving was delayed by the discovery of Joe's body and the following police circus. In *Killing Kindness*, I gave The Witch an important role in discovering the body, even though it was one of the staff. From reading the ungrateful Brenda's contributions, I wish I hadn't. I've heard The Mill's housekeeper has been signed off work, claiming to have PTSD caused by seeing a squashed and shattered corpse.

After faking distress and concern for my unborn child, the police let me leave. Worried for her life, Stevie said she wanted to go, too. Telling a detective they'd have to arrest her to make stay any longer was almost admirable.

Charlotte had more prominence in the novel than she offered in reality. The way I portrayed her in *Killing Kindness*, reflecting on Simon's disappearance in the light of Joe's death, was inspired. Events had come full circle. Charlotte considers her violent father, pathetic mother, and her unstable brother. It's a far more interesting story than what actually happened.

Charlotte

You'd have to be blind not to notice the obviousness throughout the novel. Not only did Erin make my brother a villain, but apparently I was a later accomplice. How many times in *Killing Kindness* was I acting aloof and secretive, begging readers to point the finger at me as the killer? I could be offended. I could sue Erin and win. For now, let's concentrate on this book.

Unlike Erin's portrayal, Simon didn't lash out at people in the days before his disappearance, what I know now to have actually been his death. It's a myth all children who have violent parents repeat the pattern. Some do. Most become more empathic, like Simon.

If anyone wanted to whack my father and was going to try, it was me. The bruises Thomas left on Mum's skin made me rage. When he hit Simon, I defended my brother, as he did for me. Often, we got a double beating for our trouble.

Simon told me about the plan to leave. He was going first to set up a new life, with help from Dylan's friend. He went without us because Thomas would put less effort into finding Simon than if the whole family left. We planned for Mum and me to follow eventually. Mum didn't know because it would take some convincing. Don't dare to say this means she's weak. I have prosecuted on behalf of many abused people who haven't immediately separated from their partner. Abusers are narcissists who seize power through mental and physical torture. Thomas previously told Mum his contacts would track her down and kill her if she ever left. Simon and I understood the risks of our plan, but we couldn't live in a dangerous home any longer.

Simon was so upset when he said goodbye to me on the final night. I had to convince him not to back out, promising Mum and I would be safe. Thankfully, Thomas spent more time in London. There wasn't a dramatic fight on the last day where Simon punched Thomas for assaulting Mum and me. Thomas wasn't there. Erin enjoys the misery of abuse because she's an abuser. What else is murder if not abusing the preciousness of life?

After Simon's disappearance, the police started considering suicide. At the thought of her son taking his life, Mum almost gave up. I kept her alive with a promise of eventual freedom from Thomas.

Simon's lack of contact after leaving was troubling. It took a lot of effort to believe something terrible hadn't happened to him. After a long silence, I realised I had to do something rather than wait.

Thomas's shock when I threatened to expose his criminal back-handers if he entered our house again was amazing. When he tried to gaslight me into believing I was lying, I produced the evidence.

For a while, I'd been following him, taking pictures of meetings with known criminals. Getting the photographs developed was a risk. What if someone in Boots checked them? Everyone knew and respected the kind and brilliant barrister. Thankfully, camera film was sent to a central lab for processing. Come to think of it, the same woman always came to the counter with my photos, offering a sympathetic smile. Remember, I was only a child. Without Simon, I needed those photos. When I showed them to Thomas, he never returned to our house again.

After his death, we didn't attend his funeral or send flowers. Pink tulips are banned in our vicinity. Nowadays, we prefer white roses representing loyalty, youthfulness, and innocence; everything Simon was and Erin can never be.

Erin

Unlike in the novel, I didn't ask Stevie to stay at my house because the police wanted us nearby for further questioning. I'd *never* have Stevie in my home. The idea was for her not to reach any house, let alone mine.

The evening before, Vinnie oversaw a colleague tinkering with Stevie's car. He didn't have a choice. The previous week, I'd phoned his mum for a chat. Repeating stories only a mother knows made Vinnie fear for her life. He behaved and got a discreet expert in mechanics and unlocking vehicles to do the job.

Watching Stevie's irritation at her car not starting was hilarious. I disguised my glee when offering to go to my house while it was being fixed. I knew she'd refuse to wait at The Mill, in fear of being the next victim.

It was such a pleasure being in the car with Stevie, oblivious to sitting next to a murderer. Earlier, I worried she'd come up with an alternative to travelling with me. We're not exactly close, right? To make her agree, I hammed up being a pregnant grieving woman, worried a serial killer will get her.

Before leaving The Mill, I sent a text instruction, *Now*. Then I headed for the conclusion.

Excitement thrumming in my head tuned out Stevie's chatter. Occasionally, I acted like I was listening. Adrenaline made me twitchy. My driving wasn't the best, but I stayed focused. Alertness would help find him; the man with Dylan's eyes. It was a nice touch to add it in *Killing Kindness*. Did you think Dylan rose from the dead?

At the right moment, Vinnie darted across the road. I swerved a little for effect. As Vinnie took over, I remembered why I'd been attracted to him. He wrenched the door open and shouted to get out. No knife. While he didn't want me to hurt his mum, Vinnie refused to have a weapon. Instead, he used forcefulness. On reflection, he smiled far too much when he pushed me around.

A panicked Stevie began dialling on her phone. Vinnie grunted at her to drop it while tightening the chokehold on my neck. After making Stevie join us, Vinnie held a sharpened piece of wood against her back; a pretend knife.

As discussed, Vinnie made us walk into the woods, one arm locked around my throat and the other prodding at Stevie. Masking giggles as hysterical sobs, I tried not to laugh at her being scared of a stick.

Days before, Vinnie scoped the woods and found a quiet area. I left the task to him, because killing people demands full attention. This is where I messed up. Never let anyone take over your project.

At the destination, Vinnie forced us to sit on a fallen tree. I zoned out, remembering similar woods where I killed Nick. He didn't see death coming, either. Vinnie interrupted my thinking by punching me in the stomach. That was *not* planned. Even though he knew the pregnancy wasn't real, I swear the bastard enjoyed it. The assault on a pregnant woman horrified Stevie. While I could've easily murdered Vinnie there and then, I knew I'd get my own back later. No loose ends. No Vinnie.

Dylan didn't have a brother called Wily who hurt and murdered most of The Six. Without Dylan, I needed something close to him. A brother represented the darker side I believed Dylan harboured. If he'd lived, maybe he would've shown the hidden self to me.

Vinnie tugging my hair pulled me back away from thoughts of Dylan. The increased violence was off task, but I let it go. Vinnie and I used to get rough in the bedroom. Guess who was the dom and the sub? Vinnie's strange aggression kept Stevie silent and still. I fed on her terror.

Unlike Vinnie, I brought a knife in my pocket. After killing Stevie, I'd shed some of my blood, making it look like I'd been hurt, possibly killed, too. The attacker had taken me somewhere else; the perfect way for me to disappear.

I had pink tulips and a note ready, exposing Charlotte as the killer. Who better than someone making her brother's old friends pay for not caring enough? Of course, Charlotte could eventually prove her innocence. In the meantime, it would piss off Miss Prissy Pritchard and give me time to get settled in a new hiding place.

I should've remembered Vinnie was a coward who always put himself first. Even his mum didn't matter. When he grabbed my arm as I prepared to stab Stevie, everything changed.

Charlotte

What do you want me to say, Erin? That I'm angry you were going to pin it all on me? It never would've worked. Once again you've confirmed your dreadful plotting skills.

Stevie

The confusion on your face was amazing, Erin, along with the sound of police sirens in the distance.

Erin

I escaped, though, didn't I?

Stevie

You may have more lives than a cat, but they're running out. Don't overestimate your intelligence.

Here's the rest of the story even Erin doesn't know. I met Vinnie the evening before leaving The Mill.

After spotting two men under my car bonnet, I nearly had a heart attack. The fella tinkering with the engine ran away. I was set to call the police when Vinnie fell to the ground, saying he couldn't do it anymore. I thought he was confessing to running out of energy to kill more people. Afraid he *could* do it because three times was proof, I braced to run, too. Vinnie jumped up and shouted something to me. I stopped. So would you at hearing Erin was the killer.

At a safe distance, Vinnie told me to phone Charlotte to ask her to join us and bring a laptop. After locking him in the car, I did as he requested.

When Charlotte appeared, she tied Vinnie's hands together and checked for weapons. He did everything she asked. After leading him to Charlotte's vehicle, we drove away. Charlotte's bravery in dealing with a potential killer amazed me. Later, she said she can spot a wrong 'un a mile off. Apologies Charlotte, but I wish you'd noticed it in Erin. To be fair, though, we were all fooled.

Far from Erin's sight, we parked in a nearby field. Charlotte was formidable, grilling Vinnie. We played the real version of the childhood game, goodies and baddies.

On a USB stick inserted into the laptop, Vinnie shared Erin's early draft of *Killing Kindness*. For insurance, he'd taken a copy when at her house. He said it wasn't easy, as she watched him like the proverbial hawk. Everyone needs the toilet, eventually.

Vinnie added he stole Erin's novel because he wanted something of hers to barter with. He figured if she was threatening to hurt his mum, he could threaten to give Erin's book to another author. Vinnie reflected on how it was a rubbish counterattack. He didn't even look at the novel until the night before I caught him tampering with my car.

Vinnie confessed he tried not to equate the deaths at The Mill with Erin bringing us all there. It was easier, for a while, for him not to ask questions. Thankfully, he listened to his conscience. Vinnie carried on with Erin's plan to make my car not work, but he swore that was the end. He was going to tell the police what Erin had done and show them *Killing Kindness*.

On the laptop, I skimmed through the novel, freaked out at how fiction became a gruesome fact. Everything that had happened at The Mill was there, with extra gory details. Charlotte only lost her composure once, when she read of Erin's part in Simon's death. She looked out the window while her shoulders hitched. After a silent minute, she shook her body and continued reading.

I soon skipped to the end of *Killing Kindness*. My husband is appalled by how I read the ending of books first. Now he's glad. If I hadn't learned what Erin had in store for me, I'd be dead.

We set you up, Erin. I pulled out the spark plugs to make my car seem inoperable, preparing to be with you for the final showdown. To a degree, Vinnie also went along with your plan. He knew he'd probably be convicted for aiding and abetting you. He was tired of being controlled by you.

Controversial as it may seem, I don't think Vinnie deserves to be in prison. Erin used him and scared the bloke by saying she would kill his mother. I promised to keep Vinnie's mum safe, moving her to a safe location. It's a sad day when a man's relieved his mum died of natural causes. She was no longer a serial killer's potential victim.

Pretending to say goodbye, Charlotte hugged me and whispered comforting words. She steadied my escalating thoughts. We trusted a man who'd been working for Erin. What if he turned nasty out in the woods? Maybe Erin would kill me first. I assured Charlotte my fate was in God's hands. It doesn't mean I wasn't petrified.

Charlotte waited at The Mill, ready for Vinnie to press *send* on a previously written text message to call the police. You may think we didn't need the complicated charade. We could've given the book to the police and Erin would've been arrested. It's what we should've done. Pride was my downfall.

For a while, Vinnie and I played the part of attacker and victim. He never hurt me, although I noticed he was rough with Erin.

Worried about the outcome, anxiety clouded my judgement. I didn't see it coming. If Vinnie hadn't knocked the knife out of Erin's hand, I wouldn't be writing this.

I confess I let it go too far. I should've phoned the police after Vinnie showed me Erin's novel. Charlotte and Vinnie indulged my need to make Erin feel some of the terror she inflicted on Simon, Dylan, Nick, Alex, Kat, and Joe. I also wanted Erin to think she'd won, only to snatch the victory away from her. I've got a lot of atoning and praying to do, because I still have no regrets.

When Erin realised I had got one over on her, it was amazing, until she escaped. At the sound of sirens, Erin ran to her car and sped away. Remember, she lives in the area and knows where to hide.

Erin

Round of applause, Stevie. You finally showed confidence and ingenuity. I won, though. Leave the devious plots to the experts. For the rest of your life, you'll be at the altar begging for forgiveness while I'm living guilt-free.

Well done, Charlotte. I expect this isn't the first time you've stitched someone up in your career. What's prison like, Vinnie? I'm only asking because I'll never know.

Charlotte

It's hardly a "stitch-up" if someone is guilty.

Vinnie

My conscience is clear, Erin. I'm paying for my sins. You have to live with yours. They'll catch up with you eventually.

Erin

I'm fine and dandy, living a sinful life, thank you, Vincent. More money will roll in. Millions will read my work; the beautiful fiction and shocking reality. Months later, I'm still a hot topic. Daily "sightings" are a constant source of amusement. Apparently, I'm quite the jet setter.

Stevie, Charlotte, and Vinnie, I'm closer than you think. Never stop looking. I'll always be behind you while one step ahead. My legacy is strong through this book and there's nothing you can do to stop it.

Despite what some say about the validity of the novel's title, I *did* kill with kindness. Each murder was a kindness to me; a reward for putting up with The Six, having a pathetic mother, Nick and Simon stealing love meant for me, and the lasting pain of Dylan's death. I may have killed him, but others' actions led to his death.

Every murder I committed gave me the freedom to be my true self. I don't need to live through the villains in my books anymore. I'm the real thing; a serial killer.

Killing Kindness is my greatest work. This is the end for you, dear readers, but never for me.

After the Book

6 March 2022

Erin checked the woods. Excitement and caution twisted her gut. Although she chose the location, far from her home, maybe it wasn't far enough.

The promise of signing the book contract meant she had to be there. The woods didn't spook her, even after Stevie's failed murder and Vinnie's deceit. Erin wasn't the superstitious type. Lightning never struck twice..

Erin had produced a non-fiction book in months, as Chris Palmer expected. As Erin took cover under trees, she considered Chris choosing the date as a good sign. Sealing the deal on Dylan's birthday felt right, although she'd tried to sign the contract sooner. Erin emailed Chris weekly, asking for the document. Occasionally, she threatened to stop writing. Usually, she was more savvy. Who in their right mind wrote and delivered a book before receiving a contract? The answer was an author whose only hope of being published again was with one specific publisher.

Erin suspected Chris had chosen to do business this way so they'd meet in person. Everyone was desperate to see the infamous Erin Sullivan. Being a celebrity in hiding was hard. Difficult as it was, Erin knew she had to do what Chris wanted, for now.

A name change and altering her appearance secured Erin's anonymity. There was no way Chris was welcome at her house, and not only because of revealing the location. Erin lived in a dump, full of horrible neighbours; definite characters for the next novel. A psychological thriller, based on a murderer on the run, was a guaranteed hit.

****

Chris knew the risks. Erin might have refused to meet and ended the project. Chris bargained on Erin needing to be read and heard. Chris could relate.

Reading *Killing Kindness*, followed by a factual account, was illuminating. While meeting with a self-confessed serial killer wasn't wise, Chris had to be there. Erin was unlikely to hurt anyone in public. Chris figured murdering the person publishing your book was a stupid move. Erin obviously wanted fame in print above everything else.

As she moved, Erin's coat flashed its bright colours between the trees. Being in the woods was an interesting choice, considering they were supposed to meet out in the open. Chris stood in the park while considering the next move.

From a distance, the pattern Erin wore was blurry. As Chris drew closer, pink tulips bloomed all over Erin's coat. Expectation made Chris shiver. Chris had achieved what no one else could. Erin Sullivan was no longer hiding.

A tap on her shoulder made Erin startle. She turned around, angry with herself for letting someone creep up on her.

'You!' Erin shouted.

'Me.' Charlotte smiled.

'What the hell are you doing here?' Erin moved back a few steps.

'Don't worry. We're alone.'

'I'm hardly going to trust you.'

'But you have.'

'You bitch!' Erin edged forwards.

Charlotte held out her hands, palms facing out. 'Back off. The police might be watching.'

Swallowing acidic hatred and regret, Erin checked the area.

'You're Chris Palmer,' she began. 'C.P. The same initials as Charlotte Pritchard.'

'For someone who brags about her intelligence, you're so bloody stupid.'

'Dodgy barristers obviously run in the family. Daddy would be proud. Explain why I'm here.'

'It's not only authors who create great stories. What do thriller readers expect near the end of a novel?'

Erin looked at her watch. 'Get on with it. I have places to be.'

'You're not going anywhere.'

Erin turned to a voice that wasn't Charlotte's.

'Plot twist!'

Although the speaker had aged, Erin recognised the face. She wondered if stress had caught up with her. The dead don't speak.

'Hi, I'm Chris Palmer. Not pleased to meet you… again.'

Simon and Charlotte stood side-by-side. Erin despised their impish faces; scheming sprites sharing a cruel joke.

'There is no Christine Palmer or a publishing company,' Simon said. 'When did you become so desperate?'

'Since she started living in a disgusting bedsit,' Charlotte stated. 'I loved finding out you're living in a building full of junkies. After I told Paige the truth about what you've done, she couldn't confess fast enough where you are.'

'I shouldn't have moved into the shit tip she rents out. The stupid bint!' Aware of the risk of an audience, Erin placed the hood over her head. 'Tina was right to end their friendship. Paige has always had a big mouth. Come on then, Simon. Tell me how you survived.'

Simon rubbed his hands together. 'You were so arrogant, believing I'd give up and die. You didn't bother checking. I guess you forgot me telling The Six how much I loved underwater diving.'

Charlotte smirked. 'Thomas was a bastard, but the tropical holidays came in useful.'

Simon continued. 'I threw the rocks out of my pockets, trod water, and then swam to the other side. I couldn't take the rucksack. If you returned, you'd realise I was alive. I took some stuff from it, though, and carried on with the plan I devised with Dylan. He's why we're here today. It felt right.'

'I'm aware it's Dylan's birthday. You have no claim to him.'

'Neither do you,' Charlotte added.

Erin fluttered her hand as if swatting a bug. 'Shut up and let your brother finish.'

'You've lost none of your charm.' Simon shook his head. 'Think yourself lucky I didn't tell the police you killed Dylan. I admit, for a while, the thought of you coming after me was terrifying. I stayed with Dylan's friend and found work. A few years later, I sent word to Mum and Charlotte I was alive.'

Erin grinned. 'It's almost more devious than something I'd do. You let your family believe you were dead. Pretty sick.'

'*Sick* is how you stabbed Dylan over and over, not me running away from a murderer. I had to leave because you'd threatened to kill Charlotte and Mum.'

Erin yawned. 'Does this have an interesting ending?'

'Better than the lame cliffhanger in your novel,' Charlotte replied. 'We couldn't resist making you keep it in the story, even though you didn't want to.'

'I've stayed in contact with Mum and Charlotte,' Simon continued. 'I didn't know they were having a memorial, though.'

Charlotte squeezed his shoulder. 'We wanted to join with other people in memories. Admittedly, it was sneaky setting it up and not telling you. I regret doing it now, because, well…' She pointed at Erin.

Erin bowed.

'Wow. You really are hideous,' Simon said. 'If I wasn't in America for work, I would've been there in a shot, knowing my friends were being killed.'

Erin inspected her nails. 'Not much you can do for dead people, anyway.'

'When I found out what you'd done, I had to do something. I read the copy Charlotte had of your first draft from Vinnie's memory stick.'

'Then you set yourself up as a publisher interested in my novel and adding an extra section telling the truth.' Erin slow clapped. 'Well done, but why bother?'

Charlotte lifted her nose into the air. 'You're not the only person who can mastermind a plot. Like Stevie, we wanted revenge, too.'

'How did you create the online articles about Chris Palmer's background and her qualifications?' Erin asked.

Simon smiled. 'Have you forgotten how I wanted to go into computing? For goodness' sake, you wrote about it! I'm still an I.T. geek and I have my own business. There's nothing I can't make happen online.'

'What's the matter, Erin?' Charlotte edged closer. 'You're looking a little peaky.'

'You may not care about the lives you've destroyed,' Simon began, 'but we do. We're taking something *you* love; your career, not that it was going well.'

Erin balled her fists and remained silent.

'Why on earth did you think that book could be legally published?' Charlotte frowned. 'Thanks for providing the evidence, though. The police will enjoy reading the contents, and not for your crappy writing style.'

Brother and sister closed in on their prey.

'Making other people contribute to a non-existent book is harsh,' Erin hissed.

'Careful,' Simon replied, 'it almost sounds like you care. I'm writing my own book, along with the others. It's bound to be a bestseller.'

Erin slipped the knife out of her pocket. Of course, she wouldn't meet a stranger without protection. Holding the blade near Charlotte's face, Erin imagined slicing the smugness off.

'Simon, I said your family would be in danger if you shared what happened to Dylan. It still stands. In fact, it's more important now. Never push a hunter into a corner. We always come out fighting.'

'So do the hunted.'

Charlotte stamped on Erin's foot and spun around to land a sweeping kick. Erin fell. Simon flipped her over to lie face down in the mud. It wasn't lost on him how Kat died in a similar position. He pinned Erin in place while tying her hands and feet with Charlotte's and his scarves.

Simon whispered into Erin's ear. 'Sometimes you have to be cruel to be kind. You tried to use kindness as an excuse for killing. I'm taking kindness back and rewriting the rules. It's kindness for you to be in prison. Don't worry about being bored. I'll send a signed copy of my book.'

'Shall I?' Charlotte asked.

He nodded.

She spoke on her phone. 'Come and join us.'

At first, it was a sense of foreboding. Something bad was coming. Then the footsteps sounded. Erin looked up from the ground.

A jury surrounded Erin: Stevie, Tina, Thalia, Brenda, Tim, Paige, Gemma, and Fran.

The judges, Simon and Charlotte, stood with them.

Verdict: Guilty of killing kindness.

No rewrites or different versions. Erin's story was finally over.

ACKNOWLEDGEMENTS

Thank you, Conrad and Red Dragon Publishing, for believing in *Killing Kindness*. It's an honour to work with you.

Thanks, Shelagh, for the editing and Dee for proofreading. I really appreciate your help.

Emmy, once again you've taken my idea for a cover design and created a thing of beauty.

To the friends and family who continue to support me in writing and life; you're amazing. The beers are on… you.

Thanks to The Lisa Sell Community on Facebook. You're bloody brilliant in helping me promote, and making it a group I enjoy being in. If you're not a part of it yet, come and join us!

Social media can sometimes be a terrible place. Thankfully, it's better for the lovely bloggers, readers, and authors I've met there. You know who you are because I'm probably cyber stalking you. Joke. Don't contact the police. My research history alone will get me into trouble.

For the first time in one of my books, I'm thanking my cats, Feegle and Wullie. They deserve recognition for letting me finish this book while keeping them fed, entertained, and adored.

Dave, without you, all this means nothing. I love you more than cheese.

Printed in Great Britain
by Amazon